Day Of The Dead

A University Mystery

Brenda Donelan

Day Of The Dead

©Copyright 2014 Brenda Donelan

All Rights Reserved

For Audra... after thirty years I finally followed your advice and wrote a book.

BRENDA DONELAN

Acknowledgements

A book is not written by just one person. Several others assisted me in ways too numerous to mention. Thank you to those who gave me suggestions and support during the preparation of this book and previous writing. Anna Moore Roberts, Catherine Wade, and Johnny Bryan Ward all served the roles of sounding board, cheerleader, and task-master. My beta readers, Clay Finck and Becky Kuch, provided invaluable feedback on the first draft of my book; while Alastair Stephens, my editor, polished the final draft.

Many thanks go out to my friend Samantha Lund Hilmer on the design of the book cover. I also want to recognize Jeff Fullerton for the cover photograph, courtesy of iStock.

I want to thank my parents, Lawrence and Patricia Donelan. They taught me early on how to tell a story.

Finally, Nanowrimo served as a vehicle for me to develop my writing. It was during the Nanowrimo writing programs of 2012 and 2013 that I wrote *Day of the Dead*.

BRENDA DONELAN

Contents

No one expects to die on Halloween. No one believes something truly bad will happen to them. The worst that could happen is a scare from a child dressed as a mutant monster, or being the recipient of a prank played by a mischievous group of preteens. Back in 2004, however, Halloween night and the early morning hours of November 1st proved to be nothing other than deadly for one college professor.

It was the night I died.

Chapter 1

At 6:45 a.m., Marlee McCabe roared into a nearly vacant parking lot at Midwestern State University (MSU) in Elmwood, South Dakota, where she worked as an assistant professor in the Criminal Justice Department. It was Monday, and she had two morning classes, office hours in the afternoon and a three-hour night class. Mondays were her hell days, and once Monday night class was over, the week, all of a sudden, got much better. Unfortunately, Marlee did not spend her time wisely by prepping for her classes over the weekend. Halloween fell on Sunday that year, so both Friday and Saturday were deemed "party" days, with Sunday night reserved for handing out candy to the trick-or-treating neighborhood kids.

On Friday, she got together with a few of her friends from MSU for their monthly supper club meeting. This tradition was started two years ago by Marlee and Diane Frasier, an assistant professor of speech. They invited Kathleen Zens and Gwen Gerkin, assistant professors from the Music Department. Later, Gwen's partner, Shelly McFarland, was added to the mix. Shelly also worked at MSU and was a therapist at the campus Counseling Center. The five-some got together once a month at the home of one of the members to eat, drink, and bitch about all things MSU. Initially, the group began as a way to showcase the host's cooking. Over time, the focus tended to be less on home cooking and more on social bonding, as was frequently evidenced by the empty pizza boxes and wine bottles littered around the host's home. The main topic of the lively conversation on Friday night was the new MSU President, John Ross, and how it was believed that he was running Midwestern State University into the ground with his ineptness and misguided views on education.

Marlee spent Saturday night in the company of the same people from supper club, as all five were invited to a Halloween party at the home of a political science professor. Thom Dole and his wife, Sheri, hosted an annual Halloween party, and this was the first year Marlee and her friends, all lowly assistant professors, were invited to join the festivities.

In academia, the Holy Grail is to be a professor with tenure. Tenure basically granted job security to the holders unless they committed some heinous act, such as bringing weapons to campus or being drunk in class. A few profs had affairs with students, but that did not seem to violate the norms of the campus. Hell, some thought being a professor meant open season on all students.

When starting a tenure track teaching position, one is typically hired as an assistant professor, and then promoted to associate professor and granted tenure after a few years of satisfactory performance. After another five years, the associate professor is eligible for promotion to professor. Each of these steps carried a pay raise and an increase in prestige. It was a huge honor and a sign of acceptance into the small academic community that Marlee and her friends were included in Thom and Sheri's annual Halloween soiree.

On Sunday, Marlee chose to loaf around the house and watch six back-to-back episodes of *Law and Order* followed by a long, luxurious nap. Then she braced herself for the infestation of trick-or-treaters. She used to enjoy giving candy to the cute little kids dressed as ghosts and pirates, but times had changed. Sunday night's gaggle included a preteen boy with his mom and younger sister. "What are you?" Marlee asked quizzically, surveying his purple velvet hat and jazzy pin striped suit.

"I'm a pimp," he stated with some air of impunity, while his mother giggled. Marlee handed him a couple of fun-size candy bars, and he, his mother and his sister moved on to the next house on the block. A group of four preteen girls rang Marlee's doorbell and demanded candy. One was a sexy kitten, another was a sexy cheerleader, and in a total Halloween fashion disaster that would be talked about for weeks at middle school, two of the girls were dressed in identical sexy nurse costumes. *Ohmigod!* As Marlee handed them the candy, she resisted the urge to tell them their pimp was out soliciting candy too.

The final nail in the trick-or-treating coffin came around 8:30 p.m., when two teenage boys without costumes or any receptacles to hold their candy showed up at Marlee's door and held out their hands without saying a word. Both just stared at her while she decided whether or not to give them candy.

As Marlee was placing a couple of fun-size candy bars in the hand of the shorter teen, he said, "I'm diabetic. Do you have any fruit?" Annoyed that the boys thought this was a drive-thru and she was there to take their special orders, Marlee said that she didn't, even though there were several apples and bananas in her kitchen that would probably rot before she got around to eating them. Especially since she would most likely have quite a bit of candy left over. The boy said, "Oh, well, I'll just give these to somebody else." Then both boys cut across her yard into the neighbor's and started laughing.

The little bastards, Marlee thought. After judging all the trick-or-treaters, Marlee was exhausted and decided to open a bottle of wine. She decided red wine went best with the assortment of chocolate bars still in her wicker pumpkin candy holder and uncorked a bottle of cabernet. Starting Monday, she was back on her low-carb diet, which did not include candy or wine.

Since the entire weekend was spent on relaxation and social events, Marlee knew she needed to get into work early Monday morning. Her first class was at 10:00 a.m.– Intro to Criminal Justice–and she still needed to review her notes before lecture. Her second class was Policing, which was held at 11:00 a.m. Marlee's lecture was in order for that class, but she wanted to finish grading some quizzes so they could be handed back. Her biggest worry that morning was her Criminology class that night. She had not yet re-read the chapter they would be covering and also needed to pull together some notes and devise an activity for students to use in applying the concepts they learned. Since Criminology was a three hour class, a great amount of time was invested in making sure there was enough engaging information to keep the students interested and awake for the entire period.

"Son of a bitch!" Marlee shouted, shaking her shoulder length auburn curls in disgust as she made her way toward the parking lot nearest her building. A fire truck was blocking part of the entrance to the lot, so she turned the steering wheel of her Honda CR-V into the parking lot adjacent to the Athletic Center. Even though it was a small campus of around three thousand students, everyone always sought to park in the closest lot, especially during the cold months of the upper Great Plains, which extended from October until April. On this cold and windy morning, it would have been nice to scoot right into her office building instead of trudging into the wind across two parking lots to get to Scobey Hall.

Scobey was undoubtedly the oldest building on campus. The brown brick building consisted of three floors plus a basement. The building had two separate wings that were connected by an archway on the third floor. The only way to reach one wing from the other, other than to use the third floor archway, was to go outside the building and use another entrance. Scobey Hall was called The Maze due to its narrow winding staircases, which could not accommodate two people passing each other. Students tended to avoid The Maze because they could never find the office or professor they were hoping to locate. Professors either really liked The Maze or really detested it, depending upon whether they were student-avoidant or student-enjoyant. Marlee started out her days on campus with a positive attitude toward students, but as the days progressed, she became depleted and found herself sneaking off campus in order to avoid students and their never-ending requests for extra credit, make up exams and other special considerations. *At least I had the good sense not to become a parent*, she thought, knowing that hiding from your dependents was not only looked down upon in the family-worshipping community of Elmwood, but also illegal.

Marlee parked her CR-V, flung open the door, and hopped out onto the pavement. At thirty eight years old, Marlee stood at five foot three and one quarter inches tall. She had a plump frame that had caused her much concern since she was nine years old. As she Weight Watchered, Slimfasted, and Jazzercised, the weight would drop off quickly, but return with a vengeance, along with a few extra pounds, once she returned to her default states of sloth and gluttony. Weight was a constant battle for

Marlee, but it also provided a handy excuse for her lack of steady boyfriends, occasional social awkwardness and anything else not going in her favor at the time. She was dressed in dark green slacks, a green and brown V-neck sweater with a tank top underneath to help conceal her overly-ample bust line and a brown rain jacket.

Marlee shivered and decided it might be time to retire the fall rain jacket for the season and break out a heavier coat, along with insulated gloves, and a flannel scarf. She clicked along the parking lot in her brown suede ankle boots with stacked heels, which had the desired effect of making her over five foot five inches tall. Although she loved the added height, she felt a bit like she was walking on stilts at times. An uncoordinated big girl wearing anything other than flats or a low heel was an accident waiting to happen.

Walking toward Scobey Hall, Marlee steeled herself against the biting wind and chill. As she approached the fire truck blocking the entrance to the parking lot nearest her building, she noticed additional fire trucks, ambulances, and several police cars in the background. When she had first seen the fire truck, she had assumed there had been another water main break or a fallen power line on campus, since these things happened on a regular basis. As she drew closer to Scobey Hall, her stomach began to churn as the realization hit her that something serious was going on. She noticed yellow crime scene tape about twenty five yards beyond the farthest police car. Standing under a tree at the edge of the parking lot was a man she vaguely knew from campus. His name was Earl Dingus, and he was the director of finance. The short stuffy little man in a medium gray suit made eye contact with Marlee and offered a wan smile. Marlee approached him and asked what was going on.

"They found a body," Earl said without a hint of emotion. In one minute, Marlee had gone from fretting about her class prep for the day to learning of a death on the campus that she loved. Her heart and jaw were in a race to see which could drop the farthest and the fastest.

"Who is it? What happened?" Marlee asked, clearly shocked by the news.

"The police aren't saying," replied Earl, who averted his eyes and looked into the distance at nothing in particular. A thousand thoughts hit the young assistant professor's mind at once. Her first notion was that it was a suicide since, in her mind, there were several unstable people on campus, most of them professors and several in the College of Arts and Sciences branch in which her own department was housed. It also wouldn't be too farfetched to think that a student had taken his or her own life in an act of loneliness and desperation. Then she thought of the number of middle-aged, overweight, and out of shape professors on campus that were on the fast-track for a heart attack. Perhaps a professor or janitor, working over the weekend, had fallen down the winding marble steps in The Maze and suffered a fatal injury.

It occurred to Marlee that she was not solely reliant on Earl Dingus for information on the situation since there were loads of police officers, ambulance attendants, and a few student bystanders nearby. She could approach one of the police officers for more information, which might actually work if she could find one of the officers who had taken some of her Criminal Justice classes. Earl Dingus must have read her mind. "Faculty and everyone else are supposed to go straight to the Student Union and wait there."

Frack! Well, Marlee could go to the Student Union, but take her time getting there and see what she could find out along the way. She nodded to Dingus that she understood and shouldered her brown leather book bag, clomping toward the Student Union. As she got closer to Scobey Hall, Marlee noticed that two of the police officers had protective plastic booties slipped on over their regular footwear. She knew this was to avoid contamination of crime scenes, which gave her a clue as to the nature of this incident. Obviously, it was a crime or at least a suspicious death, or else there would be no need to protect the area from contamination of whatever was stuck to the bottom of the officers' shoes. Since Marlee taught a class on Crime Scene Investigation, she knew that deaths were frequently treated as suspicious until a cause could be determined. This might be a heart attack or other type of fatal injury and not necessarily a murder.

She neared the dumpster located on the south edge of Scobey Hall and, as she did so, she noticed a sandal clad foot and bloodstains on the cement. Marlee gasped for air, and her hand flew to her mouth. She had never seen a dead body before except at a funeral, and even then she tried not to look at the corpse in the casket because it creeped her out. Viewing a dead body at a funeral always seemed a morbid way to remember somebody. She preferred remembering the deceased during better times rather than when they were heavily made up and lying stiff in a coffin.

Marlee could not approach any closer as police officers were steering away any onlookers. Other than a glimpse of the foot, which was clad in a navy blue sock and a brown Teva sandal, she had no idea who the deceased could be. Given the sock-sandal combo, she assumed it was a professor, since none of the traditional college-age students would be seen wearing that. Marlee turned to walk around the other side of Scobey Hall on her way to the Student Union. The lone car in the parking lot was an older model Porsche two-seater. The black sports car was owned by Logan LeCroix, the new French professor. Although Logan had only been on campus since late August, everyone knew his car because it looked like a toy compared to the SUVs and four-wheel drive pickups that populated Elmwood. In fact, he had even talked to Marlee about storing his car in her garage over the winter since there was no way the little two-seater would make it over the smallest of snow banks. The clearance on his car was just a few inches, and it would not be drivable after October due to the early onset of winter, marked by vast amounts of snow. The conversation had occurred a couple weeks ago at her house party when Logan began discussing buying an additional vehicle to get him around Elmwood during the winter.

Hmm. Logan must have been working all weekend, thought Marlee. *No wonder he didn't make it to Thom and Sheri's Halloween party on Saturday night.* Everyone she spoke with at the party thought this was odd since it was practically social suicide not to attend a function hosted by a tenured professor, especially since Logan was in his first year at MSU.

Marlee couldn't believe that she was thinking of the Halloween party at a time like this. Someone was dead on the MSU campus, right near the entrance to her building! She walked past the library toward the Student Union and actually brushed against Della Halter, a colleague in her department, as she exited the library.

Della was five foot nothing, but she was a force to be reckoned with. She was in her mid-50s, had short dark brown hair, glasses, and brown eyes as cold as January at the North Pole. Hailing from Mississippi, Della still retained her strong southern drawl, even though she had lived in South Dakota for over 20 years. She was clad in her usual attire, which looked as if it had been pulled from the rag bag. She wore green sweat pants tucked into black snow boots even though there was no snow or any type of precipitation on the ground. Her unzipped tan winter coat revealed a V-neck hospital-type smock with cartoon dogs all over it. Unfortunately, this was one of her better work outfits. As she turned to the side, Marlee saw that Della's hair on the back of her head stood up in a rooster tail, suggesting that she had not washed or even combed her hair that morning.

"Did you come from the parking lot?" Della demanded, standing much too close to Marlee when she spoke. Marlee nodded and asked if she knew anything about the body in front of Scobey Hall.

"It's Logan LeCroix," Della said. "They found Logan dead outside our building this morning."

Day Of The Dead

I wanted a change of pace from California, and hoped returning to South Dakota—the desolate but serene area where I spent summers with my grandparents—would be the change I was looking for. The plan was for me to start my new teaching career at MSU and, later on, my partner Joe would join me. If all went well Joe and I would look at making the move permanent.

Of course, this was contingent on the hope that Joe and I could repair our twenty-two year relationship.

Chapter 2

"How do you know it's Logan?" Marlee nearly shrieked.

"Earl Dingus told me," Della replied, obviously enjoying that she had information on the campus tragedy that Marlee did not.

Goddamned Dingus, he didn't tell me dick and then shooed me off to the Student Union, thought Marlee. It irked her that Della was able to get information from a little piss-ant like Earl Dingus when she could not.

"I saw Logan's car on campus but didn't take that to mean anything," Marlee muttered more to herself than Della. "So what happened? Was it an accident? Did he have a heart attack?" Questions were rolling around in Marlee's mind faster than she could process them. She could barely take in all the information that had developed in the past twenty minutes: a death on campus, and the victim was a fellow professor.

"I don't know what happened. Nobody knows at this point," Della said matter-of-factly, indicating that if anyone had an idea of the cause of Logan's death, she would surely know about it. She was relishing her new role as disseminator of information.

Although new to the MSU campus, Logan LeCroix had already become a well-known figure to faculty, administration, and students. Standing barely five feet five inches tall, he was a shy, introverted man with a gentle way about him. Still, he had become a fast favorite on the campus because of his kindness and willingness to help others. His short wavy brown hair set off a light brown complexion and dark brown eyes. His mannerisms were best described as effeminate and, although he never spoke of his sexuality, he fit many of the gay stereotypes. Of course, any male who does not fit the rugged manly-man type of the northern plains can, at some point, be considered a homosexual, whether he is or not.

Logan made other professors on campus appear lethargic by comparison. Not only did he teach his required four courses per semester, but he had also agreed to take on French classes at the local high school, since the long time French teacher at Elmwood High unexpectedly retired over the summer after being stricken with an undiagnosed brain disorder. Thus, the high school had an immediate opening for a French teacher, and they were unable to fill it. The principal at Elmwood High School called the MSU Languages Department to see if they had any suggestions for a last-minute French teacher. Logan had been in Elmwood for only a couple of weeks before school began and was approached about adding the two high school classes onto his already heavy teaching load. The MSU community came to realize that accepting this added load was indicative of Logan's approach to life: if someone needed help, he was there to do all he could.

Della and Marlee walked into the Student Union, a recently remodeled building which housed meeting rooms, the Counseling Center, the Nurse's Office, Student Affairs, and a variety of other offices on the top floor; the main floor was a breeze-way of sorts, allowing students to quickly move from one end of the Student Union to the other. The interior of the building smelled like a combination of fried food, stale air, burnt coffee, and body odor. In a corner on the main floor was an activity area with a pool table and several overstuffed chairs and couches. The entry and main floor served as an ideal area for Career Fairs, voter registration, bake sales, and other activities seeking the attention of as many students as possible. The lower level housed the cafeteria, dining area and kitchen, the book store, and the campus post office. Off in a corner was a large room dedicated to dances, festivals, and campus-wide meetings. It included a coffee bar and snack shop. Considering all the services provided in the Student Union, most students frequented the building daily, especially those living on campus.

Della and Marlee found their way to a table in the dining room which was already occupied by a few of the other early arrivals on campus. Their new dean, Dr. Ira Green, sat at one end of the long dining table. Dean Green, or Mean Dean Green, as he was nicknamed shortly after beginning at MSU, was an imposing figure. A loud, outspoken man, he stood six foot three and, from a side angle, was reminiscent of Yogi Bear. His large stomach was enhanced by his loose fitting tan slacks belted only slightly below his armpits. Dean Green was in his late sixties and originally hailed from New York. Most recently, he had been a professor at a large university in Ohio. He and his wife decided it was time for a change of pace, both in terms of location and work duties. When Green was hired as Dean of the College of Arts and Sciences at MSU, he and his wife were happy to make the move. He was settling in to his new role although, to some, it appeared to be a bit of a bumpy transition. Green was abrupt and frequently quite tactless, which put him at odds with many of the reserved residents of Elmwood.

"What's going on?" Marlee asked Dean Green as she strode right up to his chair. Normally, Marlee kept her distance from the dean, but this was a far from normal situation.

"LeCroix's dead," he said bluntly. "We don't know what happened."

"Was he sick? Or hurt? What do you think happened?" Marlee pushed on with her questions.

"The president's office is still trying to track down his next of kin to notify them of Logan's death. Maybe a relative can tell us if he had a heart condition, or some other type of disease," said Dean Green in his usual gruff voice.

"What are we supposed to do about our classes today?" Della asked, already angling for a reason to get out of teaching.

"Carry on as usual until we hear otherwise," barked Dean Green who was not a fan of canceling classes unnecessarily. "Keep to your regular schedules."

"Well, what do we tell our students? They'll find out soon, if they don't already know about Logan's death," Marlee said.

"We can't tell them anything if we don't know anything," Dean Green pointed out with a look that implied that "dumbass" should have been added at the end of his sentence.

"Should we refer them to counseling if they are having problems dealing with Logan's death? Even if they didn't know him, it's still a huge shock to have someone die on campus," stated Marlee.

"No, I don't think counseling is the answer here. Actually I don't think counseling is ever an answer," said Dean Green. "I went to counseling once, and it didn't do a fuckin' thing for me," he growled, looking Marlee right in the eye as if to challenge her.

Marlee backed down, realizing that Dean Green was definitely not going to be overly sympathetic towards the students, faculty or staff on campus. Perhaps he was used to dealing with on-campus deaths at his previous university and found this to be a semi-regular occurrence. Even Della, the Queen of the Inappropriate, seemed taken aback by his callous demeanor and crass remarks.

Alexander Sherkov, Professor of Russian Language and Studies in the MSU Modern Languages Department, arrived at Marlee's table and joined the group. Professor Sherkov was a tall, attractive man with a head of thick brown hair. The bags beneath his light blue eyes suggested he had pulled an all-nighter in preparing for his classes or working on a new research grant. Not the most rigorous professor in terms of making students actually work, Alexander was well liked and also had the distinction of being a tenured full professor; therefore, his lack of rigor in the classroom could be overlooked since he had already jumped through enough hoops to justify his position. He was far ahead of the pack of other professors in the Modern Languages Department in securing outside grant money and performing various types of research, which also served to keep administrators off his back. The holy trinity in the academic world is teaching, research, and service. Although MSU claimed teaching was the most valued of the three at their university, bad teaching could easily be trumped by great research, especially if it was backed up by outside grant money.

"What's going on?" asked Alexander. "I couldn't get into our building and was sent over here."

Marlee, Della, and Dean Green all took turns providing Alexander with the known details of the situation, which gave him a somewhat clearer picture of what was going on, at least as clear a picture as they had. Just then, Alice Olson walked in looking ashen and shaky. She slowly lowered her short, compact frame into a chair at the long table and rested her head in her hands, as if in disbelief. Alice was on her twelfth year as secretary for the department that housed Modern Languages, Speech, and English. She was in her late fifties with a kind nature and a naïve take on life. Alice never had a bad word for or about anyone, which endeared her to a number of people on campus. Refraining from negativity is nearly unheard of on a college campus where rumor, innuendo, and outright lies are common sport among the faculty, administration, and staff. Alice's dark brown eyes were red and puffy, and her thick-lensed glasses were smudged and sitting somewhat askew on her nose. Her graying blonde hair was cut short and was usually neatly groomed, but today it was standing up in the front, as if Alice had repeatedly run her hands through her hair in despair upon hearing the news. She and Logan were close. She was his first friend when he moved to Elmwood. Logan was forever giving Alice compliments, which meant she would move heaven and earth for him. He didn't treat her like she was just a secretary, as did many of the other faculty members. She provided hours of extra assistance in getting Logan set up in his new office, which was located just a stone's throw from her own.

Marlee noted that everyone at the table seemed to be in a state of shock, but each handled it in his or her own way. The only one of them who seemed to be acting strangely was Dean Green, but this was not out of character for him. He didn't get the nickname Mean Dean Green by being a playful little kitten.

A few more professors and secretaries joined the long table where Marlee and the others were seated. It was now nearly 8:00 a.m., so there would be the normal buzz of activity as employees arrived on campus and made their way to their offices. Students went to their early classes or to breakfast, if they were up and dared to set foot outside in the chilly morning. A few students walked by Marlee's table and looked quizzically at her and the others. Word was quickly making its way from one person to another, and soon the whole campus and the whole town of Elmwood would know of Logan's death.

Kendra Rolland, Vice President of Academic Affairs, approached the table and pulled Dean Green away for a few moments. Kendra sported a shaggy, dark brown hairdo reminiscent of the 1970s, which happened to be very "in" at the moment. She was dressed in a sage green suit and black heels. She was well-liked on campus because of her friendly nature and her diligence in getting work done, although most of her subordinates dreaded the meetings she chaired because they were unnecessarily long. Other than that, Kendra was a great spokesperson for MSU.

After she and Dean Green conferred privately for a few minutes, they approached the table of about twelve faculty and staff. Kendra and Dean Green looked at each other for a moment, and then Kendra said in a trembling voice, "The police found a gun."

I loved my students, and I loved teaching them. I gained energy from their enthusiasm, their questions, and their liveliness. Students in California had entitlement issues. They expected to be treated as a customer who had paid for a service. If they did not like their grade or the way I taught a class, they felt no hesitation in approaching me and asking for changes. The students at MSU were different. They were respectful and seemed to genuinely want to learn.

The last thing I ever wanted was for any of them to see me laying in a pool of my own blood in front of Scobey Hall.

Chapter 3

"A gun!" yelled Marlee and Della in unison. Kendra nodded her shaggy head as an affirmation that they had heard correctly.

"Where was it?" Marlee asked, quickly gaining her composure enough to realize she had someone in her presence with actual information. She wanted to get as much detail from Kendra as humanly possible before she disappeared back into her administrative bubble that was impenetrable for most faculty members, especially to assistant professors without tenure.

"We don't know yet. The police haven't released any details other than that at this time," replied Kendra. Then she turned and busily walked toward her office located upstairs in the Student Union.

Marlee and her table mates were astounded and just looked at each other for a full minute before everyone burst into a stream of questions.

"Where was the gun?"

"Who would have left the gun there?"

"Who would want to kill Logan?"

"Is there a killer out there?"

"Are we all in danger?"

"Do you think he shot himself?" asked Alexander in a tentative voice.

"What? No!" shouted Alice as she violently pushed back her chair and rose to her feet. "Why would he kill himself? He was happy, and he liked it here. He's not the type to commit suicide!" Alice was still reeling from the shock of Logan's death, the death of her friend. She could not bear to think he would take his own life in front of the building where he worked.

"Well, who *is* the type to commit suicide?" asked Dean Green in a demanding tone. Tears ran down Alice's cheeks as she struggled to make sense of what had happened on the quiet, uneventful campus where she loved working.

Everyone at the table turned toward Marlee. Not that she was an expert on suicide, but she taught in the Criminal Justice Department and had a fair amount of expertise and insight into human behavior. Marlee felt put on the spot. She was not quick on her feet when surprised with questions. She liked to have time to think about them and ponder the variety of possible answers before responding. The last thing Marlee wanted to do was to come off half-cocked like many of the so-called experts on television talk shows. Those pundits were responsible for more falsehoods and speculation than Marlee cared to think about. She knew that anything she said on this topic could be spread all over campus in a nanosecond.

Marlee cleared her throat and said, "Well, under the right circumstances, anyone could commit suicide."

"Bullshit!" trumpeted Dean Green. "I've thought about killing a lot of people in my life, but I never thought about killing myself. Suicide is for the weak, the nutcases of society."

"*Waaaaaait* a minute," drawled Della Halter in her loud, obnoxious voice. Marlee dreaded what she would say, not because it would be factually inaccurate, but because Della had the tact of a bulldozer. It would not be surprising if in her zeal to communicate facts on suicide, she inadvertently pissed off everyone at the table, including the dean. "Studies show that people commit suicide for a variety of reasons. It's not always because someone is unstable."

Alice threw her hands to her ears and shouted, "I don't want to hear any more about suicide. Logan wouldn't do it!"

Dean Green shook his head as if overwhelmed. Never mind the death on campus, which appeared to be the result of a gunshot wound, Dean Green was stymied as to how to keep the faculty and staff from the College of Arts and Sciences under control. He muttered something about talking to the president and stalked off.

Marlee put her arm around Alice's shoulders in an attempt to comfort her. "I seriously doubt Logan killed himself, Alice. I don't know what happened, but I'll bet anything he didn't commit suicide," she said intently. She didn't know where her strong resolve came from on the issue, but at the core of her being, she knew this was not a suicide.

The question remained: what happened to Logan LeCroix?

It was nearing 10:00 a.m. and Marlee's first class was coming up: Intro to Criminal Justice. She did not feel as though she could teach the class after the shock of Logan's death and the uncertainty as to why and how he died. She made her way to the Putnam Building and entered the room where her next two classes were held. Several students were already in the classroom and were discussing the death. No one knew the story, but most people had bits and pieces. Some of these bits and pieces were actually true, and some were wild speculation or altogether inaccurate. Marlee began class in her usual manner by announcing, "Okay, good morning. Let's get started." Instead of launching into a brief recap of previous lecture material or making general announcements about upcoming tests or quizzes, Marlee stated, "By now, I'm sure most of you have heard about the death on campus."

A non-traditional female student in the back looked taken aback and looked side to side to see if anyone else was shocked by the news. She raised her hand and asked, "What happened? I don't live on campus, and this is the first I'm hearing about it."

"The body of Logan LeCroix, the new French professor, was found outside Scobey Hall. The police are investigating and not much information has been released yet," recited Marlee, feeling like a news reporter reading a teleprompter. She was careful not to include any of the conjecture from her previous conversations about the incident that morning.

A male student along the east wall of the classroom blurted out, "They found a gun. I heard it was in a dumpster."

Marlee, still not willing to fall into the trap of overstating what she knew about the matter, said, "I also heard a gun was found but don't know any of the details. At this point we're just learning what happened as the police do their investigation. People like to talk even when they don't have any direct information, so you will probably hear many things about Professor LeCroix's death that may not be entirely accurate. I encourage you all to carefully weigh the information you hear, and not necessarily believe everything you're told. I also ask all of you not to contribute to the problem by adding your own version of facts and then passing on that information as if it were really true."

A shy student in the front row raised her hand and asked, "Dr. McCabe, how do we know what's true and what isn't? It's barely 10:00 a.m., and I've already heard stories that he was in the Witness Protection Program, that this was a mob hit, and that he was killed by a stray bullet aimed at someone else. How do we know what really happened?" Several other students nodded as if to say that they also had heard stories from numerous sources claiming to be factual.

"That's just it," replied Marlee. "We don't know yet. The investigation is ongoing and may not be completed for days, weeks, or even months. The police may know the cause of Professor LeCroix's death and are waiting to release the information, or they may still be trying to deduce what really happened. We just don't know. This is real life. It's not like *CSI* or *Law and Order*. The matter won't be resolved in a short period of time. Evidence needs to be collected and tested. People need to be interviewed. The detectives will search Professor LeCroix's home, office, and car. The list of things the cops have to do is endless, so we can't expect a quick result."

"So what should we do now?" asked a male student, apparently not afraid to appear vulnerable to his classmates. Marlee just then realized that although she was impacted by Logan's death because he was her colleague and new friend, the students were affected because this death happened on the campus, which was their home for nine months out of the year.

Marlee went through the safety information Kendra Rolland had provided to her and the other professors less than an hour ago. "Basically, until we know what's going on, everyone is to take necessary precautions, such as not walking alone on campus and not going out after dark unless you have someone you trust to go with you. The Vice President of Academic Affairs is planning a campus-wide meeting this afternoon to address any new police findings and also to talk about campus safety. You will be receiving emails on this shortly, as soon as a time and location have been determined. Please come to the meeting and hear for yourself what is going on. And, before I let you go for today, I just want to remind you to be safe." On that final note, the students filed out of the classroom in a state of bewilderment and uncertainty. Marlee felt the same way herself. She waited around the classroom for the next half hour until her second class, Intro to Policing, began. She then launched into a repeat from her first class and addressed very similar questions from students.

By the time everyone left her second class, it was nearly 11:30 a.m., and Marlee was completely drained of energy. She trudged back to the Student Union to find out if there was any news. She made her way to the area which now held most of the professors, secretaries, and work-study students from Scobey Hall. The increasingly large group of people had spread from one long table to several tables and chairs pulled into a middle section of the dining area. Since all of Scobey Hall was on lockdown, those who inhabited The Maze had nowhere else to go. Ella Simpson-Sampson, or Sim-Sam as she was called by her students and pretty much everyone else on campus, entered the fray at the Student Union. She was a diminutive professor in her early 40s, although she was occasionally mistaken for a student. Sim-Sam had long brown hair with a fringe of bangs. A few blonde highlights camouflaged the gray hairs that were peeping through. She wore stylish red glasses and dressed professionally. Today, she wore a black and red print skirt topped with a red blouse and a black blazer. Her high heeled, tall black boots kicked her height up to nearly five foot one inch tall. Although she was tiny, Sim-Sam could be a power house and would fight tooth and nail for something she believed in. It was not uncommon to hear her holding her own in a committee meeting dominated by men. She really was an inspiration to the female faculty, especially Marlee and her fellow newcomers.

Sim-Sam approached Marlee, Della, and a few others who were seated at a small table. She was not one to spread gossip, but by the look on her face, everyone knew Sim-Sam had information on Logan's death. After talking for a few minutes and sharing the information they all had, Sim-Sam lowered her voice and looked around to make sure no one outside the small group could overhear her. "Thom Dole was the one who found Logan. He thinks it was suicide."

Some people say you don't have feelings after you die. That's not true. I did. I could physically feel the cold early-morning air and the wind on my body. I heard the rattling of the last of the leaves that had yet to fall from the campus trees. I could emotionally feel my soul hovering over my physical self, bidding it farewell.

Chapter 4

"When did Thom find Logan? Does Thom know what happened?" Marlee's mind was formulating questions more quickly than she could spit them out. Sim-Sam was barraged by a similar array of questions from Della, Alcxander, and other professors in the vicinity.

Sim-Sam relayed the following narrative: "As I was pulling into the parking lot this morning around 8:30 a.m., I saw Thom walking through the parking lot toward the edge of campus. I could tell by looking at him that something was wrong. You could just tell by looking at his face–he looked as if he had aged twenty years since I saw him at the party this weekend, and I know for a fact it was not because he drank too much. Thom likes alcohol, but not in excess, that's for sure. I asked him how he was, and he told me that he had found Logan LeCroix outside Scobey Hall this morning and that Logan was dead. Thom said he got to work around 4:30 that morning, as he usually does since he is an early bird. Around 5:30, Cecil, the janitor, knocked on Thom's door. Cecil had found Logan's body lying on the cement outside the front door a few minutes earlier and didn't know what to do. He knew Thom always came in very early to prep for classes and grade papers, so he went to find Thom. Cecil and Thom then went downstairs and outside. Thom wanted to make sure that what Cecil had told him was true since Cecil is easily confused and not always the best judge of situations. Thom actually thought that maybe somebody had left a dummy on the sidewalk as a Halloween prank and Cecil thought it was a dead body. When they arrived at the entrance to Scobey Hall, Thom could see that it was obviously someone who was severely injured or dead because of all the blood around the head area. Thom and Cecil walked up to the body, and Thom saw that it was Logan LeCroix."

"So Logan wasn't there when Thom came in to work at 4:30 this morning, but he was there dead by 5:30? That must mean whoever or whatever killed him took place while Thom was in his office. Did he hear anything?" questioned Della.

"No, wait a minute," said Sim-Sam, holding up her hand in frustration. She was used to Della's lack of tact and jumping to conclusions and wanted to halt any misinformation that Sim-Sam knew Della would attribute back to her. "Thom came in the back door like he always does because he walks from his home to work, and that door is the closest. Logan was found near the front door of Scobey Hall, so I guess we still don't know when it happened. Or what happened."

Marlee asked, "Could Thom tell where Logan had been shot? Were there any obvious injuries that lead to the blood loss?"

"Thom said he didn't see any gunshot wounds, just a lot of blood under Logan's head and upper body," replied Sim-Sam.

"How about the gun? Was it right near Logan?" asked Della.

"No," Sim-Sam replied hesitantly. "Thom didn't say anything about a gun."

Marlee and Della looked at each other with puzzled expressions. "Then why does Thom think it was a suicide?" asked Marlee.

Sim-Sam slowly let out a breath and said, "I don't know. He didn't say. He said he thought it was a suicide, and then he started tearing up and said he needed to go home. He had been in an interview with police officers and detectives for nearly two hours and wanted to go back to his house immediately. I didn't want to keep pushing him for information."

"*Sooooo*, we don't know why Thom thought this was a suicide," Della drawled, stating the obvious.

Just then a voice boomed over the loud speaker in the Student Union, "Today at one o'clock in the Caldwell Room there will be a mandatory meeting for everyone on campus. President Ross and Police Chief Langdon will speak about campus safety and the events of earlier today. Please be in attendance." The message was repeated twice more as faculty, staff, and students all looked at each other with open mouths. What new findings would be revealed at the campus meeting?

I was truly touched by the outpouring of grief and love shown by the MSU campus and the Elmwood community. Most of the faculty did not know me, and the vast majority of the students had not been in any of my classes. People who never even saw me before my picture was plastered across the local newspaper and the local news stations were crying and hugging each other. If only we could have this kind of love and support while we are alive. If only I could have had this from everyone in my life. If only...

Chapter 5

The Caldwell Room in the basement of the Student Union was standing room only. It had long brown tables and chairs, similar to those in the cafeteria dining room. Extra folding chairs were brought in and set up in rows ahead of the tables. There were also brightly colored red booths along the north side of the wall which could each hold four full-sized adults. The chairs and booths filled up well before one o'clock, leaving most of the people to either stand or sit on the floor. Most of the students without seats chose to sit on the floor, while faculty and staff chose to stand. The Caldwell Room had an ominous feel that Monday afternoon. The chill of the day seemed to have settled into everyone's bones. They wrapped their arms around themselves and briskly rubbed up and down in an attempt to warm up. Ordinarily there was a small lunch cart near the entrance of the Caldwell Room where staff sold pre-made salads and sandwiches, desserts and hot and cold drinks. The cart had been shut down due to the serious nature of the meeting. A television camera operator and reporter came in and set up near the stage. A newspaper reporter and photographer were also in the audience in the front row of folding chairs.

Marlee sat in a booth facing the stage so she would have a good view of whoever got sent out to talk to the group. She figured it would be one of President Ross's flunkies, who would have to deliver a canned speech and field any questions. Marlee's friends were crowded into the booth with her as well. Gwen Gerken sat next to her with Diane Frasier and Shelly McFarland sitting across the table. Katherine Zens arrived later than the other four but found a chair and pulled it up to the booth. All five women were anxiously awaiting this meeting, and they looked forward to discussing the details of Logan's death afterward. Nothing helps one get through a difficult time like the support of good friends.

Surprisingly, President Ross himself entered the room at exactly 1:00 p.m., flanked by Vice President of Student Affairs, Kendra Rolland and the Elmwood Chief of Police, Bill Langdon. Other minor players in the president's cabinet followed. Earl Dingus was the last in a line of ten people who would be speaking, or were merely there as a showing of moral support. Earl looked about ready to lose his lunch. The party of ten filed up on stage with Earl doing his best to hide behind the others. It was obvious he wanted no part in speaking to the group.

President Ross opened with, "It is with the sincerest of sympathies that I must acknowledge that Logan LeCroix, a professor of French, was found on campus early this morning. Police were notified immediately, and he was pronounced dead at the scene. Detectives from the Elmwood Police Department are investigating the tragedy and have not yet made a determination as to the cause of death." President Ross tugged at his belt in an attempt to hike up his pants a bit farther. His ill-fitting charcoal gray suit had seen better days; since he lost some weight over the summer, President Ross's clothes all tended to look a bit sloppy on him now. Apparently, he was giving it some grace time before he went out and bought new clothes that fit him, just in case he gained back the weight. This was not his first trip on the diet roller coaster.

"Chief Langdon from the Elmwood Police Department is here, and I will turn things over to him now," said President Ross as he stepped to the side and handed the microphone to a nervous-looking officer of the law. Bill Langdon was in his second year as police chief, and it had been a rocky couple of years for him. His first course of action when he arrived was to do some house cleaning, resulting in four long-time police officers and detectives either quitting or being fired. Then, Langdon decided that patrol officers should work rotating shifts, meaning that one month they would work days, the following month they would work nights, and the third month they would work overnights. Drastic changing of shifts in this manner can lead to all kinds of sleep and health-related problems, not to mention problems with child care and working around a spouse's employment schedule. The result of this proposal was that several of the officers approached the city council in an attempt to have the Chief of Police fired. This attempted coup was not successful, and more officers found themselves out of work. Given the contention over the rotating shifts proposal, Langdon decided to table the idea and let patrol officers continue working their regular schedules. Even though he conceded on this point, Langdon was still not well liked by many in his department. The former officers in Elmwood had enough influence in town that they had turned support against the chief. The only public figure who vocally acknowledged support for Chief Langdon was Mayor Linski.

Langdon was in his early 50s and had worked as a patrol officer, then a detective, and then a captain at various other police departments in Montana, Wyoming, and other states. He stood five feet ten inches tall and had a medium build that had not yet succumbed to the realities of desk work and donuts. He had medium brown hair and an untrimmed brown mustache. Langdon's glasses were large-framed which called more attention to his bad habit of staring at people. He made people uneasy, as if he were trying to read their minds or figure out what color underwear they were wearing. He sported the typical non-uniformed cop attire of khaki pants belted at the waist with a cell phone holder attached to the belt, a white button down shirt *sans* tie, and a grayish sport coat.

"Ahem... I just want to begin by saying that the Elmwood Police Department is dedicating as many patrol officers and detectives as possible to this case. It is still early in the investigation, and we have not yet made a determination as to the cause of Logan LeCroix's death. We are following leads and interviewing others pertaining to this case. We are not releasing any other information on this matter until the next of kin have been notified. If you have any information on this matter, please talk to one of the many officers here at this meeting." With that brief robotic statement, which basically revealed nothing, Bill Langdon handed the microphone to Kendra Rolland and stepped back as if glad to be out of the public view.

Kendra stepped forward, calm and confident as always. She took a deep breath and pulled the microphone toward her mouth. "We are all so very sorry for the death of Logan LeCroix, and I know we all hold his memory in our hearts, even those of you that did not know him. We don't know the cause of death, but in the meantime, we wish to keep campus life as normal as possible. Classes will be held, and activities will go on as scheduled. We are instituting an escort service on campus to walk you to your classes, your car, or to the Student Union," said Kendra.

"Escort service?" smirked Marlee to the friend sitting with her. "I think they may need to rethink the name, since I assume no sex will be traded for money in this operation." Diane, sitting directly across from Marlee in a booth, looked at her and managed a small grin. Even in the toughest of times, Diane and Marlee could find some humor.

Kendra Rolland continued on with her dos-and-don'ts of campus safety and precaution. "We also want everyone to know that the police will be providing regular car patrol and foot patrol on campus during the day and in the evenings. If anyone sees something suspicious, please call 911 to summon officers right away. We are also providing cell phones for anyone who does not have one. These cell phones can be checked out at the library and used for emergency calls only. We want to make it clear that, until such time as the police make a determination as to Logan LeCroix's cause of death, we will do everything possible to ensure the safety and well-being of the students, faculty, staff, and others who live on, work at, or visit our campus. Thank you," said Kendra, stepping back and handing the microphone back to President Ross.

"As details develop, we will convey them to you as soon as possible," said President Ross. "And with that, we will conclude..."

"Wait a minute," a voice from the back interrupted. "We have some questions. A lot of information is going around campus, and we want some answers." The voice belonged to Charles Wilmhurst, a professor of business and a well-known loud-mouth both on and off campus. Even though most people did not like him much, his lack of tact and mouthiness came in handy at times like these when the university administration basically revealed nothing. Professor Wilmhurst added, "I heard a gun was found near Logan's body. Some people were saying it was suicide, but I also heard it may have been a mob hit. Can you give us any idea? I mean it makes a big difference whether Logan killed himself, or if a gun-man is out there ready to strike again."

President Ross, Kendra Rolland, and Chief Langdon all looked at each other, playing hot potato with the microphone as they passed it back and forth. Chief Langdon finally conceded that he would have to address some of these questions and stepped forward, microphone in hand. "As I said, we have yet to make a determination as to the cause of Logan LeCroix's death. As for a weapon, I have no comment on that."

Unsatisfied with a further brush off, Professor Wilmhurst countered, "Well, are you at least going to install some security cameras on campus for our safety?"

President Ross and Kendra Rolland looked at each other, and Ross nodded to Rolland. Kendra stepped forward and stated matter-of-factly, "We have security cameras all over campus now and will be reviewing the footage from them."

"Where are the cameras located? Are there any near Scobey Hall where Logan was found?" asked Professor Wilmhurst impatiently.

For the first time, Kendra actually looked nervous. She took a moment before answering but then replied, "We are not at liberty to divulge the whereabouts of any of the cameras on campus." With that statement, the microphone clicked to the off position, and the speakers all scurried off-stage, to the dismay of the crowded Caldwell Room.

The majority of the people packed into the MSU meeting room looked at each other in bewilderment. The meeting brought up more questions than answers and really provided no information. "I can't believe this! They know a lot more than they're saying," said Diane. She turned to Marlee, looking for clarification. "You teach Criminology. What do you think is going on? Could it have been a mob hit?"

Marlee took her time answering, feeling on the spot. It always baffled her that some people thought that, because she had a Ph.D. in Criminology and taught various criminal justice courses, she had a crystal ball and could clearly lay out the means, motive, and opportunity of any crime. Still, she understood that Diane was just seeking any insight into Logan's death. "One thing we know for sure," said Marlee in a measured tone "is that the less information the PD and the campus bigwigs give us, the more rumors we'll have. We're all desperate for information on Logan's death. We all want to feel safe, and we all want to know what the hell happened. Generally, when people don't have concrete answers, their imaginations go into overdrive, and all types of explanations, innuendo and rumors bubble up. Anything is possible."

"Why won't the police tell us if they know anything about a gun?" asked Kathleen. "It's a simple yes or no answer," she said, shaking her head.

"Because the police are always hesitant to offer up too much information about a crime at the beginning," said Marlee, launching into professor mode and giving her standard lecture about police procedure. "They may have a suspect or someone in custody, and by withholding details of the crime, detectives may be able to verify if a specific person did or did not kill Logan. If the PD doesn't confirm that a gun was used, and then a suspect implicates himself by talking about a gun, then they have something to hold against him. Another thing to consider is that regardless of the manner of death, the police have to locate and notify Logan's next of kin before they can release too much information. It's standard protocol to inform family of a death before releasing specific details. The last thing anyone wants is to hear of a loved one's death on a news broadcast."

"I wonder if it has anything to do with Logan being gay?" asked Diane.

"Do we know for sure that he was gay?" asked Gwen. "I guess, based on stereotypes, he might be perceived as gay, but I never heard if he was or wasn't."

The five women looked at each other, and Marlee shrugged. "I hadn't heard that he was, but I assumed so. I guess it's never a good idea to make assumptions, but I did."

At that point in the conversation, Gwen dropped a major bomb. "Well, I don't know if this has anything to do with Logan's death, but I think I might have been the victim of a hate crime last week."

"What?" shouted Marlee, Kathleen, and Diane in unison. Shelly was the only one who didn't seem shocked, but she and Gwen were partners after all, and she had probably heard all the details.

"Well, I'm not sure if it would actually be called a *crime*," Gwen backpedaled, obviously uncomfortable that she might be overstating the incident. "It was anti-gay, though, that's for sure."

"Well, what happened?" asked Marlee impatiently.

"I'm the advisor for the Tae Kwon Do Club, and we were having an early morning practice at the Bentley Center last Wednesday. When I came out of the building, I noticed a note on my car, stuffed under the driver's side windshield wiper. It said 'DIKE'. It wasn't even spelled right."

"Who do you think did it?" Diane queried.

"I have no idea. It could be anybody. Practice started at 6:00 a.m. and was over by seven, so the note was left sometime in that hour," said Gwen.

"Do you still have it?" asked Marlee.

"No, I was mad and threw it away later that morning," Gwen said, her face turning redder by the minute. "I don't know if this is related or not, but somebody keyed my car door last month. I chalked it up to somebody being drunk or just stupid. Do you think it was done by the same person who left the note?"

"I have no idea, but it seems like a strange coincidence that you would have intentional damage to your car and then, a few weeks later, get a note," said Marlee. The thing about coincidences is that they don't happen as often as we like to think."

"What do you mean?" asked Shelly.

"When things happen, it's usually not random. What are the odds that both of those things would happen to the same person in the span of a month?" asked Marlee. Have either of you experienced anything else like this since you moved to Elmwood?

Shelly and Gwen both shook their heads no, but looked at each other knowingly.

"What is it?" asked Marlee.

The couple hesitated and then Gwen said, "We haven't had anything else happen to us directly, but some of our friends have. One thing we know for sure is that Elmwood is not a gay-friendly town."

People in this remote little town are obsessed with conformity and labels. Woe to the person who is different, or doesn't fit the mold of a typical Elmwood citizen. At first, the town seems very friendly. People go out of their way to greet you and offer to help you move into your office. I was given more zucchini, tomatoes, and cucumbers than I could ever eat. Besides the generous offers of moving assistance and the gifts of homegrown produce, the Elmwood residents I met seemed to really care about one another. They were especially welcoming to me—at least, they were at first. What I learned about Elmwood, and about Midwestern State University, is that appearances can be deceptive.

Very deceptive.

Chapter 6

Sean Yellow Tail, a senior MSU student majoring in Criminal Justice and a recent hire at the Elmwood Police Department, looked a bit overwhelmed by the events of the day. Even though he stood six feet and four inches tall, he was not an imposing figure, due primarily to his baby face and the fact that he was about forty pounds underweight for his height. Although he rarely participated in class discussions or asked questions, Marlee knew that he was extremely bright, given the detailed and factually accurate responses he provided to her essay exams.

Sean was an enrolled member of the Rosebud Sioux Tribe although he had never lived a day of his life on an Indian reservation. His mother lived on the Rosebud Reservation as a child but moved to Elmwood in her early twenties and remained there to work at the local Urban Indian Health Clinic and raise her family. Sean had taken four of Marlee's classes in past semesters and was currently in her Criminology class. Since Gwen seemed a bit hesitant about disclosing her suspicions of her possible hate-crime victimizations to police officers, Marlee asked her if she would be willing to speak with Sean, since he was one of her students. Although an officer, Sean appeared less intimidating than the seasoned officers milling about the Caldwell Room conducting interviews. Gwen agreed and Marlee pulled Sean aside. She introduced Sean and Gwen to each other, and let Gwen recount her experiences with the defamatory note and the paint damage to her car. Sean Yellow Tail took copious notes during the interview and asked a series of questions pertaining to a variety of topics.

"Dr. Gerken, do you have any suspicions as to who would leave the note on your car?" asked Sean.

"No, I don't. I've never had anyone here on campus make any comments to my face about being gay. I've never even overheard any jokes or snide remarks," Gwen replied.

"Do you think the note and the scratch on the car door are related?" Sean asked.

"Well, I don't know. I don't have any proof," stammered Gwen, obviously feeling a bit awkward answering these questions. "Do you think they have anything to do with Logan's death?"

Sean looked down at his notes, thinking of what to say in response to Gwen's question. He had been on the job less than six months and had just recently returned from the police academy. Sean was still learning the finer points of interviewing and responding to questions. Raising his head and looking at Gwen with his dark brown eyes camouflaged behind tinted glasses, Sean said "Dr. Gerken, I don't know if there's any connection, but any information we get may be very important. We won't know the full story of Dr. LeCroix's death until we start putting together all bits and pieces. What you told me may have some impact on the case, or it might not. Either way, it appears that you were the victim of harassment, which is a crime in and of itself, so it's good that you made the report."

Gwen nodded and offered up a weak smile, clearly reassured that she did the right thing in reporting the matter to Officer Yellow Tail. "Do you have any other information that might pertain to the Logan LeCroix investigation?" he asked.

Shelly and Gwen again looked at each other, communicating without words. Shelly shrugged and Gwen turned toward Sean. "We have friends here in town who told us about similar notes being left on their cars in the past and some damage done to the front yard of one of their homes. Besides that, this town really isn't gay-friendly. I can get a discount at the Speedy Fitness Center through my employment as an MSU professor. It is for me and my family, but since I'm gay, they won't offer the discount to my partner, Shelly. Just me. I know they offer it to couples who are living together but not married, so it's not like it's just for married people. It seems to be a gay issue with them."

As Gwen continued her interview with Officer Yellow Tail, Diane motioned Marlee over to the side of the room. "Aren't you scared?" Diane asked. "I mean, it could be anybody that killed Logan. It could even be a professor or student who's right here in this room right now!" Diane's voice was getting louder and more intense. Marlee knew Diane was a bit skittish about living alone under the best of circumstances, but given a death on campus, she knew Diane was probably frantic.

"Diane, would you like to stay at my house tonight?" asked Marlee.

The relief showed on Diane's face as she exhaled loudly and said, "Yeah, I would. Can you come over to my place with me so I can grab some things?"

"Sure," said Marlee. They both got their coats from the booth where they'd been sitting and left the room after saying goodbye to Gwen, Shelly, and Sean Yellow Tail.

Marlee drove them to Diane's apartment which was located in the upstairs of an older home. The main floor and the basement were also converted into apartments, both occupied by young families. They walked up the steep staircase to Diane's apartment. It was then that Marlee noticed Diane's hand shake as she fumbled with the keys to open the front door. After unlocking the door and pushing it open, Diane gingerly stepped inside her small, one-bedroom apartment. *She's scared out of her wits*, thought Marlee.

Diane made her way to the kitchen and grabbed her coffee pot, coffee beans, coffee grinder, and an assortment of snack foods. Then she walked into her bedroom, quickly looking from side to side as she made her way toward the closet. With her hand on the closet door knob, Diane waited a few seconds before pulling it open as if she half expected someone to jump out at them. After gathering up her clothes and toiletries, Diane shoved them all into a dark green canvas bag with frayed shoulder straps.

Back in the car, Marlee asked, "Are you okay? You seemed really scared when we were in your place."

"I am. Aren't you? I mean, why Logan? It could have been any one of us killed on campus. I go in late at night all the time to prep for my classes. I'm a night owl, so working late at night is much more productive for me than getting to work at 8:00 a.m. My classes aren't until late afternoon or evening, so it just works better for me to go in late or stay after night classes. What if I'd been on campus that night instead of at Thom Dole's Halloween party? What if whoever killed Logan is going to kill again? What if it's a serial killer?" Diane was upset and working herself into a panic with her wild speculation.

"Diane, we don't know much of anything right now," said Marlee, "but I think the best thing we can all do for our own safety is to go places in groups or at least pairs. I'm going to stay off campus at night as much as possible from now on. We both have night classes, so we'll have to be there late from time to time, but I think working alone in the wee hours is a bad idea for all of us."

"Me too," said Diane, nodding in agreement. "Until whoever did this is found, I'm going to be watching my back!"

Within ten minutes, they arrived at Marlee's house. She had just purchased her home that August and was still getting settled into the terracotta-colored Spanish-style home. Marlee drove into the three-car garage, which was ridiculously large for her small SUV and one bicycle. It had been built in the past few years, but the small two-bedroom house was built in the 1920s. Inside, the arched doorways and rough, orange-peel texturing on the walls added to the Spanish appearance of the home. The carpet had been replaced recently by the previous owners; the flooring in the kitchen, however, was a dated pattern reminiscent of the 1970s. The dark brown kitchen cupboards were also a throwback from a previous era. The house was a mixture of old and new, nostalgia, and comfort. It was not like most homes in Elmwood, and Marlee loved its individuality and personality.

Diane was a frequent visitor at Marlee's place, so she had no trouble settling in and making herself at home. She left her coffee supplies and snacks on the kitchen counter near the sink and made her way toward the cozy living room. The overstuffed blue couch, love seat, chair, and ottoman were crammed into the space. The loveseat and big chair faced the television, while the couch was centered in front of the fireplace. Marlee loved the idea of a fireplace but was scared of having the fire overtake her home. She wasn't very handy and could easily envision the fire department responding to her 911 call when the fire jumped from the fireplace to the living room rug and spread to the furniture and walls. When Marlee had first toured the house, her realtor had suggested placing candles in the fireplace to give off a soft glow of light without the danger of a burning fire. Diane, on the other hand, was mesmerized by fire and was always encouraging Marlee to "make fire." So far, she had been able to beg off on building a fire for Diane, citing that the chimney had not been cleaned as her excuse.

Diane threw her tote bag on the floor and plopped down on the couch with a loud sigh. "Thanks for letting me stay here tonight. Hope you don't mind me camping out on the couch."

"Not at all," said Marlee. "I'm glad for the company." This was true. Although she wasn't scared like Diane, it would be nice to have someone around to talk with about the horrific events of the past eight hours. It was only 3:00 p.m., but it seemed as if days had passed since she had arrived on campus that morning. Marlee collapsed on the loveseat, propped a pillow behind her back and covered her arms with a multi-colored crocheted blanket made by her mother. The chilly weather and the death of their colleague left Marlee feeling cold and vulnerable. She was scheduled to teach Criminology at 6:00 p.m. that night but had canceled the class due to Logan's death and her own overwhelming feelings of sadness and upset.

"I can't believe any of this is really happening," said Diane.

"I know. It's all so surreal. I feel like I'm watching someone else's life on TV," Marlee replied. "When is the last time you saw Logan or talked to him?"

Diane thought for a minute and said, "I'd catch a glimpse of him all the time when I'd walk by his office or pass him in the hall, but the last real discussion I had with him was at your house-warming party. When was that, anyway?"

"I closed on my house in August and had the party at the beginning of October. I wanted to wait until I had all the rooms painted, and that took some time to get finished," said Marlee. She reflected back to the night of the party. She invited several of her colleagues from work as well as some of her non-academic friends. Since Logan's office was near Marlee's, and because he was new to the area, she invited him too. She thought it would be a good way to become better acquainted with him and for him to meet more people from campus and the Elmwood community. Marlee had been a newcomer in a few towns and always appreciated it when someone extended an invitation to include her. She assumed Logan might feel the same. He seemed genuinely flattered when Marlee had asked him to her party. She provided the directions and address and assured him he did not need to bring anything. The day before her party, Marlee left her office briefly, leaving the door ajar, and when she returned, a white box with a blue bow on top was sitting near her computer. She quickly opened it - she loved surprises. Inside was a hazelnut-scented candle, a sunflower candle holder, and a small journal. Accompanying the gift was a card from Logan which read, "Congratulations on your new house! I'm planning on attending your party tomorrow but might be a bit late. Best, Logan."

Marlee jumped up from the loveseat and marched over to the glass-fronted bookcase in the corner. From atop she grabbed a brown hazelnut-scented candle sitting on a sunflower candle holder. She showed it to Diane, and they agreed that lighting it would be a nice way to remember and honor Logan while they were processing the day's events. The soft hazelnut scent soon filled the home as Marlee and Diane reflected on their brief memories of Logan and the harsh realization that he was no longer alive.

DAY OF THE DEAD

So many rumors and so few facts are being discussed about my life and my death. Why didn't it occur to anybody to ask anything other than superficial questions about my background? Apparently anyone can waltz into this town and start teaching at MSU without much questioning.

Makes you wonder what secrets others in this town are keeping.

Chapter 7

Marlee woke up to another day of cloudy skies and a steady drizzle of rain. It was a typical November day in Elmwood. Sunshine was a scarcity in the upper Midwest during November, and Elmwood was no exception. So many people were impacted by Seasonal Affective Disorder that the local hardware store sold out of the light-therapy lamps by late October. Anyone selling anti-depressants and light-therapy lamps could make a lot of money in this town.

The weather wasn't the only thing sending Marlee into a downcast mood. As soon as she arose, she dashed to her front door to grab the newspaper from the mail slot. Of course the death of Logan LeCroix was front page news, but there was no additional information about the cause of death or any possible suspects. No details were disclosed about the gun reportedly found at the scene. The chief of police was quoted as saying that the matter was under investigation, and the manner of death was deemed "suspicious."

Marlee slammed the newspaper down on the coffee table, accidentally waking Diane who was sleeping on the couch. She groggily looked up at Marlee with a quizzical look. Slowly, it dawned on Diane where she was and why she was there. Glancing at the newspaper, she asked, "Is there anything new in the paper about Logan?"

"Nothing. Absolutely nothing! It's everything we already knew from the campus meeting and the TV reports last night. The police aren't saying anything other than it's suspicious. Really?" asked Marlee sarcastically. "The chief thinks it's suspicious. That guy's a real think tank," she said disgustedly.

"Coffee. I need coffee NOW!" said Diane, slowly propping herself up from the couch. She was wearing an oversized white Betty Boop t-shirt with a hole in the armpit and a pair of pink long-john bottoms.

"Wow, you're really styling," teased Marlee.

Diane glared at her and said, "Well, we all can't be the height of fashion like you. How long have you had that Guns n' Roses t-shirt you slept in? Or is that what you're wearing to campus today?"

"Ha ha. You're a laugh riot," said Marlee as she glanced at her black concert t-shirt and plaid flannel pajama bottoms. "Let's get some coffee and try to wake up. I think this is going to be a really long day." Diane nodded in agreement.

After several cups of coffee and showers, Marlee and Diane settled in at the oversized kitchen table Marlee used as her work desk. It was littered with books, quizzes, lecture notes and project papers, grading, several days' mail, and other assorted paper items. Beneath the clutter was a cat-hair-covered green table cloth. Marlee's grey Persian, Pippa, was mysteriously absent during the previous evening, but now she sat in a snow-boot box lined with a fuzzy black and white blanket. The snow-boot box sat on the corner of the table, well out of Diane's reach. Pippa only allowed Marlee to touch her and became downright nasty when anyone else tried to pet her or, god forbid, pick her up. Pippa appeared to be asleep, but Marlee could tell she was keeping a close eye on Diane in case she tried to sneak in a pet of her fluffy grey fur.

"What happened to the shoe box she used to sit in?" asked Diane, nodding toward the new box which had contained snow boots.

"She moved up a size," retorted Marlee with a grin. They both laughed and agreed that, over time, most gals need to move up to the next size. Marlee felt guilty because her low carb diet had been on and off since the weekend, and she needed to regain control. After arriving home the night before, Marlee and Diane tried to calm their nerves with a few bottles of wine and Halloween candy. At the time, the alcohol/sugar plan seemed to work. Now, Marlee felt hung over and bloated. Her size fourteen dress pants were feeling very snug around the waist, which is where she tended to gain most of her weight.

Since neither Marlee nor Diane had to be on campus until ten o'clock that morning, they had some time to waste. It wasn't even 7:00 a.m., and they didn't think anyone with any new information would be on campus yet. Over their fourth cup of coffee, they continued talking about Logan and the possible explanations for his death. "Anybody could've killed him," said Diane softly.

"What if it was one of us?" asked Marlee.

"You or me?" shrieked Diane, now clearly alarmed.

"No, not you or me. One of the other professors on campus. Maybe there was some type of rivalry between Logan and another professor. Maybe he got on somebody's bad side on campus," said Marlee.

"We're dealing with professors," Diane said. "We're all on somebody's bad side, on and off campus."

She has a point, thought Marlee. Professors were notorious prima donnas who believed they were the center of the universe, and that everyone else was merely a supporting player in their show. Nearly everyone on campus was disliked or distrusted by at least one other person. Competition and professional rivalry held supreme at MSU, just like at other universities all over the world. Professors and administrators were known to fight tooth and nail over complex issues like changes to the curriculum, and minor items, such as who was entitled to a new computer printer. The competition and fighting in academia were so high because most of the stakes were so low. Couple that with a campus full of over-inflated egos, and you had a recipe for conflict at nearly every turn.

Diane rode with Marlee to campus since she had left her car there the day before. They arrived in the Scobey Hall parking lot just before 8:00 a.m. and hurried to their respective offices. "Okay, so if you find out anything, call me, and I'll do the same," said Marlee, rushing toward the east wing on third floor of Scobey.

"Deal," said Diane as she scurried down the other third-floor wing.

Marlee rushed toward her office and as she rounded the corner, she realized she would be walking by Logan's office. It took her breath away as she passed the office where Logan once worked, and where Marlee would often stop just to greet him and ask about his adjustment to MSU and Elmwood. This still didn't seem real. Yellow crime scene tape crisscrossed the closed office door.

After dropping off her book bag and coat in her office, Marlee made a beeline for the department secretary's office. Everyone knows that if you want information you go to the secretaries. Plus, it was the usual gathering point for faculty. Not only did the small room house the department secretary, but the dean's office was connected. Mean Dean Green would be the best source of information, but who knew how much he would disclose. Louise, the attention-starved secretary, would be better. Not only did she have big ears and a nose for news, she was also well connected with all of the other secretaries on the MSU campus. The main problem Marlee had with Louise was that she tended to be very selective in who she revealed her information to. Normally that wouldn't be a problem, but Marlee was not one of Louise's favorites. Louise was in her early 60s and tended to have a very traditional view of women's roles. She fawned over the male faculty members, doing everything from making their copies at the drop of a hat to baking their favorite treats. The female profs received no such special attention. It was as if Louise felt they should be home making babies and supporting their husbands' careers. Louise seemed particularly put off by the unmarried female faculty in the department, of which there were several. Marlee realized her best approach to finding out additional information about Logan's death was to overhear Louise's conversations with others in the department, although it would be tough to eavesdrop in such a small office and not be noticed.

When Marlee reached Louise's office, she was relieved to see two faculty members, the dean and the janitor crowded around Louise's desk and bookcases. A somber mood hung over the room even though several people were rapidly talking at the same time. Dean Green's voice boomed over the others, causing them to become silent.

"We can't locate a next of kin," said Dean Green. "We still don't know much of anything about Logan."

"Doesn't the personnel office have some records on him?" asked Marlee. "When I started here a couple years ago, I had to fill out all kinds of paperwork that asked for emergency contact numbers and beneficiaries."

"That was the first place we looked," gruffed Dean Green. "For some reason, that information was never collected. He left those parts of the forms blank."

"I didn't realize we had an option not to list emergency contacts," said Marlee. She wasn't going to let the dean's brusque manner shut down her questions.

"The personnel office might have let him leave those parts blank with the idea that he would come back and fill them in. Sometimes people need a bit of time to decide who will be their contact person or who will receive their benefits if they die," offered Louise. Based on her answer, it was clear she had already been in contact with someone from the personnel office. Whether it was in an official capacity or for gossip was unclear.

"So what do we actually know about Logan?" asked Alexander Sherkov, the Professor of Russian.

Dean Green gave Alexander a long stare as if to decide what he would say. Finally, he opened his mouth and said, "We know he was living in California and he was teaching at a small community college there before he was hired here. After he was hired, I asked him if he had family moving to Elmwood with him, and he said he didn't. He has a Ph.D. in French from UCLA, and his educational credentials all checked out."

Alice Olson had just entered the room and said, "He had relatives in South Dakota."

All heads spun around to face Alice. Her eyes were still red from crying, and she looked just as distraught as she had at the campus meeting yesterday.

"Why are you just telling us this now?" barked the dean. "Jesus, Alice! You know we've been trying to track down any relatives of his!"

"I just remembered it this morning. We were talking about his adjustment to South Dakota, and Logan said he'd been here before. He told me that he had spent some summers with relatives on an Indian reservation when he was a kid," replied Alice.

"Did he say which reservation, or what their names were?" asked Marlee.

"No, I don't think he said anything else about it," said Alice.

"Who knows if those relatives still live in the same area or are even still alive? If Logan was a kid when he stayed with them, it would've been thirty to forty years ago. A lot can happen in that amount of time," said Alexander.

"If he does have any relatives in the state, I hope they hear about his death on the news and contact us," said Dean Green. Marlee, Louise, Alexander, and Alice all nodded in agreement. This was the first solid bit of information MSU had on tracking down Logan's relatives. Cecil, the janitor, stood in the room taking in all the information. He was the person who had originally found Logan's body and seemed to still be in a state of shock. At fifty six years of age, Cecil was the type of person who could go unnoticed in any crowd. His height, weight, hair color, and facial features were all nondescript. The best characterization of Cecil's appearance was *average*.

"What did you see when you found him, Cecil?" asked Alexander.

Cecil glanced nervously about the room, obviously self-conscious about speaking in front of so many people. "Well...," Cecil hesitated. "I saw him on the sidewalk on his back. There was a bunch of blood all around his head. When I saw Logan like that, I ran to Thom Dole's office to see what I should do."

"Did you see a gun?" asked Marlee.

"No, but I didn't stand there very long. As soon as I saw Logan, I rushed in to tell Thom," said Cecil.

A commotion in the hallway drew Marlee's attention away from Cecil. Two students majoring in Criminal Justice were making their way toward Louise's office.

They were discussing Logan's death and talking over one another. Jasper Evans and Dominick Schmidt were two lively students who kept Marlee on her toes and the class discussions interesting. Their questions and comments, while quite lively, were also fairly deep when compared to other students their age. The two were sophomores, and both hailed from small nearby towns. Even though they both gave off the air of being farm kids, they had a sophistication that only watching hours upon hours of crime shows can provide.

Dominick stood six feet and two inches and had a thin frame. He had short dark hair and a permanent half smile, as if a running monologue in his head kept him amused. Dom had a quick wit and was frequently cracking up other students before and after class. He rarely spoke during class discussions, not because he didn't understand the topic, but because he preferred to communicate in small groups.

Jasper was also quite tall, measuring six feet and three inches, but he had a stocky build and a mass of wavy blond hair. His hair was shoulder length when he took his first class with Marlee, but when he arrived on campus this fall he had a shorter style, although it was still out of control due to curls gone wild. While Dom was quieter in large groups, Jasper was an extrovert to the extreme. He loved asking questions, making comments and was a notorious practical joker. More than once Marlee had arrived in her classroom ready to lecture, and Jasper would tell her that campus was being closed on Friday for repairs. Dom would nod solemnly, and other students would follow suit. He typically pulled this stunt when the following Monday was a holiday, thus trying to score a four-day weekend for himself and others. "Really, you're not going to cancel class?" Jasper would ask. "Well, all my other professors called off class." This was a phrase commonly used by students to encourage faculty to cancel their classes. It was the equivalent of going to Mom and saying, "but Dad said I could." It didn't work on Marlee, but she knew several professors who would gladly turn a blind eye for the chance to cancel class. Although she couldn't admit it publicly, Dom and Jasper were two of her favorite students. *Their wits and personalities will get them far in life*, she often thought.

"Hey, Dr. McCabe," shouted Jasper. "We've been looking all over for you." They crowded into Louise's already cramped office. "Can we talk to you for a minute?" he asked, motioning toward the door with his eyes.

"Sure, let's go to my office," said Marlee. She didn't want to miss out on the discussion going on in Louise's office, but knew she could stop by Alexander's office later for a recap of what she missed.

The three wound through the maze that was Scobey Hall until they reached Marlee's office. She'd left the door ajar, knowing she would be back shortly. Her computer was off, and none of the answer keys or papers was in view of prying eyes, so she didn't have to move anything for fear the students would see it. Marlee's office was decorated with mementos from two trips abroad: behind her desk hung a large scarf featuring the Eiffel Tower and on the wall above two file cabinets hung a dishtowel featuring some of the castles of Ireland. The three bookcases housed an array of books on crime, criminal theory, and criminal procedure.

"So, what's up?" asked Marlee, after she motioned them to sit in the rickety wooden chairs which she had inherited with the office two years ago.

"Dr. McCabe, we've been hearing a lot of things around campus about... you know, the death," said Jasper. Although Jasper and Dom were big guys, she had to realize they were only twenty years old and, really, just scared kids. Hell, she felt like a scared kid herself since Logan's death.

"Like what?" asked Marlee.

"Well, I talked to Donnie Stacks. You know her, the kid with the bright red hair who sits in the front in Policing class and asks lots of questions." Marlee nodded, and Dom continued. "She knows somebody from the police department, and Donnie was told that Logan was shot in the head and the gun was found buried in a dumpster over fifty feet away." Dom looked at the floor, nervous and uncomfortable with the information he had just passed on. "So, it can't be a suicide if the gun wasn't even near the body," he said.

"Do you think it's a mob hit?" Jasper asked.

"I don't know about that," Marlee cautiously replied. She had to be very careful with her words to make sure she wasn't inadvertently starting a rumor. She might say one thing but the students might hear another and pass that along, attributing the misinformation to her. "Anything is possible at this point, I guess. Did Donnie know if there were fingerprints on the gun? Did the police trace the gun? Did she know if there were any suspects in custody?" The questions were flying through Marlee's head and spilling out of her mouth with the same speed.

"She didn't say anything else other than what I just told you," said Dom.

"Who's her source in the PD?" Marlee questioned. She really didn't know Donnie all that well, but it wouldn't be beyond the scope of imagination that a student could make up information as a way of feeling self-important.

"She didn't say, but it might be Sylvester Blake. I know they are friends and study together sometimes," said Dom. Sylvester Blake was a fourteen year veteran of the Elmwood Police Department. He didn't have his degree yet and was working toward it by taking one or two classes a semester. A college degree was not a requirement for employment as a police officer in South Dakota, but a degree would be beneficial for anyone applying for promotion in the police department.

Marlee's sense of Sylvester was that he liked to act like a big shot. In Marlee's classes, he frequently tried to demonstrate how much he knew on a topic. Some of the younger students seemed impressed by Sylvester's stories of life on the police force, but most saw him for the blowhard he really was. Marlee didn't mention her thoughts about Sylvester to Dom or Jasper—it just wasn't cool to gossip about one student with others.

"Have you heard anything else?" asked Marlee. Although she didn't give much credence to information attributed to Sylvester Blake, the details about the gun and the gunshot wound were the only ones that had any ties to the police department.

"Yeah," said Jasper. "We've been hearing that Dr. LeCroix was in the Witness Protection Program and he was killed because he knew too much about something that happened back in California."

"Where did you hear that?" Marlee asked. Anytime someone had a mysterious background, students tended to bring up the Witness Protection Program since it was featured on so many TV shows and movies. The reality was that very few people were in this relocation program, designed for people who had or would be providing information for the prosecution of dangerous individuals and groups, such as the mob or large-scale drug traffickers. The Witness Protection Program was administered by the U.S. Marshals Service and was top secret. Although it was unlikely a professor would be moved to Elmwood, South Dakota, to teach at MSU, it was not altogether impossible.

"I've heard it from a few different students," said Jasper.

"Me too," said Dom. "Donnie Stacks didn't say anything about it, but lots of other students are saying that's why he was killed."

"We were wondering what you thought," said Jasper. "I remember you talking in one of your classes last semester about murder and the reasons people do it. We thought maybe you might have some inside information about the case."

"I don't have any inside information from official sources," said Marlee, "but we know the main motives for murder are love, hate, money, and revenge. Based on those possible motives, who do you think could've killed Logan?"

"A boyfriend," said Jasper. "Or a girlfriend," he quickly added, not wanting to stereotype Logan as gay.

"Sure," said Marlee. "It could be a past or present love interest or someone who was attracted to Logan but he wasn't interested in them."

"Like unrequited love?" asked Dom, which earned him a laugh and an elbow in the ribs from Jasper.

"Yeah. It could be someone who was obsessed with Logan or maybe even stalking him," said Marlee. "Logan could have been totally unaware of it. It may have been going on for years."

"It might be somebody from Elmwood, or it could be someone he knew before he moved here," posited Jasper.

"Yep, that's right," said Marlee. "So how about the other motives? Who else might have a reason to kill Logan?"

"If he had any money, the person who would inherit it could be a suspect," offered Jasper. "We know he's not married, but does he have any kids?"

"I think the personnel office and the police department are still trying to track down any next of kin Logan had," said Marlee. "Anyone with a financial motive to kill Logan would be a suspect. He could have been the victim of a robbery too. Who else might want him dead?"

"Hmmm, I never knew him," said Dom "but it sounds like he was a nice guy. But maybe somebody hated him for some reason other than unrequited love or because he testified against them."

"I heard he was gay," said Jasper. "I don't know if it's true or not, but that might be a reason somebody would want him dead."

"Sad, but true," said Marlee. She knew that all too often people were targeted because of their race, religion or sexuality. Her doctoral dissertation and subsequent research dealt with hate crimes and hate groups. "Just last week I was reading about a young couple who was targeted because they were gay. They left a known gay bar in Omaha and were beaten with bats and tire irons by a group of guys as they were getting into their car. One was in intensive care, and the other had a lot of bruises and a broken leg. It's just senseless," she said shaking her head in disgust. The two students nodded in agreement.

"Is there anyone else that might hate Logan?" asked Dom.

"A student or another professor," volunteered Jasper.

"Or a neighbor, or someone he had business dealings with," said Marlee. "Of course, it could've been an accident." Both students stared at her, realizing this was an explanation they had overlooked. Anticipating their questions in advance, Marlee said, "Somebody could've been on campus just playing around with a gun, and it went off, or that person fired it on purpose. There was no intent for anyone to get hurt, but after realizing someone was hit, the shooter threw the gun in the dumpster and ran off. I suppose it could've been a case of mistaken identity. The killer mistook Dr. LeCroix for the intended victim."

"He may have been the victim just because the shooter thought he had money or something of value on him," said Dom. "He wouldn't have been singled out because he was gay or a snitch or anything else...just that he might have money. Or it could have been a thrill kill like we talked about in Intro to Criminal Justice last semester. Somebody kills another person for no other reason than they just wanted to kill."

"All are possible explanations. When I used to work as a probation officer, we had a saying: *anything is possible, but very few things are probable*," said Marlee. "In other words, the most obvious explanation is usually the correct one." After Marlee earned her Master's Degree at South Dakota State University, she worked for a few years as a probation officer, first with the state of South Dakota and then later with the federal government. While working with the feds in Elmwood, she worked on her doctorate degree in Criminology at South Dakota State University. Through hard work, determination, and a little luck of the Irish, she was able to get through the program in about five years while working full time as a probation officer. Some of her counseling classes were taken at MSU, but she had to travel over two hours away to Brookings to take most of her classes since that was the degree-granting institution. Marlee liked to bring personal stories and case examples into her classes. It helped to liven up the class discussions and also showed students the practical side, as opposed to just the theoretical side, of Criminology. She still used some of her contacts in various state and federal agencies to obtain internships and jobs for her students as well as to bring professionals into her classrooms as speakers.

"Dr. M, you knew him, didn't you?" asked Jasper.

"I knew him but not very well. His office was near mine, so I'd say hi to him almost every day, and sometimes we would chat for a few minutes, but I can't say I knew a whole lot about him. He did come to a party I had about a month ago," said Marlee.

"A party!" exclaimed Jasper and Dom in unison, looking at each other in horror. Their faces revealed that they couldn't even fathom a professor having a party, let alone inviting other professors to it.

"Yes," said Marlee, feeling a bit uncomfortable. On one hand she did not want to give students too much information about her personal life, but on the other hand she really wanted to dispel the notion that professors were alien beings who spent all waking hours grading papers and reading academic journals. On several occasions when meeting with students, Marlee had wanted to yell out, "Hey, twenty years ago I *was* you!" but she wisely refrained from doing so. She had hated being told "You'll see someday," by old fogies when she was in her college years.

"I had a little housewarming party about a month after moving to my place. Since Logan was new to campus, I invited him. He came to the party for a little bit, had a glass of wine and left," Marlee recalled. "He talked with some people he already knew from campus and met some of my other friends from campus and others who work elsewhere in town."

Again, Dom and Jasper looked at each other, mouths agape. They just couldn't picture professors in any type of social setting.

"Um, we have class in a few minutes," said Jasper, relieved to end the discussion of professors and parties. Marlee didn't have any classes that day, just office hours which she used to meet with students and catch up on her grading and class prep.

"No problem. I'll make a deal with you guys. You let me know what you're hearing about this case, and I'll do the same," said Marlee.

Both students grinned, excited to possibly have some inside scoop on Logan LeCroix's death. Marlee suspected she wouldn't be privy to any information that wasn't open to the public, but Dom and Jasper didn't know that. She wanted to keep her finger on the collective student pulse, not so much for leads on the case, but to make sure the students were effectively dealing with the campus death. As much as she tried not to, Marlee sometimes saw herself in the parental role. After all, they were just kids, and for many freshmen, college was the first time they had been away from home.

"Sure!" Jasper said with enthusiasm, and Dom nodded in agreement. They both rose from their chairs, picking up their backpacks.

While walking out the door, both Dom and Jasper said their goodbyes and promised to let Marlee know if they heard anything new going around campus. She walked them to the doorway and waved goodbye. She glanced down the hall to see if any other students were milling around waiting to talk to her. No one was in the hallway, so Marlee ventured back to Louise's office to see if there were any new developments or theories being floated about. When she walked into Louise's office, she noticed the dean's office door was shut. Muffled voices, the dean's and someone else's, were coming from behind the door. Louise was not in her office, and none of the other faculty or staff members were still there. Marlee strained to hear what was being said in the dean's office, but she couldn't make out any of the words.

Dejected, Marlee made her way back to her office. On the way, she stopped to look out the small hallway window. The day was still dreary, and the sun would probably not be making an appearance that day. What caught Marlee's eye was the tripod and camera set up on the sidewalk right outside of Scobey Hall. She shifted her gaze to the left and saw a reporter with a microphone ushering Professor Bob Ashman over to the camera. Professor Ashman had been teaching in the History Department for over 25 years. He stood five foot nothing and always wore some type of hat. Today, he sported an Indiana Jones fedora. Due to his love of hats and because he was a known blowhard by the other faculty and most of the upper level students, his surname had morphed into "Asshat."

Asshat was known for spouting off his ideas on every topic. He believed that having a Ph.D. in one subject made him an authority in all subjects. There was no subject in which he did not consider himself an expert. Asshat loved the limelight and would force his way into most community and campus discussions, regardless of the topic. He also wrote a column for the local newspaper, operated three blogs, and would give a TV or newspaper interview at the drop of a hat. For a while he had a column in the local newspaper, called *Ask Dr. Ashman*. It originally dealt with history of the area but soon delved into every topic under the sun. The column was discontinued after several readers called bullshit on Asshat's qualifications to provide information on global warming, the death penalty, and various other topics not related to history. It didn't surprise Marlee that Asshat was ready to jump in front of the camera and give his two cents on Logan's death. She cringed at what he might say. Marlee would have to tune into a local news station tonight to find out what gem Asshat had provided to the media.

Making her way back to her office, Marlee saw two men lurking outside her door. If they were reporters, she would have to shoo them away. She didn't trust the press. It seemed to her that, once words left your mouth, anything could be done with them. When working as a probation officer, Marlee saw a few court professionals get themselves in hot water by making public statements. Her personal view was to keep her mouth shut and let the MSU administration take charge in making comments. Plus, Marlee was not at all comfortable with the spotlight.

When she reached the doorway, Marlee saw that these were not reporters but police officers. The two men identified themselves as Detective Mike Krause and Detective Ted Lumar. Both men were in their mid-thirties and of average height. They were dressed in khakis with cell phones attached to their belts. Krause was a bit on the paunchy side and stretched the limits of his burgundy polo shirt. Lumar, wearing a navy button down shirt, had an athletic build and carried himself like a former sports hero. Marlee invited the detectives into her office and motioned for them to sit in the chairs that had been occupied by students not ten minutes ago.

"So, how well did you know Logan LeCroix?" asked Krause after they went through all of the background questions on Marlee's name, date of birth, social security number, address, length of employment at MSU, and a variety of other questions. Marlee repeated the story of her brief encounters with Logan on campus and his attendance at her housewarming party. She also attempted to solicit information from the detectives. They were friendly but either could not or would not provide any new details on the case.

After finishing the interview, they asked Marlee how they could locate some of the other professors in the building. She went to the department website and looked up their office numbers, phone numbers, and office hours. "You could also check their personal websites if they have them," suggested Marlee.

"Do you have a personal webpage?" asked Krause. When Marlee nodded, Krause asked if they could look at it. Sitting before her office computer, Marlee quickly clicked on the links to get to her own personal webpage. She moved from her chair and let Krause sit there and scroll through. Marlee's webpage featured a couple photos of her, the list of classes she was teaching, her office hours and contact information, as well as a listing of her previous jobs.

"Who else has a webpage linked to the MSU website?" asked Lumar.

"I'm not sure who has one. They aren't required. I just did it to give students a bit more information about me and the classes I teach," said Marlee. "If you go to the employee directory and click on names that might tell you if the prof has a personal webpage."

"Do you know if Logan LeCroix had his own webpage?" Krause inquired.

"I don't know," said Marlee, upset with herself for not checking this out on her own.

Before leaving, the detectives handed Marlee their business cards and asked that she contact them if she had any additional information on Logan's death. *I might and I might not*, Marlee thought to herself. Like her Grandma Genie always used to say, "You don't have to tell everything you know."

Like the press, Marlee didn't always trust police officers either.

Everyone's an expert. Or so they think. Teaching is a profession that values fact and empirical research, but many of the MSU professors bought into rumors and speculation just like the rest of the Elmwood community. Some saw my death as a way to garner attention for themselves.

Usually, the people saying the least know the most.

Chapter 8

Marlee spent the remainder of the morning in her office. Several students and professors dropped by to see if she had any news on Logan's death. She also stopped by the offices of other profs and went into the secretary's office numerous times trying to pick up new information. All of these discussions were fruitless, just speculation and innuendo, no real facts.

Around noon, a newspaper reporter was walking the halls of Scobey and stopped next door at Celeste Rodell's office. Celeste was a new hire in the Speech Department. Celeste hailed from Nevada, but she had a fake British affect, much like the Travelocity Roaming Gnome from the television commercials. If Asshat was the King of Bullshit, Celeste was most certainly his Queen. Standing five feet and five inches, Celeste had a sturdy, almost mannish build. Her dowdy look was complimented by high-waisted jeans, a tan pullover shirt tucked into the jeans, white socks, and black shoes. Celeste dressed like a frump most days but had a beautiful face and gorgeous shoulder length black hair. Playing the role of newcomer to the area, she continually asked, "Is this the way you people do things here?" You people! As if Elmwood were an alien universe!

Celeste got under Marlee's skin from Day One. Now, unfortunately, Marlee and Celeste shared a wall in the east wing of Scobey Hall. Celeste was ignored by some of the students, but she had a couple of groupies who frequented her office daily. Basking in the attention, Celeste held court from her office chair while one or more students sat on the area rug on the floor. She was a master at projecting her voice, so Marlee could hear every word spoken to the students. She suspected this was no accident. Although she had only been at MSU since the previous year, Celeste did not let her opinions, observations, and her version of facts go unspoken.

The reporter, a man in his mid-twenties with crooked teeth and a boyish grin, glanced inside Marlee's office. She pretended not to notice him and kept a scowl on her face as she aggressively typed, her eyes focused on the computer screen. Marlee was so busy trying to look busy that the keyboard actually jumped a couple of times as she typed. The reporter, taking the hint, moved to Celeste's office next door.

"Excuse me. I'm Russell Berg with the Elmwood Examiner. Can I talk to you a minute?" he asked, poking his head into Celeste's door.

"Of course, come in. I'm Dr. Celeste Rodell. You can call me Dr. Rodell," she said with her British affect. She motioned him to an overstuffed arm chair she had brought from her home over the summer. She usually kept it piled with books and papers to keep students from sitting in it. Marlee knew it was her nap spot. During afternoon office hours, Celeste frequently shut her door and put a note up indicating that she was at a meeting. She would turn her music on and take a cat nap for an hour or so. Sensing that this interview was an opportunity not only to pontificate on Logan's death, but also to get her name in the newspaper, Celeste quickly moved the pile of clutter from the chair to her desk.

Russell took the chair Celeste offered him. "I would like to ask you a few questions about Logan LeCroix. I see his office is right across the hall from yours. How well did you know him?"

"Well," breathed Celeste, "I knew him better than anyone else on campus. Our offices are very near each other, you see. I teach some classes at night, and he was around Scobey Hall most evenings, so we spent time sharing ideas. We planned to collaborate on a research paper and also team teach a class." Celeste sat even straighter in her chair, thrilled to share her association with Logan.

"What were the two of you planning to research and teach?" asked Russell.

Celeste was a bit flustered. She had overstated her connection to Logan, and Russell busted her on it. Most students thought she knew what she was talking about and rarely questioned her. They took at face value the information Celeste provided them, inside and outside the classroom. "Because we were both so busy, we really hadn't worked out the specifics yet," Celeste stated.

Russell let it slide and moved along in his questioning. "What else did you talk about besides your academic disciplines?"

"We spent many nights discussing religion and our views on it," said Celeste. "Logan had views very similar to mine. He did not buy into most of the conventional religions."

"What is your religion, or your belief system?" asked Russell.

"My beliefs are most closely related to paganism," Celeste stated proudly. Russell raised his eyebrows, questioning what paganism entailed. Not waiting for Russell to ask further questions about it, Celeste launched into a detailed explanation of paganism which lasted for 15 minutes.

"So, basically, it's a worship and celebration of nature?" asked Russell. He had just summarized her monologue on paganism to one statement, and Celeste was clearly not appreciative of his efforts.

"I guess you could say that, if you were trying to boil it down to its most reductive form," sniffed Celeste.

"Did Logan tell you he was a pagan?" asked Russell.

Celeste hesitated. She was busted again for overstating facts. "No, I don't think he ever really said he was outright, but based on some of his comments, I deduced that he followed the pagan traditions."

"Like what?" questioned Russell. This guy was good. He had a well-tuned BS detector.

"Um, I guess I can't recall anything specific at the moment," Celeste stalled. "This has all been such a terrible shock. I just can't believe he's dead." Celeste picked up a tissue, dabbing at the corner of her eye. She was pulling out all the stops to make sure the reporter did not find out how little she actually knew about Logan.

"One last question," said Russell. "Do you have any idea as to who might have killed Logan?"

"No, I don't," said Celeste "but I think it must be somebody from outside the Elmwood community."

"Why do you say that," asked Russell, his curiosity piqued.

"Just a hunch," said Celeste as she stood up and motioned Russell Berg toward the door.

Marlee sat in her office next door, listening to the exchange between Russell Berg and Celeste's attempts at coming off as an expert on Logan and also as his best friend, a ruse that was foiled by Russell's follow-up questions. When Celeste couldn't provide adequate detail, he realized that she was just trying to make herself sound important. Marlee rolled her eyes at Celeste's comments and smiled when Russell asked for substance to her claims.

What was she thinking, talking to a reporter? Marlee thought. *Surely no good could come out of this...* After making a few phone calls and checking in with Diane for updates, Marlee walked down to the secretary's office for the umpteenth time that morning. Passing by Asshat's office, she saw him making wild gestures and talking to Russell Berg, the reporter. She had to hand it to him. Russell sure seemed to have a knack for knowing which profs would openly talk to him on the record. Asshat let out a loud, evil snicker, but Marlee didn't hear any laughter coming from Russell. Nobody seemed to get as big of a kick out of Asshat as he himself did. Leave it to Asshat to find something funny about a death on campus, thought Marlee with a touch of bitterness.

Alice was sitting in Louise's chair when Marlee arrived in the secretary's office. She looked up when Marlee entered and gave her a weak smile, her eyes just as red from crying as they had been the previous day. "Hi, Marlee," she said. "Have you heard anything new about Logan's death?" That seemed to be the new opening line everyone uttered upon seeing anyone.

"No, I really haven't heard much else since I saw you earlier this morning. A couple of detectives stopped by, and I talked to them. Then a newspaper reporter was milling around, and both Celeste and Asshat talked to him," Marlee recounted. "How about you?"

"I talked to the Bernhart Funeral Home, and they said I could come in and see Logan one last time," Alice said, her voice quavering and tears forming in her eyes.

Marlee stood with her mouth wide open and her eyes bulging from her skull. "Do you really want to see him looking like that?" she asked, envisioning him covered in blood and riddled with bullet holes.

"They said they will have him cleaned up after the medical examiner releases the body later today. They have to complete the autopsy, and then the funeral home can pick him up and prepare him for burial," said Alice. "If that's what the family wants," she quickly added.

"Still no word on the family?" Marlee asked.

Alice shook her head. "Do you want to go with me to see Logan this afternoon?" she asked, anxious for Marlee to accept the invitation.

"I'm sorry, Alice, but I just don't think I can do it," said Marlee. Although she had worked for years dealing with people who committed heinous crimes, she didn't have much of a stomach for the blood and guts associated with the crimes. She had a hard time going to funerals and wakes, especially if the body was on view. "I'm surprised you'd be able to handle it."

"I know. At first I didn't think I'd be able to either, but I feel like I need to be there for him. Logan needs to know someone cares for him," said Alice.

Marlee felt guilty, but she knew deep down that she would not be able to handle seeing Logan dead. "You're a good person. I wish I had the strength to do it," Marlee said. Alice looked at her and shrugged, as if she really had no other option than to visit Logan.

"Why are you watching the office for Louise? Who's watching your office?" asked Marlee.

"Louise had to run to the campus post office to get the morning mail and her work-study student had to leave early. My work-study student, Jeremy, is watching my office, so I told Louise I would hold down the fort until she made it back. There have been a lot of people and phone calls in here today about Logan and the Dean doesn't want anyone to find an empty secretary's office," Alice replied.

On one hand, it was wise to have someone to field any questions that might arise, even if no new information was available. On the other hand, the dean was likely trying to make sure everyone in the College of Arts and Sciences was hard at work. With all the media attention, an empty secretary's office might reflect poorly on him.

Marlee, as well as many other professors, students, and staff, continued to circulate around campus the remainder of the day in an effort to garner new information about Logan's death. At 2:00 p.m., an email from the dean was sent to the faculty and staff of the College of Arts and Sciences. He called a mandatory meeting for that day at 4:00 p.m. in the Putnam Building. This piqued Marlee's curiosity, making her wonder what he had to report, and why it was just for their college and not the whole university. In two hours' time, she would have her answers.

At three forty-five, Marlee made her way to Room 202 in the Putnam Building, stopping by Diane's office on the way. Diane looked as bedraggled as Marlee felt. Her long blonde hair was mussed, and her black-framed glasses sat askew on her nose. It had only been a day and a half since they found out about Logan's death, but it seemed like weeks had passed. The two entered the meeting room and found a few of the other professors and secretaries already there. If everyone showed up, there would be thirty five people, but not everyone showed up for meetings even if they were mandatory. Several faculty members in her own department were well known for drumming up so-called emergencies to get out of meetings. Most meetings were dull and pointless, and Marlee herself had scheduled a couple of doctor appointments and a hair appointment at the same time as a meeting to avoid the mind-numbing tedium. Most people seemed to realize that the meeting today might shed some light on Logan's death, so it would be well attended. Faculty would not pass up an opportunity to garner information on a campus event, even when it was a tragedy like death.

At 4:05 p.m., Dean Green stomped into the room. He looked crankier than usual. The room was filled to capacity, and a hush fell across the room as he marched toward the podium. "I know some of you have been talking to the press," growled the Dean. "We need to keep quiet and let the police do their work. If you have any information on Logan's death, then you need to tell the police, not the TV stations and newspapers. There will be disciplinary action if anyone else speaks to the press. A few of you have been asking a lot of your own questions. Stay out of it, and let the police handle it!" With that statement, the dean hiked up his pants to an inch from his man-boobs and glared at the audience, defying anyone to object to his directive. The dean took the faculty's stunned silence for acceptance, and his face relaxed a bit. "Look, administration wants any information on the case to come from them. Otherwise, we have too many different stories coming from campus, and some might not paint MSU in the best light. We don't want people to be so scared for their children's safety that they withdraw them from classes and take them home or, even worse, enroll them in another university. From now on, the official word on anything to do with Logan LeCroix will come from the MSU president's office. Only the president himself or his public relations director will speak on the matter to the media. You need to get back to the business at hand, which is teaching students. Don't concern yourselves with the details of the investigation."

"Why is this such an issue?" Della questioned. "Did somebody provide false information to a reporter?"

"A few people have been approached by a newspaper reporter and television reporters. Most have declined to be interviewed, but some opened their mouths and talked about it when they really didn't have anything to say. All this does is spark rumors," said Dean Green, being uncharacteristically patient with the challenge to his directive. The dean stared long and hard at Asshat and Celeste. Looking over her left shoulder, Marlee saw them sitting a couple of rows apart from each other. Both were sitting with members of their respective departments. Celeste did not meet the dean's stare, but Asshat looked back at the dean with a defiant smirk on his face.

"Does the administration know something they aren't telling us?" asked Della, unable to let the matter drop.

"Not that I know of," said Dean Green, although Marlee sensed he knew a lot that he wasn't saying to them.

"Seems like y'all know more than you're telling us. The cops aren't saying anything. MSU administration isn't saying anything. And now, we're not supposed to say anything or even ask our own questions?" Della asked.

"Seems to me if somebody with some answers would say something, then faculty wouldn't be so quick to give interviews or speculate."

The dean stared at her, but Della would not look away. Mean Dean Green was able to cow many of the faculty members, but Della was not one of them. She held her ground while the dean thought about his response. Giving his pants another tug upward, he growled, "The fact remains that none of you are to talk to the press. Your job is to teach, not give interviews or conduct your own investigations. That's final!" He stomped away from the podium and out of the room without looking back.

Faculty and staff looked at each other. For twenty seconds it was as quiet as a tomb. Then the whole room was abuzz, processing the dean's comments and reacting to his tactless dismissal of them. They were used to Dean Green's unconventional and abrupt manner, but he usually didn't end a presentation with the "because I said so" finale that so many parents use with young children. Marlee leaned over and tapped Della on the shoulder. Della turned around, her cold eyes looking even chillier now. "I think you hit a nerve," Marlee said with a smile. Della grimaced while rolling her eyes, knowing there must have been an element of truth to what she claimed.

Diane and Marlee got up to leave, both making a face at each other in reaction to the events of the meeting. They slid into the hall without being cornered by other faculty members. "What do you make of that?" asked Diane with a level of disgust in her voice that she usually saved for lackadaisical students asking for a second extension on their speech projects.

"He knows something. This meeting was not just about public relations. Dean Green told us not to talk to the press because he doesn't want us inadvertently tarnishing MSU's reputation, but I think there's more to it than that," said Marlee. The question now was: "What was it that the MSU administration knew that the faculty did not?" Dean's directive or not, Marlee was going to find out.

Day Of The Dead

There comes a time in every mystery when someone other than the victims and the perpetrators discover what really happened. If it's not in their own best interest to reveal the truth, then they won't.

The mystery surrounding my death happened just that way.

Chapter 9

Marlee and Diane knew the safest place to have a conversation was at Marlee's house. They both drove their cars back to Marlee's home and met inside. Since Diane had shown no sign of wanting to return to her own home, Marlee gave her a key so she could come and go as she pleased during the uncertainty of the investigation. They had known each other just over a year, but Marlee trusted Diane implicitly.

It was four thirty. Marlee grabbed a bottle of wine from the refrigerator. Nothing seems to help in a crisis as much as wine. Luckily, Diane thought the same thing and grabbed two glasses from the cabinet above the sink. Diane plopped down on the couch while Marlee poured two generous portions of wine. She was not one to fill a glass part-way, so they both had to lean over their glasses on the coffee table to avoid spilling on that first slurp.

"What does the MSU administration know about Logan's death that they won't tell us?" asked Diane.

"The cops might have told them facts or suspicions and asked them not to make the information public. Or MSU might have information independent of the police. Another thing I just thought of is that MSU might in some way be in the wrong," said Marlee, sipping her wine and looking into space.

"How would MSU be in the wrong?" asked Diane.

"I think that any time a crime or an accident happens on campus, the university has to be very careful about lawsuits. When Logan's next of kin are finally tracked down, they might allege that MSU was a dangerous work environment and not everything was done to protect faculty members. Or, administration might have been aware of some safety concerns, maybe even regarding Logan, and failed to do anything about it. There are all kinds of reasons that a lawsuit might be filed. Even if it's ultimately dismissed, just the threat of a lawsuit would put administrators in a tizzy," said Marlee. "At this point, it might just be a case of CYA... Cover Your Ass."

The two continued sipping their wine until Diane spied a wicker pumpkin full of candy. "Hey, is there any chocolate left?"

"Yeah, I've been meaning to take it up to campus to give to my students. Leftover Halloween candy at my house doesn't last too long," said Marlee.

"I need some!" said Diane, grabbing for the half-full gallon-sized bowl.

Marlee was on a low carbohydrate diet but made allowances for beer and wine because not to do so would be just plain insane. Candy was another story. For the past month, minus the past few days, she had done fairly well on her low carb program and had lost eight pounds. When she could keep a rigid schedule and there were no stressors, Marlee did very well at dieting. One mild upset tended to derail the whole program and throw her back into eating carbs in lethal doses. Given the events of the past several hours, Marlee was surprised that she hadn't already devoured that bowl of candy. Diane popped a second piece of dark chocolate in her mouth as Marlee was unwrapping her first. They ate most of the candy in the pumpkin bowl, finished off the first bottle of wine and opened a second. Marlee rubbed her stomach, feeling a bit queasy from the chocolate and wine combo. Plus, the jeans she had worn to work that day were cutting into her stomach. "I think we need to eat some real food with nutrition," groaned Marlee.

"Do you have any vegetables? We could make stir fry," suggested Diane.

"Nah, let's just order pizza."

"Okay, pizza it is!" shouted Diane, easily warming to the idea.

Forty five minutes later, an open pizza box sat atop the coffee table, surrounded by paper plates, wine glasses, candy wrappers, and paper towels. "I love pizza so much. I wish I could marry it," said Diane as she stuffed a piece of crust in her mouth.

"Me too. And whoever thought of putting broccoli on pizza? It's really good. Plus it makes me feel like I'm eating something healthy," said Marlee in between giant bites of her veggie pizza. Both had changed into sweat pants, which allowed them the satisfaction of eating extra pieces of pizza without the consequence of tight waistbands.

After inhaling all but one piece of the extra-large pizza, Marlee flopped backwards on the loveseat while Diane stretched out on the couch. "Oooof, I feel sick," said Diane.

"There is a bottle of Tums in the bathroom," said Marlee. "I think I might explode from the sheer volume of food. Why do we do this to ourselves?"

Diane shrugged, rubbing her stomach. They continued to lament their overeating until the six o'clock news came on. Perhaps there would be new developments in the investigation. Right off the bat, the Logan LeCroix death was recapped without any new information; however, there was a teaser for the ten o'clock edition in which an "MSU professor gives inside details on Logan

LeCroix and his death." The image flicked to a scene of Asshat talking into a camera.

"Oh, good God!" shrieked Marlee. "I forgot about his interview. Like he has any information to add. He just loves being in front of a camera."

Diane nodded. Asshat was indeed a person with littleman syndrome. Because he wasn't much bigger than dwarf-size, he tried to make himself feel bigger by seeking out attention. Even though Marlee and Diane were thoroughly disgusted with Asshat's pathetic grab at the limelight, they both knew they would watch the ten o'clock broadcast. Not that they expected any insight to come from him, but at least they could use his interview as fodder for critiquing him. Plus, it would make for good gossip on campus the next day.

Marlee dozed on the loveseat while Diane read a novel. The television remained on, although the programming that night failed to hold their attention. When the late evening news began, both professors were sitting upright and paying full attention to the broadcast. Asshat made a series of comments that really said nothing. He talked about Logan's death being a tragedy, the matter being investigated by local police, and MSU and Elmwood being safe. Asshat reiterated Logan's brief biography, which everyone following the case knew by now. He concluded that Logan seemed like a nice guy and added that he would be missed.

"Well, thank you Captain Obvious!" yelled Marlee as she grabbed the remote control and snapped off the television. "I hate it when people talk but say nothing."

"Me too," said Diane. "I'd be embarrassed to go on TV and basically report what everyone already knows."

"I know. I would too. At least he didn't offer up any ideas that were purely conjecture on his part," said Marlee. "He didn't help anything by giving the interview, but at least he didn't put out any false information or start more rumors."

"I wonder what Dean Green will have to say after he sees this?" asked Diane.

"I don't know," laughed Marlee. "He gave the interview before the Dean held the meeting directing us not to talk to the media, so I suppose Asshat can use that as a justification if he gets called on the carpet."

"Can the dean even legally and ethically tell us not to talk to the media?" asked Diane. "It doesn't seem right."

"I don't know about the legality of it, but as dean, he can sure make our lives difficult if we cross him. We don't have tenure, and we need his positive recommendation before we can even think of applying for it. Without tenure, we're out of jobs here at MSU. So, yeah, the dean has the power to tell us what to and what not to do," said Marlee.

"Asshat has tenure and has been promoted to full professor, so there's not much Dean Green can do to him," commented Diane.

"You're right. Probably the worst the dean can do to Asshat is deny his application for travel out of state for conferences or deny his bid for sabbatical. Or, he could put him on a committee that no one wants to be on and that has very little power or status. The dean still has a lot of power, but his hold over the tenured faculty is a lot less than his grip on us newbies."

Diane grabbed the remote and turned the television back on. Pulling up a blanket, she settled back in on the couch to watch Letterman until she fell asleep. Marlee wasn't really all that tired but didn't feel like watching TV. She went to her room and resumed reading a book of short stories she had started the previous week. Short stories were perfect reading for mid-semester because she only had to commit to a few pages. If she didn't pick up the book again for another week, she hadn't lost her place. You began a new story with new characters, and all was right with the world. Marlee tended to be a binge reader. If she started a novel, she would do her damnedest to finish it. She was compulsive about finishing the story, even if it kept her up until 3:00 a.m. After doing this a few times last year, Marlee decided that she couldn't effectively teach the next day if she had only had three or four hours of rest. She self-imposed the restriction of no novels during the semester. During summer vacations, holiday breaks and the first month of each semester, when grading and class prep were at a minimum, Marlee read as many novels as she could get her hands on. Her personal record was forty books of fiction during one summer.

After page three, Marlee realized that she had no idea what the short story was even about. She couldn't concentrate on the ins and outs of someone else's life when she had so much going on in her own at the moment. Picking up a notebook and pen from her nightstand, Marlee began jotting down the facts about the case. On the second page, she made a list of the motives for Logan's death and the people who could possibly have killed him. Beginning on the third page, Marlee listed information she wanted to find out about Logan's death, other than answering the obvious questions of what had happened and why.

She put together a plan for the following day. Instead of just aimlessly wandering around and inserting herself into ongoing conversations, hoping to overhear some details from the secretary, Marlee would instead try to systematically gather information through people who might actually have some helpful knowledge on the matter. Given that she was untenured and that the dean had given a specific directive for all MSU employees to stay out of the investigation, it was risky for her to engage in her own investigation. Still, Marlee couldn't let it rest. She knew there was much more to the story than was being revealed by the PD and by MSU. She also knew that the police department didn't have a stellar record in solving what few murders had occurred in Elmwood in the past ten years. There was no way she was going to let an ineffective investigation, or a university trying to hold onto its reputation, undermine justice for Logan. Conducting her own investigation would be risky, very risky. She would have to keep a low profile.

*Pieces of the puzzle start falling into place.
One by one they begin to fit together. My life and
my death were being picked over with a fine-
tooth comb. No one wants all of their personal
information on display for the world to view.
No one.*

Chapter 10

Marlee's first order of business after waking was to check the newspaper. Maybe something developed overnight or had been uncovered by an industrious reporter. Scanning the pages of the Elmwood Examiner, it was clear to her that nothing new was being reported on Logan's death. There were short quotes from both Celeste and Asshat, but neither offered anything newsworthy. After making coffee, Marlee showered and quickly got dressed. It was a little before 7:00 a.m., and Diane was snoring softly on the couch. She didn't have classes or office hours today, so she was free to sleep in. Marlee was a bit envious until she remembered all of the people she wanted to talk to today. First up on her list was Alice Olson, since Alice went to view Logan's body at the funeral home yesterday. Marlee also wanted to talk to Donnie Stacks from her Policing class to find out firsthand the information she told Jasper Evans and Dom Schmidt. Finally, she hoped to get some information directly from an officer at the Elmwood Police Department. She had contacts in the department and needed to see what she could garner from the law enforcement angle.

Before leaving the house, Marlee jotted a quick note to Diane and taped it to the counter near the coffee pot. In a nutshell, she told Diane she was going to do some digging on her own on the case and that she would be home around five o'clock that evening. Marlee filled her travel mug with coffee and grabbed two protein bars, one for breakfast and one for lunch, as she hurried out the door. She had a bit of time after arriving on campus before Alice would be at work at 8:00 a.m. Marlee used the time to go over her notes for classes that morning and to consult her day planner about upcoming tests and quizzes. She also made a quick trip to Louise's office to retrieve her mail. Louise's door was locked, and the lights were off. Neither she nor the dean was in yet. Marlee walked to her mail box and grabbed the two fliers inside. One was from an academic publishing house and advertised new Criminology books that would be on the market later this year. The other was an intra-campus notification of an upcoming debate between the presidents of the campus Democrats and Republicans. It was open to anyone on campus, and everyone was encouraged to attend. Marlee threw both fliers in the recycling bin near Louise's chair. She had no interest in the debate and had already decided on her new textbooks for next semester.

By this time it was 8:15. Marlee hoped that she had allowed enough time for Alice to arrive in her office and get settled in a bit. Ideally, Alice would be alone in her office, and the two could chat without interruption, but Marlee knew that would be a longshot. Arriving in Alice's office a few minutes later, Marlee saw Alice sitting at her desk staring at her computer. She still wore her tan coat and had her purse over her arm. The computer was turned off. Judging by Alice's appearance, Marlee figured she hadn't been sleeping well. Her eyes were still bloodshot, and huge dark circles encased them. Alice's skin had a yellow cast to it, which may have partly been due to the harsh overhead lighting. Most likely, Logan's death was taking a toll on Alice more so than most people on campus since she knew him the best.

"Good morning, Alice," Marlee said, entering the secretary's small, cramped office.

"Oh, hi," said Alice, still looking confused and out of sorts.

"How are you doing?" asked Marlee. She was genuinely concerned about Alice. She looked worse every time Marlee saw her this week.

"I just can't get it out of my mind. Who would do this to Logan? Why?" Alice was still asking the hard questions that no one seemed to be able to answer at this point. She stood up, placing her coat on a hook behind the door and her purse in her desk drawer. She flicked the computer on and sat back down. She was operating on auto pilot, and Marlee suspected she had no recollection of just tending to her coat and purse.

"I don't know, Alice. Maybe the cops will release more information today," Marlee said, even though she held out little hope. "Did you go to the funeral home yesterday afternoon to see Logan?"

Alice nodded, tears welling up in her eyes. "They had him lying on a table, and he was covered up with a blanket. He looked like he was asleep."

Marlee didn't know how to approach the next questions without being overly graphic. Alice was clearly upset, and she didn't want to add to her trauma. "Did he look pretty bad because of the... gunshot?"

"He wasn't bloody or anything. I suppose they cleaned him up at the funeral home. I just saw a small hole on the side of his neck," recalled Alice, still teary eyed but not weeping.

"That had to be so hard for you. I know how much Logan meant to you, Alice."

She nodded, the tears now freely flowing down her cheeks. She removed her glasses and wiped her eyes with the sleeve of her shirt. Then came the sobs. Marlee wasn't comfortable with such displays of emotion and was even less equipped to deal with comforting someone in emotional distress. Nonetheless, she crossed over to Alice's chair, leaned in and gave her a small hug.

Alice smiled through her tears and wiped her eyes again. "It was so hard, but I felt like I had to see him one last time. He needed a friend."

Marlee felt guilty, not only because she hadn't gone to the funeral home to support Alice, but also because she hadn't been there to see Logan one last time. She reminded herself that people can only do what they are equipped to do, but this still didn't assuage her guilt.

"Did the people at the funeral home have any information about Logan or his next of kin?" asked Marlee.

"They said Joe Tisdale authorized Logan's body to be cared for by their funeral home. He's going to be cremated, and Joe will take the ashes with him back to California," said Alice.

"Who's that?" asked Marlee. Finally, some new information!

"It's Logan's partner from California. He's on his way here. The cops just located him yesterday. At least that's what the lady from the funeral home told me," reported Alice.

"I wonder why this wasn't in the paper this morning," mused Marlee. "Maybe the police are keeping it quiet for some reason. I wonder if Dean Green knew yesterday when we had our meeting." Every new bit of information provided more questions about Logan's death instead of answers.

Alice glanced at the clock on the wall above her desk. "I have a meeting with the dean and the other secretaries at 8:30, so I have to leave in a minute."

"Sure, thanks for letting me know what you found out, Alice," said Marlee, heading toward the door. "By the way, which side of the neck was the gunshot wound on?"

Alice thought for a minute, rubbing her temples while visualizing the dismal scene. "It was on his left side. Right below his ear."

"Okay, thanks, Alice," said Marlee. "I'll catch up with you later."

Marlee was nearly out the door when she heard Alice say, "That's how I know it wasn't suicide."

"What do you mean?" Marlee stopped in her tracks and turned to face Alice.

"The bullet wound was on the left side of his neck. Logan was right-handed," said Alice, the tears again streaming down her face.

Back in her office, Marlee shut the door and tried to make sense of everything she had just learned from Alice. She grabbed a couple sheets of white printer paper and a blue pen. She was an organized person, and putting words on paper and into charts helped her make sense of the material. First, she jotted down an outline of the information she had on Logan's death. Then she added new information, such as the location of the bullet wound and Logan's life partner coming to claim the body. Given everything that had happened in the last two days, she thought it best to start recording all information and from whom she received it. Marlee grabbed one of the protein bars she brought from home and munched on it as she moved bits of information around on the paper. Finally, she listed the possible motives for Logan's death and the suspects. Luckily, she had just discussed motives and suspects with Dom Schmidt and Jasper Evans the previous morning and had also made some notes last night, so that information was fresh in her mind. Putting information on paper kept Marlee busy until 9:45 when she had to leave for her first morning class. It was located nearby in the Putnam Building. Her second class was right after that in the same room. By noon or shortly thereafter, Marlee would be back in her office until two o'clock for office hours. Then she'd be able to do some more sleuthing.

After two uneventful classes, Marlee returned to her office and wolfed down the second protein bar she had brought with her. It wasn't a very satisfying lunch, but it stopped the hunger pangs and allowed her to focus on the investigation. *I'm thinking of this as my investigation,* she thought. She realized that she had better not make that comment aloud or there would be negative consequences for her career if the dean caught wind of it.

After fulfilling her required office hours for the day, Marlee locked her door and set out to find Donnie Stacks. Jasper and Dom said that she had some inside information from one of the police officers, and Marlee wanted to find out exactly what she knew. Donnie worked at the Student Union on campus as part of her work-study program. She tended the information booth on the lower level from time to time, so Marlee used that as her starting point. She entered the spacious Student Union, which had just been remodeled the previous year. The fireplaces provided a homey touch, although Marlee found that the over-use of gray tones gave the building too much of an industrial feel. The interior of the building was gray, and the weather was overcast and dreary much of the fall. Logan's death was the final straw in setting a dismal mood.

Her first stop was at the information desk on the lower level where Donnie usually worked. A female student with blond dreadlocks and a tie-dyed shirt was staffing the desk and looked up as Marlee approached. She had seen this student on campus but had never had her in a class. "Hey, is Donnie Stacks working here today?" she asked.

"Nah, I'm filling in for Donnie today. She's out sick," said the student.

"Is she really sick, or is she avoiding classes and work?" asked Marlee, altogether too familiar with the catch-all excuse of being under the weather. Students and faculty alike were known to employ the excuse frequently during November. Some truly were ill, while others were overwhelmed by the amount of work they had to accomplish and just needed a break. Others were taking a mental health day or accomplishing other tasks, such as working a double shift at their minimum-wage job. Nearly all of the students worked at least one part-time job. Some worked over forty hours per week, plus took a full course load. Marlee understood why a student was "sick" from time to time with all the responsibilities they shouldered. Recalling her past days as a student, she also knew that actual illness was sometimes self-induced by excessive alcohol consumption, poor diet, and lack of sleep.

The student eyed Marlee with a level of distrust. She knew Marlee was a professor and assumed she had no idea that students used fake illnesses to get out of things. Students were so naïve. They seemed to forget that professors themselves were once students and had pulled the same routine on their own profs. "Look," said Marlee "she's not in any trouble. I just have to ask her a question about something not even related to classes or work."

The student softened a bit and said, "Donnie went home to Fargo last night. She's not technically sick, but she told me she was feeling like shit because of everything going on right now."

"Any idea when she might be back?"

"No, she just told me she needed a few days back at home with her parents. I'll bet she's back on campus by this weekend, or Monday for sure," said the student.

Marlee said her farewells and asked the student to have Donnie get in touch with her as soon as she was back on campus. She could have called Donnie but felt like the conversation would reveal more if it were face-to-face. Marlee was good at reading body language and other nonverbal cues that wouldn't be revealed in a phone conversation. She was disappointed that this lead would have to wait for a few days. She pulled her day planner out of her book bag and jotted down a note to herself to look up Donnie Stacks next Monday if Donnie hadn't contacted her yet.

Leaving the gray interior of the Student Union, Marlee walked into the gray afternoon. She hopped into her Honda CR-V and drove to the Elmwood Police Department in hopes of obtaining some inside information from her contact. The parking lot to the west of the PD was full, so Marlee parked in an employee lot. She risked getting a ticket for parking there, but felt optimistic. As she entered the police station, she noticed the gray interior, which was new. The last time she had been at the PD, everything had been beige. What was it with all gray tones inside the local buildings? Although trendy, it didn't do much to improve anyone's mood. Of course, if people were at the police station, they probably weren't in that great a mood to begin with.

Marlee approached the front desk, which was covered by bullet-proof glass. Lois was the office worker with the most seniority and usually didn't handle the walk-in traffic. Her subordinates were not in the office, so Lois deigned to speak to the riff-raff that walked in requesting information and making complaints. Lois pretended she didn't know Marlee, which seemed to be part of the game they played. She had been familiar with Lois, only on a work basis, when she was a probation officer for over five years, yet Lois always acted like it was the first time she laid eyes on Marlee. "Hey, Lois. How's it going?" asked Marlee.

"Hello," she said tentatively. "Can I help you?"

"Sure. I was wondering if Officer Sean Yellow Tail was around."

"He is," said Lois. "Can I give him your name?"

Marlee sighed, then gave her name. Lois called Yellow Tail on the intercom and spoke with him in a hushed voice.

"He says to go on back," Lois reported, tripping the lock on the office door and gesturing for Marlee to enter.

Marlee made her way back to a room filled with boxes, files, and book cases. A small rectangular table was situated in the middle of the room, and two desktop computers were on it. Office chairs with wheeled bottoms were scattered across the room. There were way more chairs than was space at the table. Marlee assumed this room must be used for strategy meetings or general bullshit sessions.

Officer Yellow Tail rounded the corner and entered the room carrying a twenty ounce bottle of Mountain Dew. She guessed he was working a later shift that day since he was consuming a large amount of caffeine late in the afternoon. *He's in his early twenties and caffeine probably doesn't impact his sleep at all*, thought Marlee with nostalgic memories of her own youth. He was dressed in his police uniform and carried his sidearm. Yellow Tail grinned at her as he entered the room, clearly pleased to be seen in his official work capacity by his professor. "Hey, Dr. M. What's up?" he asked as he slid his lanky frame into one of the many office chairs, gesturing for her to sit as well.

Marlee knew she needed to tread lightly in requesting any information from Yellow Tail. Although he was her student and had some allegiance to her, he was first and foremost a cop now. He was fresh out of the police academy and had several classes on ethics and confidentiality. Marlee felt conflicted. She taught about ethics in her Policing course and didn't want him to compromise his position as an officer by disclosing information he shouldn't. On the other hand, she really needed to know what was going on that wasn't being released to the public. Marlee had a lot of respect for some members of the Elmwood Police Department, but didn't have much faith in the Chief of Police. Chief Langdon was the one who decided what information would and would not be released to the public, so she needed to work around him if she was going to figure out what had happened to her new friend, Logan.

"Hey, Sean, how's police work treating you?" asked Marlee, trying to build up some rapport before launching into her questioning.

"It's been busy. Not too many new hires get in on a suspicious death case right away," he said. "I'm learning a lot!"

Marlee was glad he had brought up Logan's death. Now that the topic had been introduced, she didn't feel quite so awkward asking about it. "I heard Logan's partner is coming to Elmwood to claim his body," said Marlee, hoping this would yield some additional details.

"Yep, his flight gets in this afternoon, and then he'll be coming in to give us some more information about Dr. LeCroix," said Yellow Tail.

"Is he a suspect?" asked Marlee, wondering if the meeting Joe Tisdale would be having with the police department would be primarily to dispense information, or if he was going to be questioned as a person of interest.

"Now you know I can't tell you that," said Sean with a twinkle in his eye. He knew exactly what Marlee was up to and seemed willing to provide a bit of information but was not going to overstep.

"Just making sure you paid attention in Policing class last year," she said with humor, and they both chuckled. "Have the autopsy results come back yet?"

"They have, and some of the findings will be made public today," said Officer Yellow Tail.

"Some, but not all?" asked Marlee.

"Right," he said. "Some of the details will be held back until we make an arrest and go to trial."

"Why is the Chief still calling this a suspicious death when it's apparent that it wasn't a suicide?" Marlee inquired.

"The investigation is still underway and no determination has been made yet as to the cause of death," said Yellow Tail, repeating the pat line officers were told to disseminate when asked a question.

"I know, but the evidence and common sense tell us that it wasn't an accident, a heart attack or a suicide. It seems the only thing left is murder," Marlee stated, wondering if there was some obvious fact she was missing.

The young officer just smiled and shrugged. Marlee couldn't figure out if Sean knew more than he was saying, or if he was only repeating what he'd been told to say. Deciding to move on to another line of enquiry, Marlee asked, "What about the gun? Were there fingerprints on it?"

"The only thing I can tell you about the gun is that it's really old. We're still trying to track down the registration for it. As for fingerprints, I can't tell you anything there,"

Yellow Tail said as he stood up. "Look, I've gotta run. My shift starts in a few minutes and I need to take care of a couple things before I head out on patrol."

"No problem. Thanks for talking with me. If there's anything else you can share, you know how to reach me," Marlee said, as she followed the young officer out the door. "Say, do you know if Bettina Crawford is around today?" She was an officer Marlee knew on a professional level. She was hoping Bettina might be able to provide her with a bit more detail on Logan's death and the chief's decisions on withholding information from the public.

"Crawford just finished her shift," said Yellow Tail. "I don't know if she's on duty tomorrow or not. You could check with Lois at the front desk."

Marlee thanked Sean again for his time and reiterated that he should contact her if there was anything new on the case that he could share. She didn't want him to violate his ethical code, but he had to know she was a professional and would be discreet with anything he told her.

Back at her vehicle, Marlee smiled as she noticed that there was not a parking ticket on her windshield. *Who says optimism doesn't pay?* she thought.

On the way to her house, Marlee reflected on the information she had garnered that afternoon. She was pleased with her conversations with Alice and Officer Sean Yellow Tail. A fair amount of information came out of both of those chats. It was unfortunate that she couldn't talk with any other officers at the PD or with Donnie Stacks from campus, but she would hit them up later in the week or early next week. After talking with Donnie, Marlee would approach Sylvester Blake to see if he had any reliable details about Logan's death.

As she was driving home, Marlee fiddled with the radio. She had been listening to a Stone Temple Pilots CD for a few days but now tuned to the local rock station. "Whiskey in a Jar," by Metallica was playing, and Marlee drummed her fingers along with the beat. A newscaster came on at the end of the song for the hourly news update. He reported that the findings from Logan LeCroix's autopsy were in, and that the coroner had ruled the death a homicide.

It's only natural to want answers. I would have liked some answers myself... and some action taken against those who wronged me. Unfortunately for me, I was new to town and gay. Two strikes against me from the very beginning.

Chapter 11

After arriving at home and parking in the garage, Marlee raced in the back door and looked in the living room to find Diane in much the same position as she was when Marlee had left hours earlier. She shook Diane's shoulder to waken her. She noticed that Diane was wearing a different shirt and lounge pants from last night, so she assumed that a shower had occurred at some point during the day. Diane turned her head on the pillow away from Marlee and groaned. Another shake to the shoulder and Diane turned back toward Marlee and opened one eye. "What?" she said groggily.

"Wake up! I have some new information on the case!" Marlee shouted, ready to reveal all she had learned that day.

Diane propped herself up on one elbow, waking up now that there was a good reason to do so. "Tell me."

"I just heard on the radio that the coroner ruled Logan's death a homicide. The Chief of Police is still calling it a suspicious death but, for whatever reason, won't rule it a homicide, at least not yet. That last part wasn't on the news. Sean Yellow Tail, a student of mine who works at the PD now, told me. You met him at the campus meeting on Monday afternoon. I'm not sure if he knows why the chief won't change the ruling," Marlee relayed. "He also told me that the gun is really old."

"Wow, you've really been out detecting today, haven't you?" asked Diane, now sitting on the couch with a gray fleece blanket wrapped around her shoulders.

"Yuppers. And, I talked to Alice Olson about what she saw when she viewed Logan's body at the funeral home yesterday. She said he was cleaned up and covered with a blanket. He had a small bullet wound on the left side of his neck right below his ear. Here's the kicker: he's right-handed!" Marlee shouted as she acted out the improbability of someone killing themselves by placing a gun on the side opposite their dominant hand.

"So, it couldn't have been a suicide. I don't watch crime shows, but even I know that no one who's set on killing himself would do that," said Diane.

"Right. Anyone who's intent on killing himself is going to make damn sure he's successful at it. If a person is suicidal, the one thing worse than being alive is being alive and in a vegetative state. There's still a lot we don't know about the gun at this point. Sean wouldn't tell me if fingerprints were found on the gun, although I think he knows. Apparently the cops are still trying to trace the gun, so we don't know if it was registered, and if so, to whom," said Marlee.

The two professors continued to talk about Logan, Marlee's findings about his death, and other campus occurrences until 8:30 that evening. Learning from their disastrous dietary mistakes the previous night, Marlee and Diane decided to take it easy on the wine and leftover Halloween candy. She hadn't been shopping in a few days but had a few basics in the cupboard and a nearly full freezer compartment. She whipped up shrimp lo mien loaded with broccoli, carrots, and peppers added in. Had it not been for the frozen shrimp and vegetables, Marlee would have only been able to serve up pasta with butter.

"So, what's up for tomorrow?" asked Diane as she twisted angel hair pasta around her fork and stabbed at a broccoli floret.

"I still need to talk to Thom Dole to find out why he thinks Logan's death was a suicide. Maybe he's changed his mind now that some of the evidence has come to light," Marlee said.

"Do you think you know him well enough to ask him about finding Logan's body?" Diane asked.

"I thought I'd start out by thanking him for inviting me to his fun Halloween party, and then say that I hadn't gotten around to expressing my gratitude yet because of Logan's death, which is actually true. That should be a good transition into the topic I really want to talk about. From there, I'll see what he has to say," said Marlee, full of confidence that her plan would work.

"Thom is on the promotion and tenure committee," reminded Diane "so you don't want to get on his bad side."

"I know," said Marlee. "I don't plan to interrogate him; just ask some general questions and see where it leads. I used to do a lot of interviewing in my previous lines of work, so I think I can get the info I need without pissing him off. At least, that's my goal," she said with a laugh as she popped a stir-fried shrimp into her mouth.

"Interviewing criminals is a lot different from trying to get information from college professors," reminded Diane.

"They're actually not that different," said Marlee, chewing thoughtfully. "Both try to gain the upper hand in an interview and think they are smarter than everyone else. The main difference is that, when I was a probation officer, I could use the leverage of the court system to entice them to tell me stuff. With professors, I don't have that advantage. Fortunately, I'm pretty good at reading body language, so I can usually tell if someone is trying to hide something."

"Who else are you going to talk to?" asked Diane, pushing back her empty plate and placing the fork on top.

"I really want to meet Logan's partner. He was flying in today, and I don't know how long he'll be staying in Elmwood, so I want to meet with him right away. The last thing I want is for him to leave before I get to talk with him. He may not know anything about the case, but he can at least shed a little more light on who Logan really was, and who might have a motive to kill him," said Marlee.

"Maybe he did it. The partner, I mean," Diane said as she scooted her chair back from the dining room table. "He could be dangerous."

"Yeah, that's true. His motives could be financial, or maybe Logan was leaving him, and he couldn't tolerate that. He could've done it himself, or paid someone else to shoot Logan," Marlee said as icy shivers climbed to the top of her spine.

"Nothing has been said about eyewitnesses to the crime," Diane said, snapping her fingers in surprise that no one else had mentioned this yet. "I know the shooting happened in the early morning hours, but, hey, we're talking about a college campus. Students are up all hours of the night. Plus, many of the athletes go for early morning training or practice. Maybe a student saw something and is too afraid to say anything for fear that he or she may be next."

"Good point, Diane!" Marlee exclaimed. "You're going to make a fine detective yet."

"Ha ha, I don't think so. I prefer the safe and drama-free confines of my office," Diane stated, pleased that she happened upon the eyewitness angle before Marlee.

"It just occurred to me that nothing else has been said about the footage from the cameras on campus. Remember, Kendra Rolland said at the meeting that there are cameras on campus and that they weren't saying where they were located? Well, I need to check to see if anything turned up on the camera footage," said Marlee.

"Do you think Kendra will tell you?" asked Diane.

"I don't know, but it doesn't hurt to ask. She's really nice and I think that if she's able, she'll tell me. Of course, she may have been sworn to silence by the police or the president. If she won't tell me anything, then maybe I'll talk to one of the guys over at the physical plant," Marlee said as she stood, clearing the dishes from the table.

Diane grabbed the empty wine bottle and threw it in the garbage. "That would be a good idea, since they probably know about any hidden cameras on campus. Plus, they like to gossip. A lot!"

"Exactly what I was thinking," replied Marlee. "I think I'll start with Stan over there and see what he has to say. As much as I detest Asshat, I think I need to talk with him too and see if he has any actual knowledge about Logan's death. It's possible that he's heard something, although I bet if he has, he would have broadcast it by now."

"Speaking of broadcasts, the ten o'clock news will be on in a few minutes," reminded Diane. "Let's see if there's anything new."

"Good idea," said Marlee as she made her way toward the living room and hunted for the remote. She snapped on the television and turned it to her preferred channel for news. *When did I become my mother?* she thought, as she realized that she had a favorite news channel. Since Marlee was little, her mother had insisted that one station in particular gave "better" news and a more accurate weather report. Marlee's reasoning for selecting KPRO news was much more scientific. She thought the weather guy was cute.

Diane and Marlee plopped down on the overstuffed furniture and settled in for the evening news. The 20-something newscaster flashed her distractingly white teeth as she began the broadcast. Logan LeCroix's death was the headliner again tonight. The report began with a brief recap of his death, followed by the announcement of the coroner's ruling of homicide. There was no announcement of any new investigative measures. No one from the police department was interviewed. The news then gave a teaser, urging viewers to stay tuned because breaking news on the topic would be forthcoming in a few minutes.

Marlee and Diane looked at each other with their mouths agape. Marlee turned down the volume as a catchy jingle for potato chips filled the room. "What breaking news do they have?" asked Marlee.

"I guess we'll see in a minute," said Diane, now on the edge of the couch, poised for the news update. She motioned for Marlee to turn the volume up again even though they were still on commercial break.

Marlee turned up the news as the toothy newscaster reappeared and announced that a Midwestern State University professor had clues to Logan's death. "What the hell!" shrieked Marlee.

The scene then turned to a pre-recorded interview of Asshat in his office. Both Marlee and Diane rolled their eyes, disappointed that it would be more of this little troll's pontificating on the topic. Asshat was sitting in his office with a television reporter sitting next to him. Asshat was wearing an Australian safari hat with one side pinned up. The videographer panned across Asshat's small office, taking in his framed academic degrees and the countless books stacked neatly in the bookcases that lined the walls.

The reporter narrated as the camera moved between shots of the office and photographs of Logan LeCroix. A brief biography on Professor Ashman was read, alerting the television audience to his academic qualifications in the discipline of History, his frequent newspaper columns and his blog. Asshat no doubt provided the reporter with his background material to lend credibility to what he was about to say.

"Professor Ashman," said the reporter, "I understand you have some new information on the death of Logan LeCroix.

"Yes. Several of my colleagues and I have been patiently waiting for the police department to announce findings relevant to the investigation. Since none were forthcoming, I called Chief Langdon myself and asked to meet with him. He agreed, and we spoke at length about Logan LeCroix's death."

"Why did he agree to talk to you?" asked the reporter.

"Because I asked," replied Asshat with an air of arrogance, which implied that no one dare turn him away when he requested information.

"What did the chief tell you?" the reporter queried.

"He said the matter was still under investigation. He said there was blowback of blood and tissue on Dr. LeCroix's arm and gunpowder residue on both hands, suggesting he had fired the gun himself," said Asshat.

"So, the chief said it was suicide?" asked the reporter.

"No, he didn't say that but, based on everything the chief told me, I think it was suicide," said Asshat, matter-of-factly, looking straight into the camera.

"What else did he reveal that led you to think Logan LeCroix killed himself?" asked the reporter, on the edge of his seat with the microphone thrust even closer to Asshat's face.

"The chief said Dr. LeCroix left his car keys and his building keys in his office when he exited the building. He was wearing a t-shirt but no jacket, and it was very chilly. It seems to me that he didn't intend on going back to his office or going home. I think he may have tried to stage the suicide to look like a murder," said Asshat.

"Where was the gun found?" asked the reporter.

"It was buried in a dumpster about fifty feet away from Dr. LeCroix's body. I asked Chief Langdon how one might be able to shoot himself, place the gun in a dumpster underneath other items, and then die in a location several feet away. The chief explained that frequently, when someone is shot, the bullet doesn't kill them instantaneously, like we see on television. I believe Dr. LeCroix likely shot himself by the dumpster, dropped the gun in the dumpster where it fell underneath some large garbage bags, and then walked about sixteen yards away where he collapsed and died," Asshat reported with a smirk, proud of himself for not only obtaining a private audience with the Chief of Police, but snaring a television interview and putting the pieces of the puzzle together himself.

The reporter scratched his chin and asked, "Assuming that your speculation of suicide is correct, why would Logan LeCroix try to make it look like a murder?"

"I don't have any inside information on that," said Asshat, "but maybe it was for insurance purposes. The beneficiary of any life insurance policies may not have been able to collect if the manner of death was self-inflicted by the victim."

"What else did you discuss with Chief Langdon?" asked the reporter.

"He said that there were other items that have come to light, but that he couldn't discuss them due to privacy concerns for Dr. LeCroix and his family. The chief also said that they are receiving help from other law enforcement agencies around the area. Besides that, they have submitted case information to a firearms expert, a forensics expert, and a specialist who deals with cold cases. Langdon said they are awaiting the findings from these three independent consultants," stated Asshat, slightly adjusting his Australian safari hat and tilting his head toward the camera in hopes of getting his best angle.

The reporter looked both intrigued and annoyed by Asshat's account of his conversation with Chief Langdon. He knew Asshat was playing to the camera and loving the attention. At the same time, the reporter was anxious to obtain any crumb of information on the matter, especially since the chief had been so close-mouthed up to this point. "So you believe Logan LeCroix's death was suicide, based on your discussion with the Chief of Police, but he is awaiting findings from outside consultants? Is that right?"

"That is correct. I believe this matter will be resolved shortly, and then we can go back to our normal routines on the MSU campus and in the Elmwood community," said Asshat.

With that final pronouncement, the interview was concluded. The reporter noted that Chief Langdon was contacted following the interview with Professor Ashman but had declined to comment. Then, the scene flashed back to the toothy newscaster, and she began talking about an international news item.

"Holy shit!" exclaimed Marlee. "Since when does the Chief of Police have private conversations with people from the community who have no involvement in a case? Why would he tell Asshat any of that information? Did Chief Langdon swear him to secrecy?"

"We know what Asshat said, but we don't know how accurately he reflected what the chief had to say," reminded Diane, always on the lookout for possibly-misconstrued information.

"That's true," fumed Marlee. "I can't believe the chief would even talk to Asshat. I'm also disgusted that what Asshat believes is a basis for a news interview. That's ridiculous! Does everyone who has an opinion get an interview now? Other professors will be lining up to chime in on what they think happened. The local evening news is nothing but a televised rumor mill."

"Well, you know the old saying about opinions and assholes," Diane reminded her with a smile.

"Yes, I just didn't think this particular asshole would go on TV to share his opinions. Asshat makes it sound like the chief thinks this is suicide too but just isn't ready to confirm it," said Marlee, attempting to process Asshat's account of his conversation with the Chief of Police.

"Is it true what he said about someone not dying immediately from a gunshot wound?" asked Diane.

"That is true. That's why police officers are trained to shoot to kill. They shoot until the person is completely incapacitated. They don't just assume that one bullet will kill a person, although much of the time one bullet is all it takes. It's all about what part of the body is struck by the bullet. If it's just a tissue wound, or if the bullet misses internal organs, then a gunshot might not stop someone at all," said Marlee, referring back to her lecture from last semester on gunshot wounds in her Crime Scene Investigation class.

"What's the likelihood that someone would kill himself and try to make it look like a suicide?" asked Diane.

"I think something like that would be very rare. There's not much sense to it. Most people who commit suicide do so out of hopelessness and desperation. They are so far down that they can't see a way up, and suicide seems to be the only solution," said Marlee.

"But why would someone do it?" asked Diane quizzically

"One reason is so that the grantor of the life insurance policy would pay the death benefits to the next of kin or whoever was named as the beneficiary of the policy. Some policies won't pay out if the person kills himself. Another reason to make a suicide look like murder is to get someone else in trouble, which requires a level of deep-seated anger that most suicidal people are beyond at that point, so it doesn't happen very often. Religion might be another reason. Some religions teach that, if you commit suicide, you will go to hell. The person who kills himself may try to disguise the suicide as a murder or accident to protect the family from scrutiny and judgment from the community and the church," Marlee reported.

"Based on what you just heard from Asshat's interview, do you think it was suicide, Marlee?" Diane asked.

"Anyone might commit suicide given the right conditions and situations, but I just don't feel this death was a suicide. The most distraught person knows that shooting himself in the neck on the left side when he's right-handed isn't the most efficient way to accomplish the goal. Sorry to be so blunt," said Marlee apologetically as she looked at Diane's surprised expression. "It just doesn't make much sense. Asshat mentioned blowback and gun powder residue on Logan's body, suggesting he fired the weapon. I would think that both of those things could be on his body if he struggled with the shooter or tried to grab the gun. Another thing that strikes me as odd is that Logan left the office without his coat, his building keys, and his car keys. It was below freezing that night. It's almost as if something or someone lured him outside.

Maybe he heard something odd and went outside quickly to check. Maybe somebody called him and asked Logan to meet up outside. Maybe Logan planned to meet someone at a designated time on campus. Maybe, maybe, maybe," said Marlee, her voice drifting off as she continued to contemplate the possibilities.

"So there's a murderer wandering around out there? Maybe someone who lives right here in Elmwood? Maybe someone who works or goes to classes at MSU?" asked Diane.

Marlee nodded. "I think so."

Day Of The Dead

Cover-ups, secrets, and unfounded speculation comprised the inquiry into my death. Much more was known by those in charge than was being made public.

Chapter 12

The next morning, Marlee was up, showered, and dressed before she thought of checking the newspaper for any new developments on Logan's case. She was so focused on Asshat's television interview last night that she even forgot to make coffee right away, part of her usual morning ritual. No new developments were revealed in the newspaper, although a front page article parroted what Asshat pontificated in his television interview the previous night. *It's sad when you have to rely on the sensationalistic media for any scrap of information about this case,* Marlee thought, as she began scooping coffee grounds from the orange Dunkin' Donuts pouch into the coffee maker. Technically, Marlee did not need to be on campus today. It was Thursday, the one day each week when she didn't have any classes or office hours. She usually stayed home in her pajamas and graded papers or prepared for the next week's classes. Today she knew she needed to get to the MSU campus quickly.

Edging her CR-V into the parking lot nearest Scobey Hall, Marlee exited her vehicle and half-jogged, half-walked to the Student Union. It was early, but Marlee knew Kendra Rolland would probably be in her office. She arrived early in the morning, left late in the evening and attended most campus events on weekends and after normal work hours. The scent of bacon and hash browns filled Marlee's nostrils as she breezed into the Student Union. A few students were holding plastic trays as they stood in line in the lower level of the building, waiting to be served breakfast. Several students sat at the dining tables eating their morning meals. Some ate alone, but most were in groups of three or more and chatted noisily above the din of the nearby kitchen. Marlee loved breakfast, and the aroma of bacon beckoned her. She knew she had a limited amount of time to catch Kendra before she was in meetings for the day, so she resisted the temptation.

Climbing the stairs to the top level of the Student Union, Marlee saw Kendra rounding the corner coffee mug in hand. "Hey, Kendra," Marlee called out.

"Oh hi, Marlee. How are you today?" asked Kendra, taking a sip from her silver, insulated coffee mug with the MSU logo. Kendra was dressed in a stylish brown pant suit and print blouse. She accessorized her outfit with gold hoop earrings and a chunky gold, brown and black necklace.

"I'm fine," said Marlee, anxious to get the mandatory pleasantries out of the way. "How are you doing? Busy, I'm sure, with all this investigation going on, huh?" She really didn't want to have this conversation in the lobby, but Kendra was hard to track down, and Marlee knew she needed to question her right then if she were to have any chance of talking to the busy administrator today.

"Very," said Kendra, dragging out the pronunciation of every letter as a way to emphasize just how busy she was.

"So, I was wondering," said Marlee, "did anyone ever review the tapes from the campus security cameras from the night of Logan's death?"

"Now, Marlee," said Kendra, with a slight level of exasperation, "you know I can't tell you anything about that. Didn't your dean instruct the faculty to stay out of any investigation that's going on in this matter?" Kendra was a genuinely nice person, but she made it very clear that any information about security camera footage would not be coming from her. Apparently, all of the campus administration was on the same page in directing faculty and staff to let the police handle all investigative matters.

Marlee was dejected. She had been hoping she could get some details from Kendra, but that was clearly not the case. "Yeah, I know. I just thought about it and wanted to make sure somebody remembered to check out the footage."

"The police are on it," said Kendra, stepping toward her office. "I have to run. There's a President's Cabinet meeting at eight, and I need to be prepared for it." Kendra gave a quick wave as she turned toward her office.

"OK, thanks, Kendra," Marlee called out. Kendra hadn't helped her at all, but it was always best to end any conversation on a positive note. Who knew when she might need information from Kendra that she was not prohibited from revealing?

Marlee exited the Student Union and made her way to the campus physical plant. The employees at the physical plant were in charge of all building and grounds maintenance, campus parking, and a host of other responsibilities. She knew one man who worked there and thought he might be able to shed some light on the camera situation on campus. Stan Shepherd worked full-time at the physical plant, but also worked in his off hours as a handyman around the community. He helped people with simple fix-it projects around their homes and yards. The majority of his clients were single female professors who owned their homes but were not particularly adept at home maintenance.

The physical plant was housed in an old, two-story brick building. The main floor held the heating, cooling, and water control systems for the various buildings on the campus. Offices were located on the top level. Marlee knew she would probably not get any worthwhile information from anyone in the offices, so she went into the mechanical room looking for Stan. She didn't see him at first, but then he peaked around the corner and grinned at her. Stan was in his early 50s and was an aging hippie. His blonde hair hung in various layers to his shoulders, giving him a surfer-dude appearance. Stan's laid back approach to life and slightly stoned demeanor added to the surfer persona. Today he was dressed in faded jeans that were a size too large and a gray Megadeth t-shirt. The t-shirt was originally black, but years of wear and washing now resulted in the faded and nearly see-through appearance of the garment.

"Hey, Marlee, what's up? Are you on your coffee break?" asked Stan. It amused Marlee that Stan just assumed everyone else on campus had official break times during the day to chat with co-workers.

"Hey, Stan! No, I don't have classes or office hours today, so I guess I don't even have to be here," said Marlee.

"That must be nice, to have a part-time job like that. I have to work full time," said Stan. If these remarks had been made by anyone else, Marlee would have known they were sarcastic. Stan was not one to use sarcasm. He assumed anyone not punching a time clock and working at least eight hours during the work week was a part-time employee. On numerous occasions, when he was at her house installing a new faucet or painting her garage, Marlee had attempted to educate Stan on the differences in work schedules between hourly employees and salaried professors. He still did not grasp the fact that most professors work well beyond forty hours in a week, and that much of that work is done after hours, on weekends, and at home.

"Stan," said Marlee, letting the part-time job comment slide, "what do you know about the cameras on campus?" Stan and the other guys at the physical plant were known gossips. If they hadn't known the whereabouts of the cameras before Logan's death, she was betting they knew about them now.

Stan opened his mouth to speak just as his cell phone rang. "Just a minute—I gotta take this," he said, reaching for the phone attached to his belt. "Yeah. Uh huh. Okay. Okay. Okay, I won't. Yep. Bye," said Stan. His conversation with the party on the other end lasted no more than ten seconds. As he was replacing his cell phone in the holster on his belt, he looked up at Marlee and said, "I'm not s'posed to say anything about the cameras."

"Did somebody just tell you that?" asked Marlee.

"Yep, it was Kendra. I'm not s'posed to say nothing to nobody about cameras or film footage. She's my boss's boss, so better keep it zipped," Stan said, as he made a zipping motion across his mouth.

"Ok, thanks anyway, Stan. I don't want to get you in trouble. If you find out something you can tell me, just let me know. You have my number," Marlee said. So far, this morning's fact finding mission was not panning out very well.

"Alrighty," said Stan. "Hey, do you want me to come over and clean out the gutters and downspouts on your house and garage pretty soon?"

"Yes, thanks for reminding me about that. You can come over whenever you have time. The garbage bags and ladder are in the garage. Just let me know when it's done so I can pay you," said Marlee.

"Okey dokey," said Stan. "Have a nice day off!"

Marlee let that comment slide as well as she made her way to Scobey Hall to talk with Asshat. He typically arrived at work early in the morning. He was old school and believed professors had to put in a certain number of hours on campus each day. Of course, there was no measurement for the amount accomplished during those hours. As long as he was there, he was satisfying his obligation to the university and the profession. Marlee and the younger professors believed in more of a productivity model. When the work was done, they went home. Or, if the work was not completed, then they took it home with them. The old guard, which consisted mainly of white males ten years or less from retirement, grumbled loudly about the newbies who didn't take their jobs seriously enough to put in a full eight hours on campus. The newer profs ignored the old guard, focusing more on the quality of teaching, research and service rather than just punching an imaginary time clock.

She wanted to speak to Asshat before anyone else had a chance. It was before 8:00 a.m. on a Thursday, and she knew that no one in her department had classes until 9:30 that day. Marlee raced to her office, removing her coat and taking her book bag off her arm in one quick motion. She didn't even need her book bag today, but it was her habit to bring it with her every time she came to campus. The coat and bag landed on the floor near her office chair. Marlee took several deep breaths in order to calm down a bit. She didn't want to march into Asshat's office and explode. She would need to keep her emotions intact if she were to gather any additional information about his conversation with the chief of police. Giving Asshat the attention he so obviously craved grated on Marlee's nerves a bit, but she knew talking with him was a necessary evil. She closed her office door and walked down the hall and around the corner to Asshat's office.

"So, did you see me on TV last night?" asked Asshat, as he adjusted his white, sea captain's hat. He didn't bother with a greeting or brief chatter before attempting to put the focus on himself and what he thought of as a coup in the information department.

"I sure did," said Marlee, not wanting to give him too much credit for his questionable antics. "Did Chief Langdon tell you to pass on the information from your discussion with him?"

"No, but he didn't tell me not to either. I just thought that everyone wants to know what's going on and since the chief isn't talking, I'll ask around and see what I can uncover. Somebody had to do it," he said, as he let out a loud chuckle.

"Do you think the police have any leads?" Marlee inquired.

"The chief didn't come right out and say it, but they seem to be leaning toward the death being self-inflicted," Asshat said, clearly pleased with his inside knowledge from the police department.

Marlee wanted to knock the smirk right off of Asshat's face. Unfortunately, she was going to have to play nice in order to get any other information from him. She believed in the old saying: *keep your friends close, and your enemies closer.*

"When did you give the TV interview?" asked Marlee.

"Yesterday afternoon," replied Asshat.

"What do you think will be the dean's reaction? If he didn't watch the interview, I'm sure he's heard about it by now," said Marlee. She wasn't proud of herself for secretly hoping Asshat would get into big trouble for talking to the chief of police and then giving a television interview about it.

Asshat rolled his eyes. "I'm sure he'll have something to say about it. I see he sent me an email already this morning, but I haven't opened it yet. I've been too busy fielding questions from everyone else," he said with an air of importance.

"Well, I better let you get back to your work," Marlee said, with an obvious note of sarcasm. Asshat would be doing little in the way of work today; he would be too busy basking in the limelight from his television appearance. He was the only one who didn't know what a joke he truly was.

Before Marlee could exit Asshat's office, a red-faced Dean Green burst through the door. His tan polyester slacks were hiked up unusually high, as if to signify his outrage. "Ashman!" the Dean roared, "I want to talk to you!"

"Uh, I was just leaving," Marlee said as she inched toward the door.

"Not so fast, McCabe!" roared Dean Green. "I want to talk to you too!"

Marlee's mouth dropped open. She couldn't fathom what she had done that would bring about this type of reaction from the dean. She thought he was probably just really upset about Asshat's interview and would be taking it out on everybody today.

"Were you both at the mandatory College of Arts and Sciences meeting on Tuesday?" Dean Green asked, glaring at Asshat and then Marlee. He knew they were both there. He was an older man, but he had an eye for attendance, especially at mandatory meetings that he initiated.

"Yeah," said Asshat nonchalantly. Marlee just nodded, tongue-tied by the dean's gruff manner toward her.

"What part of 'don't talk to the press and don't do your own sleuthing' did you two not understand?" roared Dean Green.

"But–but–but I haven't talked to anyone in the press," stammered Marlee, knowing full well he must have found out about her questioning of students, faculty, law enforcement, and others about Logan LeCroix's death.

"I know you've been talking to people on and off campus about LeCroix's death and asking a lot of questions," snarled the dean, looking straight at her. She suspected Kendra had given the dean a quick call regarding Marlee's conversation with her earlier that morning.

"Well, I guess I've been talking to some people, but everyone I know has been asking questions about Logan's death. We're all very upset by it," said Marlee, attempting to play up the sympathy factor as a way of diminishing the dean's wrath.

"Bullshit!" Dean Green yelled, as spit flew out of his mouth and landed entirely too close to Marlee's face. "Do you like teaching here at Midwestern State University?"

"Yes, very much," Marlee said nervously.

"Do you want to keep teaching here?" asked Dean Green, looking Marlee square in the eye.

"Yes, of course I do, but..." stammered Marlee, clearly upset with the turn the conversation was taking. She had never had her career threatened before, and it was a sickening feeling.

"Then no more asking questions about LeCroix's death. That job belongs to the police, not you. I take it you have enough work to keep you busy?" he asked

"Well, yes, I have plenty to keep me busy," Marlee said quickly.

"Then do your work and leave the investigation to the professionals! If you don't have enough work to keep you occupied, then I can assign you some special projects. Understood?" growled Dean Green.

"Understood," said Marlee, then she quickly exited Asshat's office and made a hasty retreat toward her own office.

Dean Green slammed the door behind her. "What the hell were you thinking talking to the chief and giving a TV interview, Ashman?" yelled the Dean at the top of his lungs. "And take off that ridiculous fucking hat when you're talking to me!" As much as Marlee wanted to stand outside the door and listen to Asshat's dressing-down, her need to get away from this situation was greater.

Plus, she still had more people to talk to about Logan's death.

DAY OF THE DEAD

*Joe was the one person in my life whom I trusted whole-heartedly. I thought we would spend the rest of our lives together.
I only wish I'd told him everything.*

Chapter 13

Since Dean Green was on a rampage this morning and was on to her investigative activities, Marlee decided it would be best to get off campus soon. She didn't have classes or office hours that day, and the dean knew she usually stayed off campus on Thursdays, so he would be suspicious if he still saw her roaming around the university. This was especially true given that he had just threatened her career as an assistant professor at MSU if she continued asking questions about Logan LeCroix's death. As nervous as she was about losing her job, Marlee just couldn't let the matter drop. Logan had been a living, breathing human being who was part of the MSU campus and the Elmwood community. The university and the police seemed more interested in keeping secrets than in actually finding Logan's killer. It had been three days since his body was found, and the police still didn't have any major details to release to the public. There was no way Marlee was going to let Logan's death go unsolved. Just because campus administration and the Elmwood Chief of Police were satisfied with keeping the death low-key didn't mean that Marlee was.

Before leaving campus, Marlee swung by Alice Olson's office on the second floor to see if she had any new information. She looked both ways before entering Alice's office. She surely didn't need the dean finding her talking to Alice.

Alice sat at her desk, absently staring at her computer screen. This time the computer was turned on, and the screen featured what appeared to be a report. The document did not seem to hold Alice's interest, and she appeared to be deep in thought. Not wanting to startle her, Marlee made some noise as she came through the doorway. "Hi, Alice," said Marlee as she walked toward her desk.

"Hi, Marlee. I was just reviewing this purchase order for supplies that the dean wants me to submit by tomorrow," said Alice, trying to cover the fact that she was lost in thought.

"Hey, did you hear any more about Logan's partner coming to town?" asked Marlee. She would have liked to visit a bit more with Alice, but knew she needed to get right to the point so she could get off campus.

"Actually, he called me. His name is Joe Tisdale, and he sounded really nice on the phone. He said Logan mentioned me quite a bit when they talked, so he wanted to speak to me. We're meeting for lunch today," said Alice, perking up a bit.

"Wow, that's great," said Marlee, trying to figure out a way to get invited to lunch with them. "I hope I get to meet Joe while he's here. I didn't know Logan really well, but I'd like to convey my sympathy." Marlee looked Alice right in the eyes, hoping she pick would pick up the hint.

"We're going to the Chit Chat around noon," said Alice, picking up the hint and running with it. "Would you like to join us?"

"I'd love to," Marlee said quickly. "Do you think Joe will mind?"

"I don't think so. He seemed to want to meet as many people as possible who knew Logan. I'm sure he'd be happy to meet you," said Alice.

"Thanks, Alice!" Marlee exclaimed. "I'll meet you guys there at noon." She tore out of Alice's office and nearly skipped out to her vehicle. Getting a chance to talk with Logan's partner, who might also have had a motive to kill him, was a major coup. This almost made up for the butt-chewing she'd received from the dean earlier.

Marlee had about three hours before lunch time and needed to get off campus. She had thirty five exams to finish grading from her Criminology class. Since she hadn't held class this Monday, due to Logan's death, she knew she would need to get the papers graded and returned next Monday for sure. Students expected profs to grade and return papers almost immediately and got angry when there was a delay. They didn't think professors had lives outside of work and couldn't understand what could possibly be the hold-up in grading their work. She knew she needed to spend some time grading, so she headed home and set up her grading station at her kitchen table. It consisted of coffee, snacks, red pens, and Pippa sitting in her snow-boot box on the corner of the table.

Within the space of a little over two hours, Marlee had graded two-thirds of the essay exams. She read some of the work from the better students first, which tended to go faster, since she didn't have to make so many corrections and comments. The last third of the essays would probably take about the same amount of time to read and grade. A portion of students in all of her classes were not strong writers. Marlee knew she could just glance at their papers, make a few comments and then assign the low grade, without putting much effort into the task. She knew several professors from a variety of disciplines that did just that. Marlee felt obligated to help make students better writers, which took much more time than simply making a couple of notations.

At eleven thirty, Marlee put the essays into a folder and prepared to meet Joe and Alice at the Chit Chat. She'd made the mistake of leaving student papers out in the past and found that Pippa had barfed up a giant hairball on them. It's hard to maintain a level of professionalism when telling students that the big brown spot on their term papers is actually a vomit stain from a cat.

After brushing her teeth and checking the scant amount of make-up she wore, Marlee left her home and drove to the Chit Chat, a local diner which featured a variety of casseroles, the common ingredient being cream of mushroom soup. Most of the locals referred to this as "hot dish" regardless of the meat, vegetables and starch involved. This type of fare went over very well in the Midwest, and the Chit Chat was usually packed at noon. The only type of food to get as good a reception as creamy casseroles were breakfast items, such as pancakes, bacon, and eggs. A large sign on the diner read, "The Chit Chat Is Where It's At!"

Pulling into the parking lot on the west side of Elmwood, Marlee did not see Alice's bright yellow SUV, which she'd won in a grocery store give-away a couple years ago. It was bright and hard to miss, even in a South Dakota blizzard, but it was free, and that trumped all else.

Marlee entered the Chit Chat, and the hostess seated her at one of the few remaining tables. She sat down, threw her coat across the back of her chair and placed her purse under the table. She smiled ruefully as she thought that, last week at this time, her biggest crime concern would have been someone stealing her purse. Today, she was trying to find out who killed Logan LeCroix.

If a Denny's Restaurant and a quirky grandma's house got married and had a baby, the Chit Chat would have been the offspring. There were plenty of decorations, and they mainly centered on the local blue-collar and farm economies. Antique wooden signs on the walls featured sayings about animals, advertisements for pop, and some home-spun logic. Marlee's favorite sign hung near the windows facing the parking lot. It read, "If you've got duct tape, I can fix it."

The tables and booths at the Chit Chat each had a small vase with an artificial flower, condiments, such as salt, pepper and ketchup, and paper placemats featuring advertisements from local businesses. Marlee read the small ads and noticed one for a funeral home. She quickly glanced up and saw that over half of the clientele had gray hair. *Looks like the funeral home made a good choice in advertising to its target audience,* she thought.

Shortly after noon, Alice entered the Chit Chat with a tall, graying man who appeared to be in his late fifties. He was slim, yet athletic. He wore dark washed jeans, a tan sweater with a green patterned Oxford shirt underneath and a brown jacket. His feet were clad in lace-up hiking boots, as if he had just come in from hiking some of the trails near the surrounding lakes. He was either an outdoorsy type or just dressed in what he thought would blend in.

Marlee stood as Alice and the man approached her table. "Marlee, this is Joe Tisdale. Joe, this is Marlee McCabe. She's a professor at MSU and also knew Logan fairly well." Marlee and Joe smiled at each other and shook hands over the table.

"It's so nice to meet you, Joe," said Marlee, looking him directly in the eye to gauge his reactions. "I just wish it were under better circumstances. I'm so, so sorry about Logan's death."

"Thank you," he said, looking down at the table and shuffling his feet. "It's nice to meet you as well."

They all sat down at the table. Marlee sat across from Joe, and Alice was seated to his right. For the life of her, Marlee couldn't think of anything to say. Joe looked around the room, taking in the local color of the Chit Chat.

"This restaurant has been in Elmwood for over 75 years," said Alice. "Well, not this exact location. It was downtown at first and then moved out to the west side of town a few blocks over. Then it burned down, and they rebuilt here about 30 years ago. My Grandpa Verlin used to bring me and my brothers and sisters here once in a while when we were kids. It was a big treat because Mom and Dad never took us out to eat. Grandpa would let us order anything we wanted."

No one was listening to Alice, but Marlee was thankful to have a chatterbox among them. It took the pressure off, since no one had to launch right into a conversation about Logan. A waitress in a gold dress covered with a white apron approached their table. Marlee recognized her from campus but was unsure of her name. Marlee felt fairly sure that the young woman had been in one of her classes, at least for a short time. It was always a worry that a student who flunked out of Marlee's class would be in charge of her food when she dined out. She hoped spit would be the worst thing that turned up in her meal.

The waitress inquired about their drink orders. "What kind of pop do you have?" asked Alice.

"Coke products," replied the waitress, counting down the minutes until the lunch rush was over and she could leave for the day.

Alice ordered a Coke, Joe had herbal tea, and Marlee stuck with water. She realized she had already consumed three large mugs of coffee that morning before she left campus and two more while she graded essay exams. Any more caffeine today and she wouldn't be able to sleep for a week. Marlee also realized that she wasn't all that hungry, which seemed odd until she recalled all the candy wrappers lying on her kitchen table when she finished grading. After serving their drinks, the waitress took their orders. Marlee and Joe both ordered the soup of the day, vegetable beef. Alice ordered the hot dish special of the day, which was a tater tot casserole made with hamburger, a few mushy canned vegetables and generous amounts of cream soup topped with a heaping portion of tater tots.

"Did you get a chance to look around campus a bit?" asked Marlee, finally regaining her interviewing skills.

"A little bit. Alice was kind enough to show me Logan's office and introduce me to some of his colleagues. I also met his dean and took a tour of Scobey Hall," Joe replied.

"The students call Scobey Hall 'The Maze' because it's so hard to navigate your way around all the twists and turns," said Marlee with a smile. "Were you able to collect any of Logan's belongings from his office?"

"No, the police have everything under seal. The crime tape is over the door, but Alice had a key and let me just peek in so I could get a sense of Logan's work space. I'll be driving his car back home. The police said it was okay if I took it, since both of our names are on the title. They already searched it for evidence and clues and didn't find anything," said Joe.

"So you talked to the police yesterday?" asked Marlee, fishing for details.

"Yes. When they notified me of Logan's death, I told them I would come to Elmwood right away. They asked that I come to the police department after my flight arrived," Joe said.

"What kind of things did they want to know?" Marlee inquired.

"The detectives asked if Logan was depressed or suicidal. They wanted to know if we were having problems in our relationship, since he moved to South Dakota, and I stayed in California. They also had a bunch of questions about my whereabouts. The detectives asked if I knew of anyone who might want to hurt Logan or who would benefit from his death," recalled Joe.

Marlee waited patiently, hoping the silence would be enough to prompt Joe to reveal the answers to some of those questions himself. When that didn't work, Marlee tried a blunt approach. "Forgive me for asking, but what did you tell them?"

"It's true that Logan and I were having some difficulties in our relationship. Every couple has times of ups and downs." Alice, married for over thirty years, nodded in agreement as Joe continued. "Logan was not happy teaching at a community college back home in Santa Rosa and had very fond memories of his childhood summers here in South Dakota. He was thrilled when he was offered a position teaching French at MSU and didn't think twice about accepting it. Being a nearly life-long resident of California, I wasn't excited about moving anywhere, especially to an area with extreme cold. I knew he was unhappy at his work, and that made him unhappy with us, so I finally agreed that I would move here with him after he got settled in. Providing he liked it here, that is," said Joe.

"So how long have you lived in California?" asked Marlee.

"Since I was a child. My family moved there before I started school, so California has really been the only home I've ever known."

"How long have you and Logan been together?" queried Marlee.

"We met over twenty five years ago and were just friends at first. We've been together since 1982, so I guess that would be twenty two years. We lived together the whole time except when he moved to South Dakota in August," said Joe.

"What do you think happened to Logan?" asked Marlee. She didn't like grilling Joe since he just lost his partner but knew he was one of the few sources of information about Logan, and that he would be leaving the area soon. Joe was a source but Marlee just wasn't sure how good a source he would be, given that he could very well be the person responsible for Logan's death.

"It wasn't suicide–I can tell you that with one hundred percent assurance!" Joe shouted, looking back and forth between Alice and Marlee.

"Do the police think it was suicide?" Marlee asked. "I don't know if you've heard or not, but a professor on campus talked to the chief of police and seemed to think he might be leaning toward the suicide angle."

"They had a lot of questions about his mental stability. It's true that Logan was on anti-depressants. He battled with depression most of his adult life and regularly sought help from a therapist, but he's never attempted suicide or even mentioned it. When he would get really down, he usually needed to have his medication adjusted and re-start therapy," Joe replied. "I can't believe the detectives are seriously considering this a suicide. The coroner ruled it a homicide, so I don't know why the police don't see it the same way."

"Logan was right-handed, as I understand it?" asked Marlee.

"Yes, he was. He wasn't at all ambidextrous, so the idea that he could use either hand to shoot himself is completely false," said Joe. Marlee was surprised by this statement. She never even considered the notion that Logan might not have had a dominant hand and could use either with the same level of efficiency.

"Do you know anything about the gun that was used?" asked Marlee.

"No, I don't. I've never seen it before. Logan hated guns, and I know it wasn't his. In twenty two years of living together, I think I would've known if he had a gun in the house," Joe stated.

"Did anyone back in California have a motive to kill Logan?" Marlee asked.

"No way," said Joe. "He was a quiet and private person. We had five couples we'd been friends with for years. Logan got along with everyone. I can't think of one person who didn't like him."

"Did he mention having problems with anyone here in Elmwood since he moved here?" Marlee asked.

"He commented about a few people giving him some trouble, but he didn't name names. Logan said there was a student in his class who seemed a bit obsessed with him. This student wasn't doing very well in the class and dropped it after a few weeks. Still, he kept bumping into Logan all over campus and all over town, which Logan didn't think was a coincidence. He also showed up at Logan's apartment a few times."

"Was this student stalking him?" Marlee asked, as she tried to maintain her composure. It wasn't typical behavior for a student to go to the home of a professor. It crossed many ethical boundaries, and most profs were good about keeping a professional distance between themselves and those they taught. If a student didn't respect these boundaries, however, a professor was somewhat limited in the action he or she could take.

"I don't know if it went to that extreme. I know this kid made Logan feel uncomfortable, and Logan said he told the kid to stop coming over to his apartment," said Joe.

"Do you know why the student went to Logan's apartment in the first place?" Marlee asked.

"He said something about wanting to get extra help so he could pass Logan's class. Logan told him they could speak about it on campus but not at his home during his personal time. Logan told me that he made it clear that he would not meet with students at home. He never did when he taught in California either. After the kid dropped Logan's class, he came back to the apartment wondering if he could have some private tutoring so he could enroll in the class next semester and have better results. Again, Logan told him they could only have contact on campus," Joe replied.

"How did the student react when Logan refused to see him at his home?" Marlee inquired.

"I guess he kept insisting that he only wanted to learn from Logan and thought he was a great professor. Logan said the kid kept trying to talk his way inside both times but finally turned away when Logan held firm."

"Do you think he had a romantic interest in Logan? Marlee asked.

"I asked him the same thing," said Joe. "Logan wasn't sure of the kid's intentions. He said the kid seemed a bit out of it at times. Logan didn't know if he was on drugs, or if he had some physical problems, or emotional issues. I wish he'd told me the kid's name, but he never wanted to breach confidentiality where a student was concerned. I always respected that about him."

Marlee nodded. This sounded just like what little she knew of Logan. He was a professor. He held students and his occupation in high regard. "Was anyone else causing him problems in town, Joe?"

"There was a guy in his apartment building who made some gay slurs right to his face and told him to go back to Fairyland," said Joe. "Logan was upset by the nasty comments and tried to keep his distance from that guy. He lived on another floor, so Logan didn't have much reason to see him. He told me the guy's first name, but I don't remember what it was. I'll have to think on it. The guy usually just ignored Logan unless he was drunk and with his buddies. Then he felt like a big man, insulting Logan when his friends were there to watch and laugh."

"Wow, having problems with two separate people in just two months seems like a lot of drama for one person to endure," said Marlee.

"It was. He had some sleepless nights over it. There were also two guys from the gay community here in Elmwood who invited him out for drinks a couple of times. He went out with them a few times but then found out that one of them was interested in him... sexually, so he didn't hang out with them anymore," said Joe.

"Really?" asked Alice, frowning and shaking her head. She couldn't understand how so many negative things were going on in Logan's life, and she didn't know a thing about any of them.

"Who were the guys he had drinks with? Did he mention them by name?" Marlee asked.

"Clyde and Darren were their names. I think Clyde was a nickname. Logan never mentioned their last names. What really bothered me about them is that Logan felt uncomfortable with them even before Darren expressed his romantic interest," Joe recalled.

"How so?" asked Marlee.

"They referred to getting beaten up and beating up other people. He was kind of scared, from a safety perspective," Joe stated.

"You mean they were victims of hate crimes and retaliated against some people who hurt them?" asked Marlee, comfortable with this topic since she'd spent several years researching various types of hate crimes. She knew violence against gays was prevalent.

"No, not hate crimes against them. Clyde and Darren talked about the violence within the gay community toward other gays," stated Joe.

"What?" Marlee asked. She was aware that domestic violence occurred in same-sex relationships just as it did among heterosexual couples, but she hadn't heard anything about violence within the gay community.

"Both of those guys talked about violence, which was basically among the males and over romantic jealousies. One guy would be jealous when someone else would become involved with a guy he was interested in, and a brawl would ensue. Sometimes it would be a group that targeted one man," reported Joe.

"Wow, I've never heard anything about this," said Marlee. Alice nodded her head in agreement. "You mean Logan could have been killed by Clyde, Darren, or some other guys who were themselves gay and sought revenge when Logan refused their advances?"

"I don't know if that's the case, but it sounds like a possibility, given what Logan told me," Joe stated.

"I don't mean to be indelicate, Joe," Marlee said, "but is it possible that Logan was involved with someone else while he was here in Elmwood?"

"No, I don't think so," said Joe. "Logan would have told me if he wanted out of the relationship. We had our problems, but communication between us was good."

"But what if he didn't want out of the relationship but just became lonely while he was here alone? I'm not suggesting that's what happened, but he certainly wouldn't be the first person to have an affair while his partner was out of the area," Marlee stated. She knew she was on shaky ground and hoped her comments wouldn't cause Joe to shut down completely.

Joe didn't speak but reached for his jacket hanging on the back of his chair. At first it appeared as though he was going to stand up and leave, but he was just reaching for his wallet in his coat pocket. He pulled out a picture of him and Logan and two giant white dogs with long wavy fur. The picture was taken outside. Both were smiling and had their arms draped around each other and the dogs. "This picture was taken at a barbeque our friends held two days before Logan left for South Dakota. He was happy. We were both happy, and I don't think he would've done anything to jeopardize that. He was unhappy with his career in California, which made him restless. I don't think he was unhappy with me or our relationship. He just wanted a new career and location." Joe looked more hurt by this line of inquiry than offended.

"I'm sorry, Joe. I just had to ask. Forgive me for being insensitive. I'm just trying to consider all possibilities," Marlee stumbled over her words.

"It's fine. I understand," Joe said, although it didn't look at all like he understood this line of questioning. "I think it's time for me to go back to my hotel and rest for a bit. It's been a tough couple of days, and I think everything is catching up to me.

"Of course," said Marlee. "You must be exhausted from the shock of Logan's death, the trip, all the questions, and everything else. You two go on ahead. I've got the bill covered."

After some initial resistance over Marlee's offer to pay the lunch bill, they both expressed their gratitude before standing and putting on their jackets. Joe extended his hand to Marlee and again expressed his pleasure in meeting her.

"Alice, you'll take Joe to his hotel?" asked Marlee, glancing at her watch and noticing it was well after one o'clock, when Alice needed to be back at work.

"No, he drove his rental car to campus, so I'll just give him a ride back to MSU. I told Dean Green that I might be a bit late getting back to the office because I was going out to lunch with you two," she said, gathering up her purse.

"You told the dean that I was having lunch with you and Joe?" Marlee asked with a catch in her voice.

"Yep, sure did. And he didn't seem to have a problem at all with me being late getting back from lunch," stated Alice.

After her warning from the dean this morning, she was not pleased to hear that he knew about her lunch meeting with Logan LeCroix's partner. *Oh, shit!* thought Marlee, wringing her hands and already making up a story for the inevitable confrontation with the dean.

*Midwestern State University and Elmwood
need a crash course in sensitivity training.
People around here describe themselves as nice.
Slurs, prejudice, and discrimination seem
anything but nice.*

Chapter 14

After paying the bill and leaving a moderate tip for the waitress, Marlee left the Chit Chat and drove home. It was early afternoon and she had time to talk with more people, but she needed to process all the information she had just learned from Joe. Plus, Diane would be returning to her house in an hour or two, and Marlee wanted to discuss her findings. It always helped to talk it out with Diane and springboard ideas off of her. As Marlee entered her house, she caught a whiff of something rotten. Nearing the trash can in the corner of the kitchen, she realized that it had been days since she'd last taken out the garbage. Her elderly neighbor next door was known to dig in the garbage bins in the area, so Marlee hauled her garbage out to the garage and would keep it there until garbage pickup day. She didn't have anything embarrassing or incriminating in her garbage, but she didn't want the old man next door to be rummaging through her rubbish.

Marlee re-entered her house and eliminated the lingering odor by spraying Febreze all around the kitchen. That was the maximum amount of house cleaning she intended to do for the day. Moving to the kitchen table, she sat down and began to compile everything she had learned from Joe. She was finishing up her notes when she heard scratching and pounding at the back door.

Nearly jumping out of her skin, she quickly made her way to the large window overlooking the deck. Perhaps she could see who or whatever was making all the racket. Marlee caught a glimpse of a tattered green bag and realized that Diane was back from campus.

Diane entered the back door with her green book bag over her shoulder, carrying two large plastic bags brimming with food. She grinned as she set the bags down by the refrigerator. "I thought I'd make us supper tonight," she said. "I hope it's okay if I stay for another couple of days."

"Hey, if you're cooking, you can stay as long as you like," Marlee said, thankful that she would not have to come up with a menu for that evening and equally thankful that the meal would consist of something other than candy and wine.

After putting away the groceries and doing some minor preparation for supper, Diane entered the dining room and sat at the table with Marlee. "Have I got some news for you!" exclaimed Marlee. "First, the dean knows about my sleuthing and yelled at me while I was in Asshat's office. He basically threatened to can me if I kept asking questions about Logan."

"Whoa! Are you serious? He really did that?" asked Diane, furrowing her brow with such force that her dark-rimmed glasses slide down her nose half an inch.

"Yep, and then he laid into Asshat after I left. I didn't hear much because I was busy getting the hell out of there. Before that, Asshat told me he thinks the police believe Logan killed himself. Of course, who knows if that's accurate, or if he just wants to think the police share his beliefs?" said Marlee. "Before talking to Asshat, I met with Kendra Rolland, and she wouldn't tell me anything about the campus cameras or the film footage of the night Logan was killed. I went over to talk to Stan Shepherd at the physical plant, but he got a call from Kendra just as we were talking. She told him not to say anything to anybody about the cameras. I'm guessing she then called the dean, and that's how he knew I'd been snooping around."

"You had an eventful morning," said Diane as she shifted some of her books from her book bag to the table.

"That's not the half of it," said Marlee, surprised that she hadn't led with the most important information. "I met Logan's partner, Joe Tisdale. He was meeting Alice Olson for lunch, and I tagged along.

"What was he like?" asked Diane as she pulled her chair up even closer to the table, intent on catching every detail.

"Seems like a nice guy who is genuinely upset at the death of the love of his life. I think he knows more than he told me, but I didn't get the sense that he had anything to do with Logan's death. Of course, I could be completely wrong on that. He may just be a very convincing liar," said Marlee as she recalled the lunch time conversation.

"What did he have to say?" asked Diane. "Tell me everything!"

"He said they had a strong relationship and the only reason Logan left California was because he was unhappy teaching at the community college where he worked for a few years. He wanted his career to advance, and he had positive feelings about South Dakota since he spent some summers here with relatives as a child," recalled Marlee.

"Did Joe seem believable?" Diane asked.

"He did. He seemed really sincere. Joe also said that if things worked out here for Logan, career-wise, then he was going to move to Elmwood too," said Marlee.

"What kind of work does he do?" Diane enquired.

"Geez, I guess I didn't get around to asking him about that. I'll check with Alice later. She probably asked him," said Marlee, upset with herself for overlooking such an obvious question. Regaining her train of thought, Marlee continued on. "Joe said Logan had problems with three different people or groups since he moved here. The first one he mentioned was a student who seemed somewhat obsessed and went to his apartment a couple times."

"Wow. That does seem odd. I've never had anyone from classes just show up at my door. Have you?" asked Diane.

"Nope. That would really creep me out if a student showed up. Logan was creeped out too, according to Joe. He told the kid to only approach him on campus. The second questionable thing that Logan told Joe about was a neighbor who hurled some gay slurs at him. Joe said the guy was drunk and with some of his buddies at the time. I'm not sure if it was a one-time deal, or if it happened more than once," Marlee said, wishing she'd asked Joe more about it.

"That's horrible. It's bad enough that some people have negative attitudes about gays, but then to say something right to Logan's face is even worse. Coming from California, he was probably used to a lot more tolerance than he faced here," Diane said, with a look of disgust.

"No shit. He probably thought he'd fallen into a reverse time-warp and ended up in the 1950s. Joe said another group made Logan feel really uncomfortable too. Some guys from the gay community asked Logan out for drinks a few times and talked about beating up other gays and being beaten up themselves," said Marlee.

"You mean like a gay fight club?" asked Diane, trying to get her mind around the concept.

"No, it's more like if one person feels romantically rejected by another guy, then the first guy and his friends go beat him up," said Marlee, hoping she had completely understood this absurd story that Joe had revealed to her.

"That happens on a regular basis around here?" asked Diane.

"Apparently so," said Marlee. "The whole thing made Logan nervous, especially after one of the guys expressed a romantic interest in him."

"So, Logan thought he might be assaulted for not returning the interest?"

"Yeah, that's what Joe made it sound like. Weird, huh?" Marlee said, shaking her head. "I've never heard of a group regularly using physical violence against someone who isn't interested in one of them."

"Me neither. Maybe you should check with Gwen and Shelly to see if they've heard anything about this practice," suggested Diane.

"Great idea!" exclaimed Marlee as she quickly walked into the living room toward the telephone. She grabbed her small address book which contained the telephone numbers of her family and friends. Punching in Gwen's home number, she waited for an answer. The answering machine came on, and Marlee left a brief message asking Gwen to call her as soon as possible. Then she hanged up and called Gwen's campus offices number. Marlee was unsure of Gwen's teaching and office hour schedule, so she wasn't hopeful that she would reach her. She was relived, when on the fourth ring, a female voice answered. "This is Dr. Gerken."

"Gwen, hi. This is Marlee. Do you have a minute for a quick question?"

"Sure, what's up?" asked Gwen.

Marlee briefly relayed parts of her conversation with Joe, and then asked if she knew anything about groups of gay men beating up other gay men in town.

"What?" asked Gwen. "I've never heard of anything like that anywhere. Of course, lesbians tend to live a much different life from gay men, so maybe it goes on, and I just don't know about it. I'll ask around and let you know what I find out."

"Thanks, Gwen. Also, do you know of any gay men here in town named Clyde and Darren?" asked Marlee. "Joe said they invited Logan out for drinks, and they were the ones who brought up the thing about assaults. Darren also seemed to have had some romantic interest in Logan, which made him really uncomfortable."

"That's understandable. I don't recognize the names, but I'll check on that too. Gotta run. A student is waiting outside my door to talk to me," said Gwen quickly as she hung up the phone.

"Thanks," Marlee said to an already dead line. She reported to Diane the conversation she just had with Gwen, and they both sat down in the living room wordlessly.

Two hours later, Marlee rubbed her eyes upon hearing some banging and clanging of pans in the kitchen. Thinking about all of the events of the day had turned into a nap. A long nap. Now, Diane was in the kitchen making supper. "Hey, why did you let me sleep so long?" asked Marlee as she trudged into the kitchen, stretching her arms above her head.

"I fell asleep too and only woke up about a half an hour ago. You were snoring like a buzz saw, so I figured you must be really tired," Diane said with a laugh. "When I got up, I knew I needed to start supper, since this dish takes a while to cook." Diane chopped carrots and threw them into a pile along with diced onions and celery.

"What are you making?" asked Marlee, confused as to how it could be nearing meal time.

"It doesn't really have a name. I just put a bunch of vegetables and chicken in a pan with some broth and seasoning and bake for an hour. It's really good, plus it's low carb," she said.

Marlee assisted Diane with the remainder of the meal preparation, and then they retired to the living room to drink wine and talk more about the case. It was nearing 6:00 p.m., and Marlee knew Alice Olson would probably be home from work by now. She gave her a quick call. "Hey, Alice, I just wanted to thank you again for letting me tag along at lunch. I'm really glad I got to meet Joe and find out more about Logan. I hope I didn't upset him too much with all my questions."

"No, I think he was just tired. He's been through a lot in the past few days. He didn't say anything to me about being upset by your questions," said Alice.

"By the way, did he ever tell you what he does for a living?" asked Marlee.

"He's some type of engineer, but he lost his job a couple months ago and hasn't found a new one yet," said Alice.

Marlee's mouth dropped open as she considered the new twists that Joe's unemployment placed on the case. She realized that she hadn't talked to Joe about money and assets. If Joe was unemployed and had fallen on hard times, then he had a financial motive for wanting Logan dead. And if he didn't have a job in California, what was keeping him from moving to Elmwood?

People see what they want to see and people think what they want to think. As the old saying goes, "If you're looking for something, that's probably what you'll find."

Chapter 15

The next morning Marlee awoke to her alarm clock beeping at an obnoxious decibel. It occurred to her that this was the first morning since Logan died that she hadn't woken up on her own. She hit the snooze button and laid in bed, pondering the investigation and her role in it. Marlee knew that she owed it to Logan to find out as much as she could about what had really happened to him. Whoever killed him deserved to be brought to justice and incarcerated. Since the police department and the university seemed to be taking a lackadaisical approach to the matter, Marlee felt it landed on her shoulders to determine the cause of Logan's death. After nine minutes, the contemplation was over. The alarm sounded again, and she needed to get her butt out of bed and ready for work.

Marlee got to her office around 8:00 a.m., although her first class wasn't until ten. She wanted to do a bit more sleuthing but needed to keep a low profile so the dean couldn't berate her further for her independent investigation. Marlee quietly entered her office, leaving the lights and the computer off. Any glow of light under the door would be a tip-off that she was there. After getting her notes together for her two classes that morning, Marlee walked to Thom Dole's office. She hadn't caught up with him yet, which was important since he was one of the first people to see Logan's body.

Thom Dole was in his office down the hall with the lights off and his door slightly ajar. He was short, with an athletic build and a mop of unruly brown hair that always looked as if he had just come in from a wind storm. He had a quick wit and a loud voice, both of which added to his enthusiastic telling of any story. Marlee knocked on the door frame, startling him as he sat reading from his computer screen. His usual jovial mannerisms had been replaced by a somber appearance and large dark circles beneath his eyes.

After exchanging pleasantries and complaining about the dismal weather once again, Marlee asked Thom about finding Logan's body on Monday morning.

"Technically, I wasn't the one who found him. Cecil, the janitor, did. He ran to my office to tell me right after he found Logan. Cecil knew that I'm an extreme early bird and like to come in around 4:00 a.m., so he knew I'd be here. About five thirty, Cecil pounded on my door and told me somebody was lying on the sidewalk with blood around him. I ran down and saw that it was Logan. I could tell he was already dead, but I felt for a pulse anyway. Then I called 911," Thom recalled, with a pained look on his face. He was reliving the scene as he retold it.

"Did you see the gun or anything else that might have been used as a weapon?" Marlee inquired.

"I didn't. All I saw was Logan on his back with blood underneath him, especially around his head," Thom reported.

"Did he have any belongings with him, like a backpack or a briefcase?" Marlee continued.

"Not that I noticed, but it was such a shock that I really couldn't take it all in at the time," Thom said apologetically.

"That's completely understandable. When I talked to Sim-Sam that day, she said you told her that you thought Logan committed suicide," stated Marlee, anxious to get to the part of the conversation she really wanted to have with Thom.

"Yes, I thought that because, really, who gets killed on a college campus in South Dakota? Nobody. Suicide seemed like the only logical answer," said Thom.

"Do you still think it was suicide?" asked Marlee.

"I'm not so sure anymore. It doesn't make much sense for Logan to kill himself in that way. Plus, I don't really think the gun would have been in the dumpster several feet away if he had shot himself. I've been through it in my mind, over and over. I just don't know what to think," replied Thom with a woeful expression. The death had taken a toll on everyone on campus, but Thom and Cecil had felt the worst of it since they had seen Logan after he died.

"Thanks for talking to me about this, Thom. I just wanted to follow up on what I heard from Sim-Sam. I thought you might have some inside information that wasn't released to the public," said Marlee, relieved to hear that Thom was no longer sticking with his claim of suicide.

"No, I only know what I just told you," Thom said. He looked at her quizzically and asked, "Why are you wondering about this?" It was well-known on campus that Marlee had a background in probation and many ties to local law enforcement. Thom seemed to be inquiring if she was officially helping out on the investigation.

"Just trying to make sense of everything," Marlee said, lying only a little. Thom nodded, accepting her brief explanation. Marlee thanked him for his time and waved as she backed out the door and into the hallway. She heard the dean's booming voice around the corner and knew she needed to make herself scarce before he saw her. She quickly ducked into the supply room and pushed the door partly shut. She crouched down behind a stack of boxed copy paper until the dean's voice faded away, and she could make a safe exit to her office.

Marlee's two classes were largely uneventful that morning, and she gave her lectures on auto-pilot. She was so familiar with the information in both Intro to Criminal Justice and Policing that she only half-way needed to keep her mind on the topics. As Marlee walked from the Putnam Building back to Scobey Hall after her last class at noon, she spied Donnie Stacks walking across campus. "Donnie! Hey, Donnie!" she yelled, waving her arms.

Donnie looked toward Marlee and stopped. Recognizing her professor, she walked toward Marlee with a slow, deliberate gait. "Hey, Dr. M. What's up?" she asked casually, running her hand through her short red hair.

"You're just the person I was hoping to see," said Marlee, relieved that she could finally have a follow-up conversation with this student. After agreeing to chat, Donnie followed Marlee up to her office in Scobey Hall. Marlee closed the door behind them, just in case the dean was patrolling the halls again. She didn't want him or anyone else listening in on this conversation.

Donnie disclosed that she'd been having a rough time since Logan's body was discovered on campus. "I had nightmares and started worrying that a killer was lurking on campus. Plus, I had some papers due in a couple classes and couldn't concentrate on them. I was talking to my mom about all of this, and she said I should come home for a few days. I'm glad I did, because I feel much better now. Plus, I actually finished both papers." Donnie smiled, but underneath the cheerful expression, it was obvious there was more on her mind.

"I was talking with Jasper Evans and Dom Schmidt on Tuesday, and they seemed to think you had some information on Logan's death from a police source," said Marlee.

"I heard about the gun being in the dumpster over fifty feet away from his body," Donnie replied, not disclosing her source of information.

"Did this come from Sylvester Blake?' questioned Marlee, knowing the two of them often sat together in her classes.

Donnie looked around uncomfortably, not wanting to answer the question but also not wanting to avoid a direct question from her professor. Finally, she nodded and looked down at the floor.

"Look, I know you don't want to break a confidence, but if you tell me what he told you, I'll keep it hush-hush," Marlee assured Donnie.

"Yeah, it was Sylvester. He didn't say much more than that. The last I knew, they hadn't found any fingerprints on the gun and hadn't been able to trace it. Please don't let this leak out. I'm not that great of friends with Sylvester, but his wife and I have known each other since elementary school. If he finds out I blabbed this, my friendship with his wife will be over. He has a way of turning his wife against people he's upset with," Donnie reported.

"Mum's the word," said Marlee, as she thanked Donnie for the information. "Wait, do you know anyone in Dr. LeCroix's French 101 class this semester?"

"I'm in it. It's a good class, and I really liked Dr. L. a lot," said Donnie, with the woeful look returning to her face.

"Is there a male student who maybe sought a lot of attention from Dr. LeCroix before or after class?" Marlee inquired.

"Nate Krause. He's this weird guy who always makes a lot of comments in class, but they don't make much sense. I've been in a few classes with him, and he usually makes an ass out of himself and then just stops going to class," reported Donnie.

"Did he talk a lot in Dr. LeCroix's class?" Marlee asked.

"Yeah, he made the usual dumb-ass comments in class. He was always up at Dr. L.'s desk before class and then would stick around after the rest of the students left. There's something wrong with that guy," Donnie answered.

"What do you mean?" Marlee asked, her curiosity piqued by Donnie's statement.

"Well, he seems to be obsessive and won't let things drop if he still has questions. I remember, at the beginning of the semester, Nate had questions about the Provence region in France, and Dr. L. kept putting him off saying that we would be covering it later. Nate wouldn't let it go. He kept asking and interrupting until Dr. L. just gave in and answered all his questions. It put us behind in class, and some of us were so mad at him," stated Donnie.

"Mad at...?" asked Marlee, unsure if Donnie was referring to Logan or Nate.

"Mad at Nate. He's such an idiot. Not that he's dumb, but he doesn't have any social skills and doesn't have any friends either. We call him Creeper because he's always in the Student Union, just staring at people," said Donnie, with a shudder as she thought about Nate Krause.

"Did you get the sense that Dr. LeCroix was afraid of Nate?" Marlee asked.

"No, not afraid, just annoyed. Dr. L. never said anything negative to Nate in class, but I could tell he was irritated by him. I don't know what was said after class when they were the only two left in the room," Donnie stated.

"Thanks for the help, Donnie. I'll check over at the Student Union for Nato and talk to him one of these days," Marlee said, standing up and moving toward the closed door.

"If he's not in the dining area of the Student Union, you might check with the counseling office upstairs," said Donnie, as she slung her backpack over her right shoulder, then slid her left arm into the remaining strap.

"The counseling office? Here on campus?" Marlee asked.

Donnie made her way toward the door and said over her shoulder, "Yeah, I heard he's required to go see a counselor there at least three times a week. Like I said, the guy has some serious issues."

People are singled out in society because of their differences. Instead of understanding and embracing the differences, individuals and groups are stigmatized and punished. Punishment takes many forms. One of the most hurtful is exclusion.

Chapter 16

The November wind of the Dakotas whipped across the MSU campus. Marlee, like the other residents of Elmwood and the surrounding area, knew it would get much, much colder in the next few months. As a way of pacing herself for winter, she did not wear her heavy winter coat until at least December. If she gave in and wore her winter coat too early, then the winter seemed longer and harsher. It was a stupid game, but one she played every year as a way to psychologically deal with the oncoming winter. Her reward was beating Mother Nature again. And a damp chill down to her bones that she just couldn't shake.

Marlee zipped up her unlined fleece jacket and exited her office, looking both ways to make sure the dean wasn't lumbering down the hall. She made her way out of the building and over to the Student Union. Due to privacy laws, Marlee knew she wouldn't be able to get any information from the campus counseling center about Nate Krause or his condition. She might, however, be able to bump into him if he was just hanging around.

The Student Union was busy with a late lunch crowd. Marlee passed several tables occupied by groups of students. The chatter from the tables took on similar themes: Logan LeCroix's death and the investigation, unfair assignments from professors, and upcoming parties that weekend. She waved at two separate tables of students as she hurried through the dining area. If she didn't locate Nate Krause, she might circle back and talk to the students to see if they had heard any new rumors. She had learned early in her career as a probation officer that just because something is a rumor, doesn't automatically make it untrue. There was often a grain of truth in many rumors, which made it worthwhile to listen.

As she climbed the stairs to the second floor, Marlee saw a young man sitting on a couch staring at all the people walking by. Before Donnie left her office, Marlee had asked her to provide a description of Nate Krause. This student fit the description to a tee. He was of slight build with long, dirty blond hair, which was partially covered by a black stocking cap. Donnie said that Nate wore the same clothes every day: an oversized black sweater and baggy jeans that were black in previous times but had now faded to a dark, grainy gray. His wire rimmed glasses sat askew on his face, as if he absentmindedly put them on after waking up and never readjusted them.

Walking slowly toward the young man, Marlee put on a smile and said, "Excuse me, are you Nate Krause?" She needed to approach him with care, not that she was fearful of him, but because he might not be very forthcoming with information.

"Yeah," he said looking up at her, diverting his gaze from the groups of students walking past him. "Why?"

Marlee introduced herself and identified that she was a professor on campus. She thought it might put him at ease knowing she was not a detective. "I was a friend of Dr. LeCroix's, and I understand you had a class with him this semester. I was wondering if you had any thoughts as to who might have killed him."

"Why would I know?" asked Nate, with an air of contempt.

"I've been talking to a lot of students who were in his classes," Marlee fibbed. "I'm wondering if any of you students have some thoughts on the investigation that the police hadn't thought of." She wasn't sure if buttering him up would work, but it was worth a try.

"Don't know nuthin'," Nate muttered, his gaze returning to others in the open seating area.

"I heard you were sort of close to Dr. LeCroix. Some students said you talked to him before classes and then stayed after class to chat some more." Marlee didn't want to overplay her hand but this kid needed some coaxing.

"Sometimes we talked," Nate stated, not offering any details.

"What did you talk about?" Marlee quizzed. "I'm not trying to be nosy. I just want to find out as much as possible about Dr. LeCroix, you know, before he died."

"Mostly how I could do better in his class. He was a good teacher, but I just couldn't concentrate on French. It's confusing. Dr. LeCroix said he would help me," said Nate.

"How was he going to help you?" Marlee asked. She hoped he would disclose going to Logan's apartment. She eased into a chair near Nate in an effort to give a more informal feel to the conversation.

"He met with me after classes in his office a few times and went over some pronunciation and vocabulary," stated Nate.

"Did you ever meet anywhere else?" Marlee continued.

"I saw him in the library a couple times and asked him questions. He started to get tired of helping me," said Nate, warming to the conversation a bit.

"How do you know he got tired of helping you learn French?" Marlee asked. "Did he say something to you?"

"Because I went to his apartment one night just to ask some questions about an assignment, and he sent me away. He was kind of grumpy about it," disclosed Nate. "I went to class a few more times after that but couldn't get the hang of it, so I dropped out."

"Have you gone to other professors' homes for help with your classes?" Marlee asked, anxious to see if this was typical for the student, or if Logan had been the only one.

"No. Most don't seem all that excited to help me. Most profs just want to teach during class and then not have anything to do with me after that. I can tell they don't really like me. Dr. LeCroix was different. He seemed to really care," Nate reflected, with a sad face.

"What do you think happened to Dr. LeCroix? I mean, who would have had any motive to kill him? He seemed to be very well liked by his students and the other profs," said Marlee.

"I don't know who would want to hurt him. I dropped his class, but I was going to take it again next semester. I was even trying to practice my pronunciation now so it wouldn't be so hard when I retook the class," he said. "I heard some people talking in one of my other classes. They said it might have been a mob hit."

"What do you think of that idea?" asked Marlee.

"Sounds a little crazy to me. Sounds like something Hollywood would cook up for a lame movie," Nate stated.

"So, are you waiting here for your next class?" asked Marlee.

"Nah, I'm meeting my counselor at two o'clock," said Nate.

"Oh, you go to counseling," stated Marlee. "I know a lot of people who go to therapy and have been helped by it. How often do you go?" she asked, knowing she was on shaky ground.

"Three times a week. On Mondays, Wednesdays, and Fridays. I don't think I need to go that often, but my probation officer says I do. He gets on my ass if I don't go," Nate replied nonchalantly.

Have prejudice and discrimination really decreased in the past decade, or have they just gone underground? From my short time in Elmwood, I can confirm that a look speaks a thousand words.

Chapter 17

The shift change at the Elmwood Police Department happened at 4:00 p.m. Marlee knew that the best time to talk with her contacts within the department was right before they went on duty or right after they finished their shifts. She rolled into the parking lot and went to the glass front window. "Hi, Lois," she said, thinking this might be the one time Lois would remember her.

"Hello. Can I help you?" Lois asked. No such luck in being remembered.

After re-introducing herself for the hundredth time, Marlee asked if Bettina Crawford was on duty. Lois gave her the stink eye for twenty seconds before contacting Bettina on the intercom. A few minutes later, Bettina walked to the front security door and motioned Marlee inside. When they got to a back office corner, Marlee grumbled, "Geez, why does Lois always act like this is the first time she's met me? I've known her for umpteen years."

"She thinks that if she's too chatty, then people will start to ask her for favors and inside information," said Bettina, shuffling aside some papers. "So, what brings you to the PD?"

"Um, I need a favor and some inside information," Marlee said with a mischievous smile. Maybe Lois was on to something with her chilly reception. Bettina raised her left eyebrow and gave a quick grin. Marlee had first met Bettina Crawford years ago when she was a federal probation officer and Bettina was an officer with the Sisseton-Wahpeton Tribal Police Department. Marlee frequently traveled to the Lake Traverse Reservation in Sisseton, because tribal land fell under federal jurisdiction. This meant that, if a felony, such as an assault, happened on tribal land, the investigation and prosecution of the crime fell under the auspices of the federal system. This was a major bone of contention since, often times, the federal sentences were more severe than the sentences handed out in South Dakota state courts. What this meant was that a Native American convicted of committing an aggravated assault, such as beating another person with a baseball bat, would end up in an automatic eighteen-month federal prison sentence. If that same person had committed the exact same crime in South Dakota, but off tribal land, then that person might not receive a prison sentence at all and just be placed on probation. Probation allowed for a person to remain in the community without serving prison time. This resulted in two very different systems of justice in South Dakota: one for Native Americans and one for everyone else.

When Marlee traveled to the reservation to meet with people on her probation caseload, she sometimes had trouble locating them. Bettina was a good source of information; she knew if anyone had moved, if they were fighting with parents or spouses, or if they were attending a local festival or a funeral. Since she was an enrolled member of the tribe and a life-long resident of the Lake Traverse Reservation, Bettina had her finger on the pulse of the town of Sisseton and the outlying tribal housing districts on the reservation. On one occasion, when Marlee believed that there might be some type of trouble in one of her probationer's homes, Bettina accompanied her to the home and provided back-up. Although Marlee had a gun and had passed all required examinations through work to carry the weapon, she almost never took it with her. She hated guns and felt more at ease when she didn't carry it. Bettina, on the other hand, was required to carry a firearm as a police officer. Marlee didn't like guns, but if she thought she would be facing a combative probationer or be walking into a house where many of the occupants were drinking, she was more than happy to take Bettina and her side-arm with her for protection.

When Bettina had decided to apply for a police officer position off the reservation, Marlee was only too happy to provide her with a much-deserved glowing recommendation. After Bettina moved to Elmwood, she and Marlee had become even better friends. Bettina was separated from her husband and had two small children, so that restricted her social life since moving to town. Now that Marlee was a professor, she and Bettina had even fewer opportunities to cross paths.

"My shift ends in about twenty minutes and, for once, I'm actually caught up on my paperwork. How about we get a beer and we can talk in private?" suggested Bettina. She knew the line of questions Marlee had and didn't want to be overheard by one of her fellow officers or the chief of police.

"It's not even four o'clock yet," said Marlee.

"Do you have a problem with that?" asked Bettina with a chuckle. "Oh, and you're buying. And, I'm going to want supper after we have some drinks. You're buying that too. And, it better be somewhere good. Don't be thinking you're just going to buy me something from the dollar menu. I have some stuff to tell you that I think you'll find very interesting."

"Sure! Let's meet at Apollo's at five?" Marlee suggested. That would give Bettina time to go home and change out of her uniform before going out on the town.

"See you then. And bring your checkbook, because I'm really hungry and thirsty," Bettina said as she strolled out of the room, smiling.

At 5:00 p.m., Marlee entered Apollo's. It was part of a regional chain and considered the nicest place in town. The dress was casual, but customers could be seen dressed in anything from fancy evening attire to sweat suits. The restaurant was decorated in dark greens, browns, and burgundies, which added to the overall coziness of the dining experience. Apollo's was split into four seating areas. One consisted of a bar, which was quite popular during happy hour. It was separated from the other three rooms. The remaining dining areas were hooked together but kept individual by cleverly placed walls. Marlee suspected one reason for walled-off rooms was to shield diners from noise. Elmwood was a very child-friendly town, and people often took their young kids out to eat. Dining with kids typically involved some degree of chaos, so sectioning families off in a separate area was good business. The second area tended to be for large groups, such as family reunions, prom dinner dates, and the like. A large fireplace was in the largest of the dining rooms and was the preferred seating area. Tables of varying sizes were located in the middle while large booths lined two of the walls. A small partition enclosed two other booths at the far end of the restaurant. Marlee always suspected this was for private meetings or people having affairs.

When she arrived, Marlee found Bettina already seated in a booth behind the partition. She was thankful for this seating arrangement so that no one could see or hear them talk. Bettina was already drinking a tall Bud

Light tap with tomato juice and green olives. Marlee ordered the same thing as she slid into the booth. The concoction was the source of amusement by newcomers, but it was a standard drink in South Dakota and it was delicious!

After exchanging pleasantries and inquiring about each other's families, the two got down to business over their second beer. "So, what can you tell me about the Logan LeCroix investigation?" asked Marlee. She knew Bettina trusted her to keep the information secret and Marlee would fulfill that obligation.

"The chief thinks it's a suicide and is about to release that finding to the public," said Bettina.

Marlee was dumbfounded. She had suspected that Chief Langdon was heading down this path, but it still shocked her to hear it was true. "Why? What makes him think it was suicide?"

"He can't find any leads that suggest anyone else," said Bettina, as she rolled her eyes, clearly not buying into the chief's theory either.

"So, because the case is taking some time, and a suspect hasn't been located, he thinks it's acceptable to rule it a suicide?" Marlee inquired, more than a little bent out of shape.

"Apparently so," said Bettina. "He's explaining away the gun in the dumpster by saying Logan threw it in there after he shot himself and then walked away. Since the bullet didn't hit a major artery, he didn't fall to the ground right away. Basically, everything the history prof from your department said on TV the other night was an accurate depiction of the chief's thoughts on the case. What is it that you call him? Assmunch?"

"*Asshat* is what the students—and well, everyone—call him. If the chief is so committed to his theory of Logan's death, why hasn't he made an announcement yet?" asked Marlee.

"Because he's waiting for some outside consultants to finish their reports. They are reviewing the investigative materials, forensics reports, autopsy, and anything else in the case," Bettina reported.

"Who are these outside consultants?" asked Marlee.

"I don't know specifically who they are, but one is a firearms expert with the FBI, one is a forensics specialist, and another is a former detective turned private investigator. I think some of them are from out of state," Bettina said. The chief talked to all of them this morning, and they all gave verbal confirmation that they believe it was a suicide. He's just waiting for their written reports so he can make an official announcement."

The waitress appeared at their table, interrupting their discussion. Both ordered another red beer, and they decided to share some mozzarella sticks. Nothing goes with beer quite like deep fried cheese. After the waitress was out of earshot, Marlee asked, "What in the hell is it that makes them all think it was suicide? Do you think the suicide theory holds water?"

Bettina thought for a moment as she sipped at the last of her beer. "Well, it's possible," she said, hesitantly. "It just seems to me that it's being tied up in a neat little ball without enough time and investigation. Personally, I don't buy it."

"That's what I think too. It seems that the chief and MSU administration just want to have this ruled a suicide and then forget about it," said Marlee, upset that anyone would make this type of ruling just because it was an easy answer. "The PD comes out looking good, since there's no unsolved murder in Elmwood, and MSU doesn't have to report any murder statistics to the parents of current and prospective students. It's win-win for both parties."

"It's a complete injustice to Dr. LeCroix," said Bettina angrily. It was no secret that she wanted to be a detective. She had over ten years of policing experience with the tribe but had only been with the Elmwood Police Department for two years. Her newbie status prevented her from climbing to detective any time soon. She had to prove herself in Elmwood before she could even be considered for a promotion to detective. Marlee realized Bettina was taking a risk with her career by meeting with her and sharing information that had not yet been released to the public. "I really don't know how much effort the detectives put into the case. Logan was gay and part Native American, so he had two strikes against him right away."

"What do you mean?" asked Marlee.

"It's no secret that the chief doesn't have time for homosexuals or for minorities in this town," she said bitterly. "I think he probably decided to rule this a suicide as soon as no likely suspect turned up. He doesn't want to waste his time or ruin his reputation further with an unsolved murder on his hands. Especially since he's in so much disfavor already."

"That's right," said Marlee, recalling the pressure some of the Elmwood residents had placed on the mayor and the city commission to oust Chief Langdon just a few months prior. "Have things started to settle down in the department yet?"

"A bit, especially after the chief backed off his idea of mixing up shifts. Once officers realized that they wouldn't be forced to rotate shifts, then everything calmed down a bit. Logan LeCroix's death has caused quite a bit of contention in the department. We all know the chief's thoughts on the case, but a lot of us don't believe it was a suicide," said Bettina. "The chief doesn't want to hear about our thoughts, and anyone who disagrees with him on this gets a strike against their record."

"Really?" asked Marlee. "So there's a good deal of support in the department for the theory that this was a murder?"

"Yes, there is. I'm new here, so I can't say much without it coming back to haunt me. Several of the patrol officers and a few of the detectives don't buy the suicide theory," said Bettina.

"Who's been questioned as a possible suspect in the case?" asked Marlee.

"Logan's partner, Joe Tisdale, was questioned. His alibi checked out. He was with some friends on an extended weekend getaway back home in California. They didn't return from the park where they were camping until Monday around noon. Logan's body was discovered very early Monday morning, so he couldn't have done it," reported Bettina.

"Anything to suggest he might have hired someone?" inquired Marlee.

"Not so far, but Krause and Lumar are still checking on it. At one time, I heard that one or both of them might be going out to California to do some interviews of neighbors, friends, and others, but now that the chief is ready to announce this as a suicide, it won't happen," said Bettina.

The waitress delivered the mozzarella sticks along with ranch dressing and pizza sauce. She set down their beers in front of them and whirled off to accommodate another table. "Who else was questioned?" asked Marlee, grabbing the first mozzarella stick and dipping it into the warm pizza sauce.

"The only other person I know of who was seriously considered a person of interest was Nate Krause. Do you know him? He's a student at MSU," said Bettina.

"Funny you should mention Nate Krause. I just met him and talked to him a bit this afternoon," said Marlee. "Why was he interviewed? Did he make any threats against Logan?"

"No threats that I've heard, but he seemed a bit obsessed with the professor. Students we talked with said Nate spent a lot of time before and after class talking to Dr. LeCroix," said Bettina.

"That's what I heard too. I met Joe Tisdale yesterday and had lunch with him and one of the secretaries from campus. He said that Logan told him a student came over to his apartment twice and tried to talk his way in. I talked to Nate, and he confirmed that he was over there once asking for additional help with French," stated Marlee.

"Hmmmm... that adds even more twists to the case. I know this kid is disturbed. He has a history of mental health issues and has been in the psychiatric ward of the hospital numerous times," said Bettina.

"Do you know if he's dangerous?" asked Marlee.

"Well, he's on probation right now for an assault on a former high school classmate. I'm not sure if he has a tendency toward violence, or if this was just a one-time thing. His probation officer is Vince Chipperton. You might talk to him for more details," said Bettina.

"Sure, I know Chipper. I'll check with him and see what he can tell me about Nate's background and mental illness." Marlee was already anticipating her meeting with the studly probation officer.

"What complicates the case even more is that Nate Krause is the little brother of Mike Krause, one of the lead detectives on the case," said Bettina.

"What? Isn't that a huge conflict of interest?" questioned Marlee, knowing that detectives should not interview their own friends and relatives whenever possible.

"I guess Lumar is the one who interviewed Nate. Still, Lumar and Krause are partners, so there's some sharing of information," said Bettina.

"Do you think there's any attempt at some type of cover-up by Lumar and Krause?" asked Marlee, knowing that this wouldn't be the first time that law enforcement officers covered for their family or the relatives of their partners.

"I've wondered about that myself," said Bettina "but I don't know of anything specific."

The waitress came by and took their orders. Marlee requested blackened walleye, and Bettina ordered steak, medium rare. "So if you had to, who would you guess killed Logan?" asked Marlee.

Bettina grabbed the last cheese stick and swirled it around in the remaining ranch dressing. "I don't know for sure. I've been going over it in my head. Who would want him dead? We've all heard the rumor about the Witness Protection Program and the mob hit, but those don't really hold water."

"Do you know for sure that he wasn't in the Witness Protection Program?" asked Marlee. "When I was a probation officer, we knew that there were some people in the program that were relocated to South Dakota, but we didn't know who they were or the details that got them relocated here. The U.S. Marshals were the only ones who knew. Is it possible that he was in Witness Protection, and it just wasn't common knowledge in the PD?"

"Well, that could be, I suppose. Although I think it would've come out by now, since his death, if he had been in Witness Protection. I'll do some more asking around about that," said Bettina.

"Could he have been killed as an accident?" asked Marlee. She was aware of a story going around campus that Logan was killed by a stray bullet. This seemed a bit far-fetched as she hadn't heard of random gun shots on campus in the year she'd worked there.

"It was hunting season, so there were more people in the area with guns, but I really don't think it was an accident. Besides, the gun used was not for hunting," replied Bettina.

"What can you tell me about the gun? The last I heard it was unregistered and untraceable," said Marlee.

"That's right. One of the outside consultants on the case is a firearms expert. He looked at not only the gun, but also the angle of bullet entry and the wound. So far nothing has been discovered about who owned it. There was some blowback on the gun itself, which was shown to be Logan's blood and tissue. I think that's one of the main reasons it's suspected a suicide," said Bettina, clearing away her utensils so the server could set down her plate of food. "Mmmmmm... I love a good juicy steak."

"OK, no more talk about forensics stuff while we eat," suggested Marlee as she picked up her fork and sized up her blackened walleye. The fish was accompanied by garlic mashed potatoes and a sautéed vegetable medley.

Bettina nodded as she cut into her steak, the pink juices running in various directions on the large serving plate. The two ate in silence for a few minutes, enjoying the elaborate entrees set before them. "Is there any kind of financial motive?" asked Marlee, finally breaking the silence.

"I think Logan and Joe were financially stable and actually, quite comfortable. I don't get the sense that Logan was rolling in the dough," replied Bettina.

"He was a professor at a community college, so I can't imagine he was earning all that much. Did he have any type of savings or inheritance?" asked Marlee.

"None that I've heard about. They co-owned the home they shared in California, but there was a mortgage.

There were a couple of life insurance policies, and Joe was the beneficiary of both of them, but I don't know the values," said Bettina, brushing her dark bangs away from her forehead.

"Will he be able to collect on the policies if Logan's death is ruled a suicide?" asked Marlee.

"I don't know. It depends on the specifics of the policies," said Bettina.

"Have you heard anything about gay men in Elmwood getting together in a group and beating up a person who rejected the sexual advances of one in the group?" asked Marlee.

"No, I haven't heard of anything like that. I know of specific gay couples in which one or both have been violent toward another person or each other, but I've never heard anything about groups being organized to beat up someone," said Bettina.

"Do you think domestic violence happens more in the gay population?" asked Marlee.

"I don't know that it occurs any more regularly," said Bettina "but I think we talk about it more because there's still a stigma placed on homosexuals."

Marlee nodded. "Do you know about any hate crimes here in town?"

"There are plenty of crimes where homosexuals are the victims, but I don't think any of them are officially classified as hate crimes. Like I said before, the chief isn't overly sympathetic to gays, lesbians, or racial minorities," Bettina reported.

"But the prosecutor could step in and charge it as a hate crime," Marlee said.

"Right, but one of the problems with a hate crime is proving intent," Bettina stated.

"Yep, prosecutors have to show that the offender selected the victim based on something specific, like race or sexual orientation," said Marlee. "I spent several years researching this very topic for my dissertation and some research papers. Some have suggested that one reason more crimes aren't prosecuted as hate crimes is because it's tantamount to punishing people for thoughts, like hate."

"I've heard that too. I went to police training in Albuquerque a couple years ago where one of the speakers referred to hate crime as thought crime. Obviously, she wasn't a big believer in charging someone with a more severe crime and giving them a harsher penalty just because they hated the group the person belonged to," said Bettina.

"What's interesting about hate crimes," said Marlee, stepping into professor mode, "is that the perpetrator doesn't have to hate the victim or the group. What constitutes a hate crime is that the perp selected the victim based on actual or perceived group membership. In other words, somebody might assault a person believing they are gay but not have any particular hatred toward them. Or, the perp might assault someone believing they are gay, but in fact, they are not."

"I didn't realize that. I thought all perpetrators hated their victims in a hate crime," said Bettina.

"Often they do, but it's not a requirement. Let's say there's a group of five guys who decide to beat up a gay person. Two of the members might actually hate gays while the other three in the group agree to just go along with it. They participate in the assault, but they don't truly hate gay people. Everyone involved in the assault, except the victim, can be charged with a hate crime. The actual feelings toward the target don't matter. What does count is that the victim is targeted due to his or her sexual orientation, race, or whatever. Sorry to launch into a lecture," said Marlee, suddenly feeling a bit sheepish about her speech. She was passionate about the topic and had been involved in studying and researching it for years. In fact, she was in the process of putting together a proposal to teach a class on hate crimes in an upcoming semester.

"No, I get it," said Bettina, pointing to her dark-skinned forearm. "Obviously it's an interest area for me too."

"Have you been a victim of hate crimes?" asked Marlee, realizing that for her Native American friend this topic was much more than just an academic discussion.

"I've been called names, followed around in stores to make sure I'm not stealing anything and stuff like that. As far as being assaulted or robbed or anything like that, no, I haven't," said Bettina.

"Have you experienced a lot of racism since moving to Elmwood?" asked Marlee. "My students who come to MSU from other states frequently tell me this is a really racist town."

"I don't know if I would say a lot, but some, that's for sure. Most of what happens isn't even spoken. When I came into this restaurant today and asked to be seated, the hostess gave me a funny look, like she couldn't believe I would have the money to eat here. Then, when I ordered a beer, I got a look from the waitress like, 'Here's another alcoholic Indian.' You could drink twice as much as me tonight, and the waitress and hostess will only notice what I drank. They want to believe the stereotypes of the drunken Indian and go out of their way to look for it, meanwhile ignoring the same behavior in their own race," said Bettina.

Marlee felt her face flush. She didn't have to worry about being prejudged or stereotyped based on her race, and she was sad that Bettina had those experiences. Even more, she was infuriated that this subtle racism occurred in Elmwood in this day and age. The two of them were dressed similarly in jeans and sweatshirts, but Marlee knew others in the restaurant would judge Bettina more harshly for dressing casually.

"What do you do when these types of things happen?" asked Marlee.

"What can I do? Technically, nobody says anything. It's all in the way they look at me. It's hard to confront someone based on their expression or how you think they perceive you. I can say that things have gotten better here over the years. When I was a kid, we would come to Elmwood from the rez to do some shopping once or twice a year. Back then, I remember being called names in the parking lot and being followed around in stores by employees to make sure I didn't steal. Another time, we went to eat at a café, and the manager came over and asked us to pay for our meal before it was served. He assumed that we wouldn't have the money. I didn't see anyone else paying before they ate. Just us. It was so humiliating. I never went back there. Those types of things haven't happened to me in Elmwood in a long time. Now, I just get looks from people," said Bettina.

"Maybe things haven't gotten any better. Maybe people are harboring the same attitudes but just know it's socially unacceptable to say anything," commented Marlee. "By the way, what café did it happen at?"

"The Chit Chat," stated Bettina.

"Whoa! I had no idea. Well, they just lost me as a customer," said Marlee.

"It was a long time ago, and they probably have different managers and policies now. Still, I can't get it out of my mind and have never wanted to go back," Bettina was lost in thought for a moment before she mumbled, "Too many bad memories."

"I don't blame you," said Marlee.

"Let's switch topics for a minute. Did you meet the new social worker in town, Tim Deal?" asked Bettina.

"No, why?" asked Marlee.

"Well, he asked me out, and we have a date tomorrow night!" Bettina exclaimed.

"Hey, that's great! Do you have a babysitter lined up?" Marlee asked, hoping that Bettina wasn't going to ask her to watch her children for the evening. Not that Marlee had a problem with Bettina's kids. It's just that she really wasn't a kid person. She liked being around little ones for brief periods of time but had no desire for any children of her own.

"Yeah, my neighbor is going to watch them for me. We trade off babysitting for each other. I trust her, and we have similar ideas on how to raise kids, so it works well for both of us. Plus, she actually likes kids," said Bettina with a smile. Marlee did a mental happy dance since she wasn't being called upon to babysit.

"Well, are you ready to go? I'll get the check," said Marlee waving over the waitress.

"Um, not until I get dessert. You know I'm gonna have to eat like a bird tomorrow on my date, so I need cheesecake tonight," said Bettina.

"Well, cheesecake does sound good. I suppose I should have some too so you won't have to eat alone." Marlee's low-carb plan was now a distant memory. As they were finishing their desserts, Marlee and Bettina returned to the discussion of Logan LeCroix's death. "Joe Tisdale told me that Logan said someone in his building had made some negative comments about his sexual orientation. He didn't know the guy's name, but knew he lived in Logan's apartment building on another floor. Had you heard anything about this?"

"Joe told us the same thing. The detectives were supposed to follow up on it, but I don't know if they did since the chief is set on the suicide ruling," said Bettina. "Do you know if anything was taken from Logan?" asked Marlee.

"We don't know for sure. His wallet was at the scene, but there wasn't any cash in it. His driver's license, credit cards, and MSU identification card were all there. His backpack was there too, but nothing of significance was inside. Something, like money, might be missing, but we just don't know," said Bettina.

As the two were preparing to leave, Marlee took note of their waitress and the hostess. Just as Bettina said, they both gave her a disapproving look as she exited the restaurant. Marlee met their looks with a cold stare and raised her eyebrows. She wanted them to know that she knew what was going on. It probably wouldn't do any good, but it made Marlee feel a bit better knowing she was not tolerating their behavior, albeit in a very small way.

As Bettina opened her car door, she shouted her thanks to Marlee for the meal. Marlee called out, "No problem. Thanks for the help. Let me know how your date goes." As she hopped in her Honda CR-V, she realized that she was a bit jealous of her friend. What did she have to do to get a date in this town?

Kindness and understanding can be found in the strangest places. They can also be absent in places you would expect to find them. Boardrooms, chatrooms, classrooms, and courtrooms exemplify both extremes.

Chapter 18

When Marlee arrived home that evening, she found a note from Diane indicating that she felt safe now and had returned to her apartment. Marlee flopped down on the couch. Now who was she going to chat with? She had no intention of ever getting a roommate, but it had been comforting and even fun at times to have Diane stay with her. She knew Diane was probably getting tired of sleeping on the couch and would be anxious to return to her own home. Pippa ambled over to the couch and rubbed against Marlee's leg. Picking up the giant fur ball in her arms, Marlee said, "Well, it's just you and me now." Pippa looked up at her and started to purr.

The weekend was fairly uneventful since there were no classes or activities going on at MSU. Marlee made good use of the time to prepare for her classes in the upcoming week and to grade the rest of the essay exams. Mondays were always busy for Marlee, but the upcoming Monday would be particularly hellish. Not only did she have her two morning classes and her three-hour night class, but she also had to attend a mandatory meeting called by the dean. She knew she wouldn't be able to sidestep him any longer and was mentally preparing her defense if he cornered her again about talking to people about the investigation.

After cleaning her house and doing a load of laundry, Marlee made a trip to the grocery store and stocked up on vegetables and plenty of protein sources. She was committed to making this a better food week than the last. She knew it would be easier without Diane around. Not that Diane was the source of Marlee's poor dietary choices, but she found it easier to fall off the diet wagon when she was around others. Plus, the Halloween candy was gone, and they had polished off the last of the wine. It was a good time to recommit to her low-carb plan.

Monday's morning classes came and went. Although she had had a restful weekend, Marlee still felt like she was teaching on auto-pilot. She vowed to kick it up a notch during class that night. She hung out in her office until two o'clock when the mandatory meeting was scheduled to be held. Marlee made her way to the meeting room at 1:59 p.m. She didn't want to get there early and risk being called out by the dean before the meeting. She knew an ass-chewing was coming. She just hoped it would be in private, after the meeting, and not in front of her colleagues.

Marlee sat in the second row along the west wall in the classroom. From lecturing in that room in previous semesters, she knew from personal experience that it was an area she didn't focus on when she was at the front of the room. Hopefully, this was the tendency with most speakers in this room. The dean entered the room with his usual fanfare. He stomped to the front and scowled as he surveyed the room, noting who was and was not present.

It was surprising that Dean Green didn't even mention Logan LeCroix, the death investigation, nor the role that any faculty and staff had played in doing their own investigations, or providing information to the various news outlets. Instead, he focused his remarks on recruiting new students to MSU and retaining the students who were already enrolled. Dean Green provided slide after slide of data showing how many of the students who came to MSU for tours eventually enrolled. He also had data on the drop-out rates for freshmen, sophomores, juniors, and seniors at MSU. The dean emphasized how important it was to recruit and retain students so that MSU could increase its enrollment. As one of the smaller public institutions in the state, there were always rumors afloat that the Board of Regents wanted to close MSU. Some professors who had been there for over ten years expressed repeatedly that MSU's closure had been a hot-button topic since they had begun teaching, and it had not come to fruition thus far, so they didn't give the whole matter too much credence. The dean exploded and insisted that, if everyone didn't get on board with getting more students to enroll and keeping the ones already in attendance, MSU was doomed for closure. He concluded the meeting with comments about the development of a new committee to deal with an increase in cheating and plagiarism at MSU. After the doom and gloom meeting, Marlee filed out of the room along with the other professors from the College of Arts and Science. Dean Green hadn't looked at her even once during the meeting, so she figured someone else must be on his shit list now.

After the meeting, Marlee went home to rest up a bit before her evening class. She took a short nap and then had an early supper before she drove back to campus. She arrived in her office at five thirty, which was enough time for her to center herself and mentally prepare for the three-hour class ahead of her. Marlee organized her notes and quickly reviewed the material she intended to cover that evening. The class was Criminology and was one of her favorites to teach. Tonight, unfortunately, they were scheduled to discuss murder and non-negligent homicide. She would need to tread carefully with this topic, given Logan's death only a week ago. Marlee knew she wouldn't be able to just talk about murder in an abstract way. Even if she tried, students would ask questions about Logan's death. They were anxious for details and answers, just like she was.

The classroom where she taught Criminology was equipped with theater seating. The stage where she lectured was at the bottom of the room with eight rows of graduated seating that looked down at the stage. Off to her right was a large screen. The projector sat atop the computer station at the front and was what she used to transmit her notes onto a large screen for the students. Most chose to write down what was on the overheads, but some chose to just listen to the lecture and get the notes from another student or forego the notes altogether. Marlee was a visual learner and, as a student, had written down every word that her professors had put on the overheads. Since becoming a professor herself, she had learned that some students learned best while listening, and some learned best by applying the knowledge during activities or discussions. She tried to provide all three types of learners with an adequate means of processing the material she presented in class. Of course, the students were supposed to have read the chapter before lecture, but she knew that rarely happened.

The first hour of the class was spent discussing the different types of murder and non-negligent manslaughter, the elements that distinguished one type from another, and the penalties associated with each. The next half hour focused on perpetrators, victims and how they were associated, if at all. Students frequently raised questions during the lecture, mostly seeking to make sense of the material as it pertained to Logan LeCroix's death. "So, how is a first degree murder different from the other types? I just don't completely understand that part," said a frustrated student in the middle of the room.

"There are a lot of different ways I can word this, but the easiest way to understand is that first degree murder is intended, and there is some degree of planning. Let's work on an example together. Let's say you are the perpetrator. You absolutely hate your roommate and want to kill him or her. You also want to get away with committing the murder. How would you do it?" asked Marlee.

"I would use poison," said the student who asked the first question. A few in the room laughed at the speed at which she voluntccrcd the answer.

"How would you carry out the murder, Angie?" asked Marlee.

"I'd sneak a poison into her coffee," said Angie.

"OK, let's go with Angie's poison angle for our example. Poisoning someone requires a degree of planning, right? I mean you have to figure out what you can slip into the victim's drink, food, toothpaste, or whatever. You also have to determine what type of poison will go undetected by the victim and, hopefully, by the coroner and detectives. What else is necessary for our perpetrator?" asked Marlee. The more students became involved in the discussions and examples, the more they tended to enjoy class and learn the material.

"The perpetrator would not want the poisoning linked to her," offered a male student in the back row.

"Exactly! So what would Angie do to ensure that she got away with it?" questioned Marlee, winking at Angie. "Is it okay if we use you as our poisoner, Angie?" The student smiled and nodded, eager to play along in the example.

"She would have to make sure that she had an alibi for the day and time the victim was poisoned," offered a student in the front row.

"Good. But what if the poison takes several days or weeks to work? Some poisons need to build up in the system before they become deadly," said Marlee.

"I would wipe off my fingerprints and plant the poison bottle in someone else's home or car. That would throw the suspicion onto a completely innocent person and off of me," said Angie.

"Yep, but let's say you've anticipated that you'll be a suspect, and the alibi thing won't work out. What else could you do?" questioned Marlee.

"After poisoning my roommate, I could skip town or flee the country," said Angie. "It would look really suspicious to the police, but maybe I could hide out on an island in the South Pacific and change my name."

"Sure," said Marlee. "And if it's a country that doesn't support the death penalty, then that country might give you asylum. Now, let's get back to the poison itself. How does Angie know what poison to use, how to administer it, how she can get the victim to drink it, and how to keep the medical examiner from discovering it?"

A shy kid sitting to the far left of the room raised his hand and said, "All of that information is available online. All she would have to do is spend some time researching different types of poisons."

"Yes, or she could even go old school and read books about poisons in the library. Regardless of how she gets her information, what must she remember to do?"

No one answered, and the students looked at each other. Finally Marlee said, "Angie would have to make sure she didn't use her own computer to do the research. Even if she erased the browser history, forensic computer specialists can still uncover searches that were performed on a computer. If Angie read about poisons in library books, she shouldn't check them out. She also needs to be sure no one sees her reading books about poison." The students nodded, grasping the idea that the cover-up was important in avoiding arrest.

"So, does it make sense how this would be different from a murder in which two people were drinking at the bar, got into a fight over one spilling beer on the other, and one killed the other?"

Angie was first to speak, proud that she now fully understood how first degree murder could be distinguished from other types. "The poisoning was intentional, not an accident. And, I took steps to plan it out, throw suspicion on someone else and try to go undetected."

"Bingo!" exclaimed Marlee. "The poisoning was intentional and planned. The spontaneous fight between two drunks, in which one dies due to the injuries, is not planned, and the person who won the fight may or may not have wanted the victim dead. It depends on the circumstances of the crime."

By this time, the students were anxious to apply some of the information they learned in class to Logan's death. "So, was Dr. LeCroix's death a first degree murder?" asked Angie.

"We don't fully know the circumstances of the crime yet," replied Marlee, feeling uncomfortable in discussing such a personal situation in such an academic way. "It's possible, but the police are still investigating." This last part was probably a fib, since Bettina Crawford from the Elmwood PD told her that the chief was already inclined to rule it a suicide. She fielded a few more questions regarding Logan's death and then gave the class a ten minute break. Marlee learned long ago that, if students didn't get a break halfway through class, they would not be able to pay attention. Some would start to nod off, and others would slip into a daze, not hearing most of what was said.

Following the short break, Marlee reconvened class and broke them into small groups. This allowed everyone in the group to have a chance to participate without the worry of speaking before the whole class. She provided each group with four scenarios and had them identify which were first degree murder, second degree murder, voluntary manslaughter, and involuntary manslaughter. In addition to distinguishing between the types, the students also had to identify what information in the scenarios made it obvious that it was a particular type of murder or manslaughter. When the groups were finished, Marlee involved the whole class in a discussion on the types of murder and manslaughter. When that discussion was complete, she had about fifteen minutes left of class, just enough time to talk about the test they had taken two weeks prior and to pass back the exams.

When the exams were returned, and she had fielded all the questions about grading, Marlee excused the class at 9:00 p.m. Niles Barkley, the shy student who had provided information on poisons during the class discussion, waited in the classroom after everyone else left. Marlee was packing up her bag and powering down the computer when she noticed he was still there. Niles was a non-traditional student in his mid-twenties who had recently returned from service in Iraq as a military police officer. He stood five feet ten inches tall and had muscles on top of muscles, which he maintained through regular work-outs at the campus gym. She'd initially had a negative impression of him on the first day he attended class. Marlee assumed that, since he was non-traditional and a war veteran, he would be a class know-it-all. Instead, he turned out to be very respectful and quite knowledgeable. Niles was most interested in learning new things, not showing the class how much he already knew.

"Do you have a question about your exam, Niles?" Marlee asked, secretly praying he didn't because she just wanted to go home and relax after her big day.

"No, I was just wondering if you wanted me to walk you to your car," Niles said.

Marlee was touched. Niles thought she might be scared to walk into the dark parking lot by herself after class and was offering to escort her safely to her vehicle. She thanked him for his kind offer, but indicated she needed to go to her office to first drop off some books and would not be leaving campus for a bit. Niles nodded with a smile and left the room. Marlee was pleased that someone had taken the time to worry about her. She went to her office for a half an hour and realized that she couldn't concentrate. She was fried. Marlee walked out of the building, looking both ways as she exited. She walked right over the very spot where Logan LeCroix's body was found last week.

In uncertain times we often find a quick answer will substitute for a correct answer.

Chapter 19

Tuesday morning brought a jolt to Marlee and the rest of the Elmwood community. Around 11:00 a.m. she was in her office meeting with some of her advisee students about the classes they would be taking next semester. All professors were advisors to some of the students in their respective departments and were expected to help students navigate their way toward an eventual graduation. Marlee had just finished mapping out a spring semester schedule for a student who was struggling to get through the required class of English Literature. This would be his second attempt at the class, and Marlee reminded him that showing up for class, reading the text, and turning in all of the assignments were the three missing pieces of the puzzle in his quest to actually pass the damn course. As he walked out the door, she shook her head at needing to point out the obvious. Sometimes it wasn't that a student didn't know what to do but needed encouragement or just a butt-kicking to get motivated. Putting her counseling skills to good use, Marlee provided a bit of both.

She answered her phone on the second ring. The caller did not self-identify, and it was impossible to tell if the call came from a male or a female. The caller whispered, "The police chief is making an announcement on campus at noon about LeCroix's death in the Quinn

Building." Then there was a click, and the line went dead before Marlee could respond. She had no idea who the caller was. Someone from the police department? Or could it have been an employee on the MSU campus? What if it were someone from the community? Maybe the caller was someone she hadn't even thought of talking to so far. She pondered the caller's identity while sorting through important and non-important email messages. At eleven forty-five, she put a sign on her door canceling her office hours for the rest of the day and made her way over to the Student Union.

Walking into the cavernous classroom, Marlee wasn't sure if she really wanted to hear what the chief of police had to say. The room held over 250 people with graduated seating looking down at a stage with a podium. She sat near the middle of the room behind two professors from the Art Department; one, a young blond man dressed in jeans and an MSU sweatshirt, and the other a woman in her 50s wearing a turban and African tribal dress, which highlighted her Midwestern pallor. Marlee didn't know either of them well, but leaned in to ask what they knew of the case and of the upcoming meeting. Neither had any information, and the blonde man said that the only reason he knew about the meeting today was that he was in his department secretary's office when she scheduled the room. The three looked at each other, then settled back into their seats. About 15 other people showed up by noon, the majority of them professors. *Why aren't there more people here?* Marlee thought.

At noon President Ross, flanked by Kendra Rolland and Chief Langdon, entered the door at the front of the room and stood before the group. All three wore somber expressions, and Kendra looked at the floor. President Ross approached the podium and gently touched the microphone to ensure it was on and working. The slight screech ensured all systems were operating at full capacity.

"Thank you all for being here," said President Ross to the room of twenty people as he pulled the microphone closer to his face. "We are here today so that our Chief of Police, Bill Langdon, can make a statement regarding the death of Dr. Logan LeCroix. With that, I will turn it over to Chief Langdon."

Bill Langdon approached the podium and moved the microphone toward his mouth. He looked as if he would rather be anywhere than where he was. He cleared his throat and recapped the details of Logan's death. Then he launched into a brief synopsis of the investigative work which had been done to that point. "Based upon the evidence at the scene, an investigation into Dr. LeCroix's background, interviews with numerous people, forensic examination of the firearm, and the opinions of outside consultants, I am ruling the cause of death as a self-inflicted gunshot wound." A collective gasp echoed in the large room.

When it appeared that Chief Langdon was not going to make further comments, the art professor with the turban asked, "Can you give us some details as to what led you to that conclusion?"

"Uh, sure," Langdon said, shuffling his feet. "The ruling is based on..." His eyes caught sight of someone who had entered the back of the room, and he appeared even more ill at ease. "Uh, it was based on all those things I just mentioned."

Marlee looked toward the rear of the room to see what had further stymied the police chief. Five people were standing along the back wall. Marlee recognized three of them as students: Donnie Stacks, Dom Schmidt, and Jasper Evans stood side by side watching as the chief spoke. The other two individuals appeared to be students as well, as they were in their early twenties, carried backpacks, and were casually dressed in jeans and sweatshirts.

"But, what about the specifics of who was interviewed and what the evidence revealed? Also, what was the background information on Logan you mentioned?" persisted the turban-clad art prof.

"Due to privacy concerns for the deceased and the deceased's family, I cannot go into Dr. LeCroix's background information. As far as the evidence, it was collected and sent to the state crime lab for testing. The gun was found in a dumpster near the body and could not be traced. I'm not going to get into any more details of the case at this time," said Langdon as he backed away from the podium and edged toward the door.

"Was there a suicide note?" shouted Marlee. The chief looked at her but did not walk back toward the podium to answer her.

President Ross approached the microphone, again adjusting it to his height. He didn't answer Marlee's question either and moved on to further announcements. "I would like to extend MSU's thoughts and prayers to the family of Dr. Logan LeCroix. Also, a memorial service will be held this Friday at 4:00 p.m. If you would like to speak at the service, please contact Kendra Rolland, as she is organizing it. Thank you for coming today." With that brief statement, he snapped off the microphone, and the three of them walked out the back exit.

Jaws were agape in the oversized classroom. People looked incredulously from one person to another, seeking some meaning in what had just been said or unsaid. All at once, the room exploded as everyone began talking to those near them.

"How can it be suicide?" asked the blond art professor. "We've all heard the gun was buried in the dumpster, which was several feet away from Logan's body. I just don't buy that someone could shoot himself, hide the gun, walk away, and then drop to the ground and die." The other professors around him were shaking their heads in disbelief.

"Why wasn't this meeting announced through campus email?" asked Marlee. "And why aren't the local TV station or the newspaper here covering it?"

"It seems like the chief and MSU wanted as little notoriety at this point as possible," said the turbaned art professor. Marlee and the blond prof nodded in agreement.

"Seems to me like both offices just want this whole thing swept under the rug and forgotten," said Marlee, disgusted and ashamed at both her police department and her university.

Attendees from the meeting left the room and gathered in small groups outside the meeting room to further discuss the bombshell that was just dropped. Although Marlee had heard from numerous inside sources that the chief would be ruling this matter a suicide, she was still in shock. There were too many questions and no acceptable answers.

Jasper, Dom, and Donnie found their way over to Marlee and began talking at once. Marlee raised her hand to stop them. "I can't understand you all when you're talking at once. Do you guys have class or have to be at work now?" They all shook their heads, indicating that they didn't. "Good. Let's get off campus and have some lunch. My treat." The students' ears all perked up when they heard the offer of free food. They agreed to meet at Pizza Ranch in ten minutes.

Marlee parked her car in the lot at the buffet-style restaurant which offered not only pizza, but also broasted chicken, potatoes, gravy, vegetables, ice cream, and dessert pizza. There were large and small rooms for birthday parties and company meetings, upon request. Marlee was the first to arrive and requested a small room in the back after she paid for their four buffet lunches. The room was separate from the main dining room, away from the buffet stations and out of earshot of the kitchen and bathrooms. She knew that if they closed the door, their conversation would not be overheard. Marlee waited in the back room and peaked out occasionally until she saw the three students walk in the front door. She waved them to the back and they hurried over.

After filling their plates, getting their drinks, and settling down in the private room, Marlee began to speak. Her plate was heaped with mashed potatoes, gravy and a giant broasted chicken breast. She had already consumed several forkfuls of potatoes and gravy and nearly three cups remained on her plate. The low-carb program was not going well today. "How did you guys all hear about the chief's announcement today?"

"Sylvester told me, and I told Dom, who told Jasper," said Donnie. "Guess he heard about it during the morning shift change meeting at the PD."

"Did any of you call me?" asked Marlee, still wondering who placed the anonymous call to her tipping her off about the meeting.

"We tried your office right before noon, but there was no answer," said Dom. "But we were relieved to see you when we got there. How did you find out about it?"

"Somebody called and told me. I have no idea who it was because the caller was whispering and disguising his or her voice," Marlee reported. "I thought it was really strange. I'm not sure if it was someone from the PD, from MSU, or someone else."

The three students looked at each other and shrugged, not aware of who may have placed the call.

They continued to shovel in the free food and went back for seconds and thirds. Marlee was content with one plate which, in truth, probably held enough food for a small family. During the meal, they all shared the information they knew about the case. Marlee was careful not to disclose any information she promised the source that she would keep confidential. Some information she could share but could not attribute to Bettina Crawford or Sean Yellow Tail for fear of getting them in trouble if it came out that they were the leak in the police department. All of them were outraged at the police department's conclusion that Logan's death was a suicide.

"It just doesn't make sense," said Donnie Stacks for about the fifth time.

"I know. It really doesn't add up with the evidence. Did Sylvester mention, or even give a hint, that there might be evidence we don't know about?" Marlee asked Donnie.

"No, not really. He doesn't give out a lot of details, just a few tidbits. Next time I see him, I'll see if I can get a bit more information from him," said Donnie.

"Why didn't the chief or President Ross answer your question about a suicide note?" asked Dom.

"I'm wondering the same thing. It seems it would be a fairly easy question to answer. They wouldn't have to go into any detail on it, just put it to rest one way or another–was there a note or wasn't there," said Marlee.

"What's your feeling on it?" asked Jasper.

"It seems to me that, if they are ruling the death a suicide, they would confirm the presence of a note. It would prop up their theory and investigation and take some pressure off them. My guess is that, since they refused to answer the question, there is no note," stated Marlee matter-of-factly.

"Is there some legal reason that they couldn't confirm or deny it?" asked Jasper. "The chief said they want to protect the privacy of Logan and his family, but how would confirming a note be a breach of privacy any more than a suicide ruling?"

"Good point, Jasper," said Marlee. "The only thing I can think of is that maybe MSU or the PD is afraid of a lawsuit by Logan's family or partner and don't want to discuss any more details than necessary. One thing I do know is that there's a lot more information on this case than what is being shared publicly. And I really don't think it's a suicide. If there were a note, then the PD wouldn't have been interviewing people or have the gun tested. There might not have even been an autopsy."

"I don't believe it either," said Jasper. "Let's say he did want to kill himself. Why would he do it on the sidewalk at campus?" They all shook their heads, trying to make sense of the facts before them and attempting to figure out what really happened and why the police and MSU didn't want everyone to know.

Marlee did not glean much new information from the students. They all weighed in on Nate Krause, the student from Logan LeCroix's class who went to his home on more than one occasion. "I don't think he's really a bad guy," said Jasper, "but he's odd and it makes people scared of him."

"Yeah, he doesn't really have any friends. When he talks to anyone in class, they usually move away from him or make sure not to sit near him in the next class," reported Donnie. "It's kind of sad, now that I think of it. I always just thought of him as a nuisance because he took up so much of Dr. L.'s time in class, but I guess maybe he was just lonely." Donnie looked down at the table, reflecting on some of the interactions she and other students had had with Nate this semester. A look of sympathy and regret crossed her face as she contemplated Nate's isolation and rejection by fellow students. Jasper and Dom nodded their heads in agreement, also realizing that Nate was a person with feelings, and not just someone to be mocked or avoided.

"Have any of you seen Nate be violent or out of control?" Marlee asked. The three students shook their heads that they hadn't.

"He was just odd and kind of a pest, but I never saw him threaten or hit anyone. I never felt like he was dangerous," said Jasper.

"Well, I actually remember hearing that he beat somebody up last year. I think it might have been self-defense, though," said Dom. "I don't know anything other than that about it. I don't even remember who told me."

The group agreed to keep in touch and alert each other to any further happenings in the case. Donnie said, "I don't mean to be rude or tacky, but it's kind of fun for all of us to get together and discuss the case. I wish it weren't someone we knew. I wish no one was shot on campus, but it does help to talk it out. Plus, I'm learning a lot more about how the criminal justice system really works." Dom and Jasper nodded with enthusiasm.

"Well, there's no reason we can't get together periodically to discuss this case or just matters that generally pertain to criminal justice. I could see about starting up our Criminal Justice Club again. We used to have one, but then membership dwindled and the faculty advisor for the club resigned and no one else took over. This was all before I got here in 2002," said Marlee.

"Yeah, that would be great!" exclaimed Jasper. "I know a lot of students who would be interested in it."

"Great. I'll do some checking around to see what needs to be done to get it going." On one hand, Marlee was just as excited as the students were to have a forum in which to discuss criminal justice matters that were happening locally or nationally. As an officially recognized club at MSU, they would be able to receive funding, which would provide for food and drinks at their meetings and, most importantly, for travel funds so that some students could go to local, regional, and national conferences. On the other hand, she knew that there would be some level of university involvement which would limit their autonomy. Any time a group went from an informal to a formal status at the university, a number of limitations and responsibilities were placed on the group. She would have to fill out reports, attend meetings, put in requests for funds and justify what the club was doing with said money. Marlee would need to figure out if the benefits of reviving the Criminal Justice Club at MSU would outweigh the cost of the restrictions they were sure to face. As good of an idea as the Criminal Justice Club was, the dean would have to be involved in the implementation of the group. His participation and input were things Marlee could do without.

Day Of The Dead

You'll never know unless you ask...

Chapter 20

After lunch with her students, Marlee returned to her office. She had cancelled her office hours for the day but decided to return to do some class prep for the remainder of the week. She was bloated and groggy due to the vast amount of potatoes and gravy she'd consumed at Pizza Ranch. She wasn't at her most alert in the afternoon anyway, and piling on the carbs only increased her desire for a long nap. As she sat in front of her computer, struggling to find the words to reply to an email request from a colleague, there was a sharp knock on her partially closed door. "Come in," Marlee said, as she swiveled her chair away from her computer and toward the door so she could see who wanted to speak to her.

Stella DeVry, a professor of chemistry, stood in the doorway. "Hey, Marlee. I've got some really exciting news!" Stella was in her late fifties, was athletic, and had a high level of energy. She was a senior professor and had taught at MSU for over twenty years. Stella was well liked by her students and was rigorous in her expectations of them. She mentored many of the students who would go on to medical school. Stella could, however, be a bit hyper. She frequently sounded off in faculty meetings about things that were not always the main topic, earning her the dreaded label of "flake" from some of the other faculty members, mainly the male faculty members who were at the same level. Marlee thought Stella was very intelligent in matters related to her field but was a bit out of touch with reality when it came to most other topics. Of course, this was an accurate blanket statement of most of the professors at MSU, and of professors in general.

"What's got you so excited?" asked Marlee. Coming from the previous careers of probation officer, social worker, and federal investigator, Marlee tended to have a somewhat skewed idea of what constituted excitement. In her past careers, excitement usually dealt with the more horrific aspects of life, such as murder, rape, and assault. In the academic world, exciting news could be applied to something as mundane as getting a new office chair. Marlee didn't feel the need to brace herself for Stella's news.

"Well," she said, pausing for effect, "I have lined up a speaker to come into my Criminalistics class tomorrow and I was wondering if you'd like to attend."

"Who is it?" asked Marlee. Stella had a flair for the dramatic, so the speaker was probably just someone from the local hospital coming in to discuss laboratory hygiene or something equally fascinating.

"It's Bill Langdon! The Chief of Police! He's going to talk a bit about the Logan LeCroix death investigation," exclaimed Stella, proud for achieving such a coup.

"What?" shouted Marlee. "He's coming to your class?"

"He sure is," Stella said, with a wide grin. "I just called him up and asked if he would be willing to come to my Criminalistics class to discuss some of the details of the LeCroix investigation."

"And he agreed to it?" Marlee asked, incredulously. *What was up with this guy?* she thought. On one hand, he seemed very uncomfortable making public statements about Logan's death, but when professors called him up to discuss the case, he was a regular Chatty Cathy.

Stella nodded. "He has some stipulations. First, the only people that can be there are you, me, and the ten students in the class. He didn't want anyone from administration or the press there. We can't invite other students to attend either. Second, what we discuss in that room has to stay in that room. Chief Langdon doesn't want any information he gives us to leak out. Third, he won't be able to answer some questions for us for various reasons, like privacy."

"Why is he willing to do this?" Marlee inquired. She couldn't believe he was going to open up and share additional information with the class, information which was not made public.

"He is doing it to educate the students on the testing of crime scene evidence," Stella replied, moving from foot to foot in excitement.

"Do you think he'll tell us something that hasn't been released to the public?" asked Marlee. She seriously doubted he would do so, but then remembered how he opened up to Asshat when they had spoken about the death investigation the previous week.

"I hope so," said Stella. "There still seem to be a lot of unanswered questions."

Marlee nodded in agreement. "Can we ask whatever we want, or are there areas he has already limited us to?"

"He didn't put any limitations on the discussion when I talked to him, but he might before he starts his talk tomorrow. I guess we'll just have to play it by ear," said Stella.

"Well, you can definitely count me in for this!" said Marlee, anxious for the chief's presentation and wondering if she would be able to wait until tomorrow.

She was already going over the questions in her head that she intended to ask.

After Stella left, Marlee could no longer concentrate on anything related to her classes. She decided to go home and make a list of the questions she would ask Chief Langdon tomorrow. Marlee knew he would have some pat answers that did not reveal anything, so she intended to catch him off guard with a few inquiries. He was trained in interviewing, but Marlee had a good interviewing skillset herself, thanks to over ten years of previous experience in the criminal justice field. She was used to getting information out of people who had a vested interest in keeping secrets.

Before going home for the day, Marlee decided to go to Logan's apartment building. His apartment would probably still be sealed, but she wanted to be able to visualize where Logan lived during his short time in Elmwood. During the course of her own questioning, she learned that he lived in the Newsome Apartments, located near the mall on the east side of town. She didn't know what floor he lived on but figured it would be easy enough to find out.

Arriving at the apartment building, she parked along the street, since the sign behind the building threatened that those not living there would have their cars towed if they parked in the lot. She eased out of her vehicle, watching for traffic. Last year a man was killed in town when a car clipped him as he was exiting his vehicle on a side street. This town was small, but there were a lot of bad drivers of all ages, evidenced by the long court column in the newspaper dealing with traffic offenses. The young drivers put the blame on the large elderly driving population, while the older folks held the young whippersnappers accountable for the numerous infractions and accidents around Elmwood. The middle-aged contingent was noticeably quiet on the debate, probably because they had children in the youth group and parents in the elderly group. Regardless of your age or belief in who was causing the accidents around town, everyone had to look out for themselves.

The Newsome Apartments building was a reddish-brown brick and had seen better days. It was three stories high and included over forty apartments. Most had two bedrooms, but there were a few single-bedroom units as well. Marlee wasn't sure what floor Logan lived on, or if he had a one- or two-bedroom apartment. When Marlee was a probation officer she had found that the best way to find out information about people was to ask their neighbors. Frequently, people were more than willing to provide information about those who lived near them. Older people and others who were at home during the day were prime sources of information. They had time on their hands and were likely bored and looking for some excitement. Marlee's elderly neighbor who lived to the north side of her house was brimming with information about the comings and goings of the other neighbors. Herman had apparently figured out her schedule, to some degree, as she often found him waiting in his back yard when she arrived home from campus. He was always ready to volunteer everything he'd seen and heard that day. Because of Herman, Marlee learned that one of her neighbors was having an affair and another had an online shopping addiction. Both female neighbors tended to their proclivities during the afternoon hours while their husbands weren't home.

When Marlee arrived at the front entrance to the apartment, she was glad to see that it did not have a security door. This meant that anyone who chose to could enter the building at any time of day or night. While this was good for Marlee's fact-finding operation, it was a concern from a safety perspective. The locked mailboxes were just inside the front entrance and some were marked with full names, some with just first initials and last names. Other mailboxes were not labeled at all, either because the apartment was vacant or the tenant hadn't labeled it. Unfortunately, neither Logan's name nor his initials were on any of the mailboxes. She would have to go old school in locating his apartment.

Marlee decided to start with the first level. Faded green carpeting covered the floors of the entrance and the hallways. The walls were painted a light color, which had yellowed with age. She meandered down the hall, looking at the names and door hangings on the doors. There was nothing to pinpoint Logan's apartment on the first floor, so she climbed the back stairs to the second floor. She caught her shoe on a tear in the carpet on the rear stairway and stumbled, breaking her fall against the wall. That was a lawsuit waiting to happen if it didn't get fixed soon. Continuing her quest to find Logan's apartment, she heard the creaking of a door behind her. Marlee turned to see an elderly woman in a flowered house dress peering out with caution. She quickly smiled at the old woman and the smile was returned with a quick slamming of the door. Marlee made note of the woman's apartment number just in case she needed to knock on the door later for information. Given the old lady's initial behavior, Marlee wasn't expecting much cooperation from her. Having no luck identifying Logan's apartment on the second floor, she climbed to the third floor and had the same result.

Even though it was not her first choice, Marlee decided to knock on the door of the old woman who had peeked out at her and then slammed the door. She rapped on the door with her knuckles and the door immediately opened. The woman had been standing at the door, probably peering out the peephole the whole time. Marlee smiled brightly, introduced herself to the woman and indicated that she had worked with Logan LeCroix at MSU before his death. The old woman responded with a shy smile and motioned for Marlee to enter her apartment. The overwhelming smell of animals hit her hard as she entered the unit. In the corner hung an empty bird cage. As she entered the apartment, three small Pomeranian dogs bounded up to greet her. The apartment furnishings were straight out of the 1970s. The furniture, a couch that sagged in the middle and a matching orange flowered chair, was clustered in the center of the room. Two wooden end tables flanked the couch, and each held a large table lamp with plastic covering the shades. The carpet was variegated green shag while the refrigerator and stove were a coordinating olive green.

"I'm Rose, and I knew Logan. He just lived across the hall from me in 4B," said the elderly woman. "I met him on the first day he moved in. After that, he would come over from time to time. He brought me cookies once, and another time he helped me carry some trash out to the dumpster. Logan was a sweet boy." Rose looked down, and Marlee thought for a second that she might start crying. She pulled a tissue from the sleeve of her house dress and proceeded to dab at her damp eyes. Then she got up from the arm chair and bustled to the kitchen. She insisted on serving Marlee a snack even though she was still bursting from her enormous lunch. A few minutes later, Rose returned with two cups of instant coffee, that she had heated up in the microwave, and slices of banana bread, which had been defrosted in the microwave.

Marlee took a bite of the stale banana bread, which had been frozen after it had already gone bad. She tried to swallow it but it stuck in her throat like a lump of cement. She reached for the coffee cup and took a sip. The coffee was strong enough to peel paint off a house, but it did help to dislodge the banana bread from her throat. "Rose, I suppose you heard that the chief of police ruled Logan's death a suicide," said Marlee, taking another nibble of the banana bread in an effort not to be rude.

Rose nodded. "I had a nephew who killed himself with pills a few years back. We all knew he was crazy. I thought it was just a matter of time before he hurt himself or someone else. When my brother called to tell me the news, I was shocked but not surprised. I knew something bad was going to happen with Ricky; I just didn't know what or when. I never had that feeling about Logan at all. He seemed to have his life together."

"Do you have any idea of who might have wanted him dead?" asked Marlee, as a small parakeet flew by her head and landed on the arm of the chair where Rose sat.

"I know he was a gay and some people don't like the gays," Rose replied. She used her index finger to gently pat the parakeet's head.

"Do you know anyone specifically who might have wanted to hurt Logan because he was gay?" Marlee inquired.

"No, I don't know anyone who wanted to hurt him. There's a guy up on the third floor who used to give Logan a bad time about being gay. He thought he was being funny, but I know it really hurt Logan's feelings. I don't think Al, that's his name, Al Haskell, would have actually hit him or tried to kill him, but I guess you never know," Rose responded.

"You don't think Al's a violent type?" asked Marlee.

"He's a loud-mouth, especially when he's drinking with his buddies, but I don't think he'd hurt anyone when he was sober and by himself. Who knows what he'd be capable of when he's drunk and with those other idiots he hangs out with. They are always making a lot of noise in the hallways and out in the parking lot," Rose reported.

"Did you hear Al or his friends make anti-gay comments to Logan?" Marlee questioned.

"No, I never heard anything personally, but Logan told me about it when he came to visit one evening. I don't think he was scared of Al and his friends, but his feelings were hurt," said Rose.

"That's completely understandable," said Marlee. "It must have been difficult enough being in a new town, then to be tormented for being a homosexual."

Rose nodded in agreement. She had a fondness for Logan and it was clear she missed him. "Rose, how long have you lived here?" asked Marlee.

"Since my husband died in 1975, so I guess it's been almost thirty years," she replied. "It doesn't seem that long, but I guess it is. I used to be a bookkeeper and retired in 1994 when I turned 70. I don't have any children, so it gets a bit lonely here for me. Logan was so nice and kind, and I sort of felt like he was my son. I miss him so much already." Rose dabbed the corners of eyes again with a tissue.

"Did you ever see anyone come to visit Logan at his apartment?" Marlee asked.

"He had some deliveries from UPS, and one time a scary-looking kid came to his door. I don't like to be nosy, but the kid was making a lot of noise and Logan was trying to quiet him down. They talked for a minute or so at the door, but the kid didn't go inside. Logan never talked about it and I didn't ask," Rose said. She looked a bit sheepish to have just admitted that she spied on her neighbors.

"Oh, I totally get it," said Marlee. "If there were a commotion outside my apartment, I'd be looking out to see what was going on too." She didn't want Rose to clam up out of embarrassment or in an attempt to save face. By admitting she would have done the same thing, Marlee hoped to put Rose at ease. Rose smiled and nodded.

"There was a tall, slim guy who came to visit him once around the beginning of October, and I think he may have stayed with Logan for a few days, because I saw him walking out the front entrance a couple days later wearing the same clothes I saw him in when he came to Logan's apartment a few days earlier. Logan never mentioned having guests, and I didn't want him to think I was spying on him," said Rose.

"Can you describe the guy?" asked Marlee. As Rose launched into a detailed description of the man and his clothing, Marlee began to suspect it was Logan's partner Joe, or someone who looked a lot like him. She found this very curious. She'd been under the assumption that Joe had never been to Elmwood before. Had Joe told her this was his first trip to Elmwood? Marlee couldn't recall, but she knew for sure that he never once mentioned coming to visit Logan since he had moved there in August.

Marlee thanked Rose for her time and the heartburn-inducing refreshments. She also exchanged telephone numbers with Rose and encouraged her to call if she recalled anything else about Logan or anyone who might have visited him. Rose beamed as she wrote down her phone number on a scrap of paper and handed it to Marlee. This was the most excitement she'd had in a long time. As Marlee was leaving the apartment, she noticed the window behind the couch where she was sitting. It was cloaked in dark multi-colored curtains held back by burgundy ropes. She walked toward the window and peered out. Rose had a perfect view of the parking lot. This was likely where she learned a lot about Logan, in addition to spying on him through the peephole.

As Marlee left the apartment building, she realized she needed to talk to Joe again to question him about visiting Logan in early October. She hoped he hadn't already left to go back to California. This was not a conversation she wanted to have over the telephone. She needed to look Joe in the eye and read his body language when she questioned him. It was the middle of the semester and there was no way she would be able to take time to fly to California to talk to Joe in person, so her only hope was to speak with him before he left town. He clearly had more information than he had previously provided, and Marlee aimed to find out what it was.

My family was made up of more than those who shared my blood. My true family loved and supported me unconditionally. Family is made up of those you choose to surround you.

Chapter 21

It was late afternoon, and Marlee was exhausted, both from the enormous lunch and from the amount of information that had come her way that day. She replayed her conversation with her students, Rose from Logan's apartment building, and with Stella DeVry, trying to think of additional questions for each person. Her mind was a bit foggy and she was feeling overwhelmed by all the information. When she returned home, she pulled out the notebook containing her notes on Logan's death and recorded what she had learned earlier that day, and the questions that were still unanswered.

As far as Marlee knew, Joe Tisdale was still at the Ramkota Hotel. She called the hotel desk's main line and asked to be connected to Joe's room. She was put on hold while they contacted his room and Marlee's spirits soared. That meant he was still in town. On the second ring, Joe answered the phone. After exchanging pleasantries, Marlee asked Joe if he would like to meet for supper that night. He readily agreed, anxious to get out of his hotel room and have a conversation with someone, even if it was a person he didn't know very well.

Marlee stretched out on her couch and covered herself with a fleece blanket made by one of her friends. It was patterned with a variety of cartoon cats in humorous poses. As soon as she settled in for a short nap,

Pippa jumped on the couch, looking for some attention. Padding her way from the foot of the couch to the pillow where Marlee rested her head, Pippa meowed repeatedly with each meow growing louder and more desperate. She petted Pippa and scratched behind her ears for a few minutes until she settled down on Marlee's stomach and went to sleep.

A loud beeping noise jolted Marlee awake, and Pippa rocketed off the couch. At first, she thought it was the smoke detector, but soon realized it was the alarm she had set before taking her nap. Marlee had wrestled with insomnia since her mid-twenties. It often took her a long time to fall asleep, even for naps, but then she would sleep deeply for hours. She had learned long ago that naps required a wake-up time or she would miss out on anything else planned for the day. Marlee ran to her bedroom with Pippa underfoot the whole way. She turned off the alarm and noted that the time was 5:00 p.m. That gave her an hour and a half to wake up and get ready to meet Joe for supper.

After a quick shower and clean clothes, Marlee felt fully restored. She brushed on a layer of brown-black mascara and added a little brown eyeliner. Then she pulled out a tube of clear mascara and applied a layer to her eyebrows. She didn't want to look like her maternal grandfather or any of his brothers, as they were widely known for their overgrown, out-of-control eyebrows. She dotted concealer on her blemishes and blended it in to match her naturally light skin tone. It puzzled her how she could have acne and wrinkles at the same time, but she knew she wasn't alone based on the conversations she'd had with several of her female friends in the same age bracket. It just wasn't fair. The final touch was a coat of Burt's Bees tinted lip balm. This was pretty much her usual regimen. With each passing year, she subtracted one or two steps from her beauty ritual.

Joe was waiting in the lobby of his hotel when Marlee arrived. She suggested picking him up and he had readily agreed. Elmwood was not a large town by any stretch of the imagination, but Marlee thought Joe might be getting tired of constantly asking for directions and trying to navigate his way when he had so much on his mind right now. He was wearing dark blue Dockers, a pale blue Oxford shirt underneath a navy print cardigan. He wore the same hiking boots and coat that Marlee had seen him in a few days earlier at the Chit Chat.

Joe hopped in Marlee's vehicle, and they sped off to a small restaurant a few miles outside of town. The Dockside was located on the western bank of Richmond Lake. Summer was the busy time for the restaurant due to tourists and local boaters, but The Dockside remained open through Christmas to accommodate hunters and those wanting to hold holiday parties at the establishment. In the summer, Marlee liked sitting out on the deck overlooking the river. That would not be an option today, since it was only 25 degrees and had been dark for nearly an hour, thanks to the recent Daylight Saving Time change. On week-day nights in the fall, the main dining room was closed, but there was ample seating in the bar. The Dockside featured a variety of food choices, from standards like steak, chicken, and pasta, to local favorites like walleye, venison, and pheasant. She chose this restaurant so that Joe would have a chance to try some of the local fare if he chose or he could fall back on dishes he was familiar with, if he didn't feel like experimenting with something new.

They were seated at a table in a corner of the bar, away from the rest of the crowd. The hostess must have assumed they were a couple out on a date, or perhaps a married couple getting away from the kids for a few hours. Marlee appreciated the hostess' consideration, since she didn't want everyone in the restaurant to be privy to their conversation. The waitress, a weary looking woman in her late forties with wisps of black hair falling out of her ponytail, brought them menus and glasses of water. They considered the menu, and Marlee answered a few of Joe's questions about the food options. When the server returned to the table, Marlee ordered her favorite dishes that The Dockside offered: grilled walleye and sweet potato fries. Joe was up for a culinary adventure and requested the smothered pheasant. Not only did Marlee not find the dish appetizing, but the name did not whet her appetite either. She suspected it was pheasant cooked in a crock pot with cream of mushroom soup and served with a side of potatoes. She hoped Joe would not be disappointed with his choice.

The two chatted comfortably while they waited for their meals to arrive. Both ordered a small dinner salad and those arrived within minutes. Marlee decided not to apologize for the questions she had asked during their previous meeting, since it might just dredge up bad feelings. Joe seemed relaxed and ready to talk and she did not want to ruin it. He brought up the issue of the police department's finding of suicide in Logan's death.

"I just can't believe it," Joe said with a grimace. "Suicide is out of the question. Plus, the evidence just doesn't measure up!"

"I know. I think everybody was upset to hear that ruling from Chief Langdon. How did you hear about it?" asked Marlee, realizing for the first time that Joe was not at the meeting earlier that day.

"The chief called me at the hotel around two o'clock and told me. I'd been napping and was a bit groggy when he called, so I didn't have a lot of questions. Now I do!" said Joe.

"He didn't call you until two o'clock?" Marlee asked incredulously. "He made the public announcement at noon, although no one from the press was notified of the meeting. I guess they were given the details afterward–very few details, by the way. The chief said that was out of privacy for the family. What do you think that means?"

"It's inexcusable that he made the announcement before he notified me. What if I had heard about it when I turned on the TV?" Joe asked. No matter what the final ruling was, Marlee could not imagine hearing such an announcement from a news source rather than directly from the official in charge of the investigation. Chief Langdon showed little sensitivity when dealing with victims and their loved ones. This level of impropriety was but one of the reasons Marlee disliked and distrusted Chief Langdon. At this point, she was not sure if the insensitivity had to do with a lack of compassion or a dislike of homosexuals.

"He didn't say anything about a suicide note," Joe continued. "I don't know what he's withholding that he thinks would be upsetting to the family. What could be more upsetting than a ruling of suicide when it's clearly a murder?"

"Do you think the chief could be referring to Logan's depression or the therapist he's seen in the past?" Marlee inquired. This hardly seemed like information detrimental to the family. Many people Marlee knew suffered from depression or other types of mental illness. There was still a stigma, but she didn't think it was something the police would consider extremely sensitive information in a death investigation.

"He never said one word about any sensitive information," said Joe.

"Do you plan to follow up with the chief with some of your questions?" inquired Marlee, finally picking up her fork and digging into her salad. She was anxious to hear what he had to say but did not want to be too pushy.

"You know, I really would like to talk to him one-on-one and find out exactly what made him go with the suicide ruling." Joe's lower lip began to tremble, but he regained his composure quickly. "At this point, I guess it doesn't matter what I say. Chief Langdon won't change his mind, I'm sure."

"Joe, I don't want to be pushy, but I would be willing to go with you to meet with the chief if you'd like. Do you just want to think about it and let me know?" asked Marlee.

"No need to think about it. I would definitely like you to go with me. Maybe tomorrow?" asked Joe, raising his voice and seeming a bit hopeful for the first time that night.

"Tomorrow would be fine, as long as we can schedule it after 2:00 p.m. He is actually a speaker in a chemistry professor's Criminalistics class tomorrow at one o'clock, and I was invited to attend. I would like to see what information I can get from him during the presentation before I go with you to meet him," said Marlee.

"Ah, you think Chief Langdon might be telling me one thing and people in the community another?" asked Joe, crunching into a radish slice from his salad.

"I'm not saying he is, but it is possible. After all, you aren't from around here. What are the odds you would be talking with a local?" Marlee posited, holding her fork in midair. "Maybe I'll learn something that we can use in speaking with him in private that he didn't intend for you to know."

"Good idea!" exclaimed Joe. "I'll schedule an appointment for after two o'clock tomorrow. I won't tell him that you're coming too."

The waitress cleared their salad bowls and came back with two scorching plates. Marlee's walleye was cooked to perfection, and Joe seemed to be enjoying his smothered pheasant. Just as Marlee suspected, it was covered in cream of mushroom soup or some other creamy sauce. Instead of potatoes, it was served with a side of white rice and green beans that looked as if they had been boiled for hours.

After they finished their food, the discussion again turned to the investigation of Logan's death. "Joe, how many times did you visit Logan after he moved here? One of his neighbors was telling me about a man she saw him with, and the description sounded like you," said Marlee. She knew this could be a hot-button topic, especially if Joe had never actually visited Logan in South Dakota.

"Just the once," Joe said without hesitation. "We had an argument over the phone and I thought we needed to talk in person, so I flew here on stand-by. I was only here for a couple days in October, but it was enough to work out our issues."

"If you don't mind me asking, what were the issues?" asked Marlee.

Joe looked her square in the eyes. "Normally, I would mind if someone asked me a personal question like that, but I understand there are special circumstances here. Logan really liked teaching at MSU and living in Elmwood. He wanted to stay here and I was waffling about pulling up roots and moving to South Dakota. We had a big argument one night on the phone and it ended badly. I flew here the next day and we settled it. I decided to give it a try here in Elmwood. We would give it a few years and then if one or both of us were unhappy, we would move somewhere else."

"Thanks for telling me, Joe. I know you've had a lot of people prying into your private life and it must be uncomfortable, to say the least." Joe nodded as Marlee spoke. "What were your main concerns about moving to Elmwood?"

"This is going to sound silly, but one thing I was worried about was the cold weather. I've lived most of my life in California and I'm used to very mild winters. I was also afraid that South Dakota might not be very tolerant of someone who is gay. In California, Logan and I had a wide circle of friends. Some of them were gay, and the ones who were straight didn't care about our sexuality. And, we didn't care about theirs. It was a non-issue for all of us," said Joe.

"As it should be. South Dakota has a long way to go in accepting differences, but it is getting better compared to when I was growing up," said Marlee, recalling the numerous gay slurs that were part of everyday conversation in her high school. "Speaking of differences, I understand that Logan spent some time on the Rosebud Reservation as a kid, and that he's part American Indian."

"Yes, he told me about his summers there as a kid and the great times he had. His grandfather was well-known in the community and several people would come to his home for advice. Logan also told me they went to powwows and a lot of community gatherings. His grandmother, who was a white woman, was into herbal remedies. Logan said she could cure about any ailment with plants naturally growing in the area. He really had a fondness for both of them," said Joe.

"Did he stay in contact with them or any other relatives from South Dakota?" Marlee asked.

"No, he wasn't close with any aunts, uncles, or cousins. When his grandparents died, he lost contact with that whole branch of the family. I think he had some regrets in not keeping in touch. It wouldn't have surprised me if he had decided to look up some of his cousins eventually," said Joe.

"Do you know any of their names?" Marlee asked.

"No, he never mentioned them by name, just grandpa and grandma," said Joe.

"Are you sure they were actually related?" asked Marlee. "Often, Native Americans refer to elders as their grandparents even when there's no blood relation between them."

"Hmmmm... I never thought about that. When he said they were his grandparents, I just thought he was speaking about the parents of one of his parents. I don't even know if they were his maternal or paternal grandparents," said Joe.

"What about his parents and siblings?" asked Marlee.

"Well, his parents are both dead and have been for many years. They were deceased before we met. Logan and his sister have been estranged since before his parents died. He wouldn't talk about it, so I don't know the nature of the relationship. I never had the impression that there was animosity between them. It was more like they just didn't have anything in common and never stayed in touch," said Joe.

"Yeah, I guess that happens in some families," said Marlee. "How about you? Are you close with your family?"

"It was a little rough when I first came out, but after some time, both of my parents came around. They realized I was the same person they had always known. Mom died about ten years ago, and Dad passed away two years later. They both loved Logan, just as I do. I mean did," said Joe, tearing up and rubbing the corner of his left eye with the sleeve of his sweater.

"Do you have siblings?" asked Marlee.

"Two sisters. They both accepted that I was gay immediately. I think they probably knew before I even understood what was going on. Sara and Marta are both several years older than me and always protected me. The three of us are still very close. Logan and I got together with them and their families all the time. We all live about an hour apart, so that makes it easy to plan get-togethers," said Joe.

"When I talked to Alice Olson, she told me you were looking for work. What line of work are you in?" asked Marlee, attempting to get some answers about his employment status and then lead into questions about finances. She found herself liking Joe more and more, but she still hadn't completely ruled out the notion that he could be behind Logan's death. From her experience as a probation officer, Marlee knew very personable people were capable of some terribly heinous acts. Evil frequently wore a mask.

"I'm a mechanical engineer. I worked for the same company for twelve years, up until a few months ago when I was let go due to downsizing. Another company bought the company I worked for and there were two of us doing the same job. The people in charge had to decide between keeping me or the guy from the other company and he won out. I haven't been able to find work in my area since the lay-off," said Joe.

"That's too bad," Marlee said with sympathy. "It must have been difficult, financially, to be out of work and maintain two households with Logan living here in Elmwood."

"I received a nice severance package when I was downsized, so we were doing fine. Neither of us were big spenders. We lived comfortably and had our toys, like our sports car that Logan drove and our boat, but we put quite a bit into savings for a rainy day," said Joe.

Marlee was relieved to hear that Joe was not in dire financial need. "So, were you going to look here in Elmwood for work?"

"That was the plan. If Logan liked it here, then I would move here and look for work. Like I said before, I had some hesitation about moving here, but we came to an agreement that I would at least try it for a while," said Joe.

"Was there something Logan knew about that might make someone want to silence him? Or did he have something that someone else might want?" asked Marlee, grasping at straws.

"I don't think so, but I guess I don't know for sure," said Joe.

"Any detail could be the key to Logan's death, so if you think of something, let me know," said Marlee. Joe nodded in agreement as Marlee wracked her brain trying to figure out what Logan knew or had that could have brought about his death.

After dropping Joe off at his hotel, Marlee was deep in thought as she drove home. Tomorrow promised to be full of surprises, since she would be attending Chief Langdon's speech in Criminalistics class and also visiting with him and Joe.

Questions and answers. They don't always go together.

Chapter 22

Marlee tingled with excitement all morning on Wednesday thinking that she might glean more details on Logan's death from the chief of police. It would be nearly impossible to change his ruling of suicide, at least at this point, but she hoped to eventually gather enough information to refute the chief's ruling. There were several lingering questions that Marlee wanted answered as soon as possible. First, who was responsible for Logan's death? More than anything, she wanted the name of the killer revealed and the person brought to justice. At this point, there were no strong suspects, but Joe Tisdale, Nate Krause, and Logan's homophobic neighbor were all contenders.

First, There was also the possibility that the shooter was someone she had not yet considered.

Second, what was the motive for the killing? Love, hate, and money were the most common reasons for murders, but there were other possibilities in the case of Logan's death. Also, it could also have been an accident or a crime of opportunity.

Third, why did the chief of police believe that Logan's death was a suicide, especially since the coroner had labeled it a homicide? There was no indication of a note. There did not appear to be a history of mental instability. Logan battled depression but was on medication and was frequently seeing a therapist, so his depression seemed to be under control. Did the chief have proof that it was a suicide, or did he just use that finding since the investigation hadn't produced any strong leads or suspects? Was this a face-saving move by Chief Langdon as a way to overcome his negative perception in the community? If so, Marlee failed to see how claiming a murder which was actually a suicide would benefit the chief's reputation, especially since the evidence pointed to a shooter other than Logan. Why had the outside consultants concurred with the chief's belief in suicide?

Fourth, what was MSU's role in Logan's death? Why was he killed on campus during the very early hours of November 1st? What did the administration at MSU know about his death, and why were they so anxious to keep faculty and staff quiet?

Fifth, why wasn't Logan carrying the keys to his office, the building, or his car? Why wasn't he wearing a jacket in the cold weather? Had someone summoned him outside? Was anything taken from him?

Sixth, had the firearm used in the shooting been traced yet? Did the police look into more seriously than just as a preliminary measure, or had they disregarded it after the chief's conclusion of suicide?

Marlee was sure there were many more questions than these that needed answering, but her head was swimming from her consideration of just these six issues. At one o'clock, Marlee entered the classroom where Dr. Stella DeVry held her Criminalistics class. The students and Stella were all seated and looked up expectantly when Marlee walked in. "Just me," she said cheerfully, realizing they were all anxious for the chief to arrive. Marlee had no sooner sat in a chair at the back of the room than Chief Langdon entered through the side door. His face was deadpan as usual - no emotion whatsoever. Stella greeted him and introduced him to the class. Since there were so few people in the room, the chief sat in a chair at the front, and his presentation took on more of an informal conversational approach. Stella and the students moved their chairs and were seated in a haphazard semi-circle before him, ready to listen to what he had to say and hit him with questions of their own.

Chief Langdon appeared much more relaxed than on the two previous occasions he appeared on campus to make statements about Logan LeCroix's death. Marlee guessed that he felt he could side-step any questions from the students and two professors that he didn't want to answer. He began his talk with an overview of the case, starting with the time at which the police were notified of a dead body on campus. He talked about the investigation of the crime scene in chronological order and detailed the efforts of the police officers in securing the scene from outsiders to limit contamination of evidence. Chief Langdon then spoke about the steps taken by the detectives in collecting evidence at the crime scene. None of this was new information to Marlee. She taught a class on crime scene investigation and knew the proper procedures for roping off the scene of the crime and maintaining its integrity. She also knew the various ways to collect and store evidence and then maintain the chain of custody so that the evidence was never unaccounted for. Any evidence that was not in someone's possession or in a locked area could be tampered with. Although this was unlikely, it was possible, and defense attorneys could get the evidence thrown out based on sloppy detective work. Even if the evidence was not excluded from trial, juries would be very suspicious and hesitant to convict someone when evidence was not in the custody of the police or the laboratory at all times.

The students listened politely to Chief Langdon for thirty minutes as he detailed the investigation. Finally, one impatient student raised his hand and asked, "If the gun was in the dumpster several feet away from the body, how could it be a suicide?"

"Most people get their knowledge of guns and gunshot wounds from television. On TV, a person gets shot once, and they die. In real life, that doesn't always happen. In Dr. LeCroix's case, the bullet didn't hit a major artery, so he lived for a brief period of time after the bullet entered his neck. He had enough time to throw the gun in the dumpster, which settled to the bottom underneath other trash items, and then walk several steps before collapsing to the ground and dying," stated Chief Langdon.

"What do you know about the gun? Was it registered? Were there fingerprints on it?" asked a female wearing a ball cap and a blue North Face parka.

"We weren't able to trace the firearm," Chief Langdon said. "It was manufactured back in the early 1900s, so there was no serial number. We interviewed several people and did not find anything to indicate who owned the weapon. Dr. LeCroix came into possession of it in some way, but we don't know how."

"Did you have any suspects before you ruled it a suicide?" asked the girl in the blue parka.

"We interviewed a number of people we thought might have information on the case. None of those leads produced a suspect. We ceased interviewing people when it became clear that this was a self-inflicted gunshot wound," Chief Langdon reported.

"If it was a suicide, do you think Dr. LeCroix intentionally tried to make it look like a murder for insurance purposes?" asked Stella.

"Just because someone kills himself does not mean that his beneficiaries will be denied life insurance benefits. That's another misconception from TV crime shows. It actually depends on the policy. In many cases, if the insurance policy was written over a year before the suicide, then the beneficiaries can still collect the money. In this case, regardless of whether it was a suicide or a homicide, Dr. LeCroix's beneficiaries should be able to collect the life insurance," said the chief.

Dr. Stella DeVry was now standing and hopping from one foot to the other. "What made you conclude it was suicide? Was there a note?" she asked.

"No, there wasn't an actual note," the chief said, not meeting Stella's gaze. "There were no fingerprints on the gun, but we did find blowback on the gun."

Stella turned to her class and said, "We just studied blowback last week. Does someone want to summarize it for us?"

The female in the blue parka raised her hand and began speaking as soon as Stella nodded in her direction. "Blowback is blood, hair, or tissue that literally blows back on the person who is firing a weapon. The force of the bullet entering the body causes skin and blood to displace onto the firearm itself, or onto the shooter."

Chief Langdon nodded and said, "That's correct. We found all three of those things—hair, blood, and tissue—on the gun in the dumpster. All belonged to one person: Logan LeCroix."

"Well, if he used the gun to kill himself, why weren't his fingerprints on the weapon?" Marlee asked from the back of the room.

"The weapon was not wiped clean of fingerprints. There had been prints on the firearm, but they were smudged. The forensics lab could not get any clear prints, even partials, from the gun," said Chief Langdon, clearly not pleased to see her in the room and actively participating in the discussion. "Because of TV, everyone thinks all fingerprints are clear and easily obtained from any surface that we touch. Nothing could be farther from the truth. Our findings indicate that Dr. LeCroix most likely handled the gun and his fingerprints were smudged during the shooting and subsequent disposal in the trash dumpster."

Marlee was seething inside. The chief's condescending answer insinuated that she knew no more about fingerprints than the average person who watched crime shows for entertainment. The two of them served on a committee together in the community and he well knew of her current and past work experience. She didn't like being talked down to, but there was really no benefit to putting him in his place, other than restoring her ego. Marlee chose to let the comment slide, for the time being. Still, she could not completely resist poking the bear. "Chief, one thing I noticed about the crime scene that day was that the area grew larger over time. When I first arrived on campus that morning around seven o'clock, the crime scene tape covered a specific area. When I left campus that afternoon, the crime scene tape included a much larger area. Can you tell us about that?"

Frowning as he looked at Marlee, he said, "The first responders were patrol officers. They roped off the scene immediately after checking to see if Dr. LeCroix was still alive. When detectives arrived a short time later, they determined the crime scene should be expanded. They based that decision on their investigation."

"Did they find something that made it necessary to enlarge the crime scene?" Marlee asked, not willing to let this line of questioning drop. One of the first rules in securing a crime scene was to start with a larger area than needed and then reduce it as the investigation progressed. This procedure reduced contamination of the scene.

"I'm not getting into the specifics of the investigation," Chief Langdon stated.

"The reason I was wondering is that a fair amount of contamination of the scene could have occurred between the time the initial scene was roped off and when it was later expanded. There were people all over, walking across the area. Footprints, garbage, or anything else that was found could have been left after Logan died," said Marlee. She knew she was being a jerk, but loved rubbing the chief's nose in it, especially after his condescending comments to her.

"Look, we could play *coulda-shoulda-woulda* all day, and it won't change a thing!" the chief barked. "Next question."

Stella asked, "If Dr. LeCroix did shoot himself, then why wasn't there a blood trail between the dumpster, where you think he shot himself, and where his body was found? Wouldn't lack of a blood trail indicate that he didn't move after he was shot?"

Chief Langdon shook his head from side to side. "Not at all. Dr. LeCroix shot himself at the dumpster, threw the gun inside and then took steps until he collapsed and died. The bleeding that occurred would have been light or nonexistent in those first few moments. Someone who is shot doesn't automatically drop several pints of blood. It takes time for someone to bleed out."

"Why would he shoot himself outside the building where he worked? Why not his office, or apartment, or car?" Marlee couldn't make any sense of Chief Langdon's conclusions. The chief merely raised his eyebrows and shrugged.

"Did you find blowback on Dr. LeCroix's body?" asked blue parka girl.

"We did. Tissue, blood, and hair all belonging to Dr. LeCroix were found on his hand," answered Chief Langdon.

"Which hand?" asked Marlee. Logan was right handed, and the bullet wound was in the left side of his neck.

"I believe it was the right hand," replied the Chief of Police.

"Doesn't it seem strange that someone would commit suicide by shooting themselves in the opposite side from their dominant hand?" Marlee pressed on.

"Stranger things have happened," said Chief Langdon, brushing off her question and pointing to a male student in the middle wearing an MSU sweatshirt and gray sweatpants.

"Couldn't Dr. LeCroix have blowback on his hand because he was fighting with the person who shot him?" asked the male student.

"Possible, but not probable," stated the chief. His answers were getting more and more abrupt. "We found no evidence to suggest someone else fired the weapon."

"When you searched his office and apartment, did you find clues suggesting he was going to kill himself?" asked Marlee.

As the chief looked toward the floor, searching for answers, Marlee knew she had hit upon something with her question. "No, we didn't find any actual physical evidence," said the chief, still avoiding the eyes of his audience.

Marlee's bullshit detector was bleeping like a fire alarm. She could feel that, although the chief may have told the truth when answering her latest question, it was not the whole truth. "What about his office and home computers? Did you find anything on either of them?" Marlee persisted.

Chief Langdon stared straight at Marlee, his mustache twitching at the left corner. "I wasn't going to say anything about it, but I guess I will since you asked me directly. Our computer technicians found a short story on Dr. LeCroix's computer which details the death of a college professor in a manner very similar to how he actually died."

A hush fell across the room as everyone attempted to make sense of the information just revealed to them. The girl with the blue parka was the first to speak. "Was it on his home or office computer?" she asked.

"At this point, I'd rather not give out any details. What I will say is that we believe the short story was written by Dr. LeCroix himself. Although a suicide note was not found, this short story is very similar to Dr. LeCroix's life and how he died. We think it was autobiographical, and in a way, it was his suicide note," said Chief Langdon. "Other than that, I really can't give out much more detail on the story or the investigation. If you'll all excuse me, I have an appointment back at the station in ten minutes."

The chief stood and started walking toward the door. Stella DeVry jumped from her chair and quickly gained enough composure to thank Chief Langdon for his time as he marched through the door. A faint sound of halfhearted clapping came from the classroom as he made his way down the hall.

Stella leaned against the classroom wall, partially covering the periodic table while the students sat with their mouths agape. The girl in the blue parka turned toward the male student in the MSU sweatshirt. "What the hell was that?" she asked.

It's more of Chief Langdon's half-truths. That's what it is, Marlee thought.

*When the right questions are asked, those
with something to hide become
nervous. As they should...*

Chapter 23

Marlee would have loved to hear Stella DeVry and the students process the information Chief Langdon had just delivered, but she needed to rush to the Elmwood Police Department and sit in on Joe Tisdale's meeting with the chief. She ran from the room and hurried to the parking lot to find a folded piece of paper under the driver's side windshield wiper of her CR-V. She assumed it was from a campus group advertising their upcoming event, or a local pizza establishment providing coupons for special deals. Marlee was in a hurry, so she grabbed the folded paper and threw it on the passenger seat. She sped to the police department, hoping to have a minute or two to chat with Joe before their meeting with the chief.

Joe stepped out of his dark blue rental car just as Marlee screeched into the police department parking lot and parked her vehicle. "It should only be another day or two, and then they'll release Logan's car to me, and I can drive it home," he said, motioning to his rental.

Marlee nodded and quickly changed the subject. "Joe, did the police say anything to you about a story on Logan's computer that they think he wrote?"

"No, I don't recall anything being said about that," he said. "Why?"

"Chief Langdon just spoke in Dr. DeVry's Criminalistics class and said that, during the investigation, they found a short story they believe was written by Logan. It was about a college professor who kills himself on a college campus, and many of the details apparently mirror Logan's actual death. They are considering it a suicide note, of sorts," Marlee said, words spilling over each other as she rushed to get them out.

"Nobody said anything about that to me!" said Joe. "Why would they think that was a suicide note? Logan wrote a lot of short stories about a variety of things. It was his hobby."

"You have to admit, it does seem strange that he died in a way very similar to his short story. That seems really odd," admitted Marlee.

"Now you think that it's suicide because of some story Logan wrote?" asked Joe, taking a step away from Marlee.

"No, I don't, Joe. But I do think it's odd that Logan died in much the same way the story played out," said Marlee.

"Did the chief show you a copy of the story or let you read it?" Joe inquired.

"No, he didn't. And he didn't provide a whole lot of details other than to say it was remarkably similar to Logan's real death," Marlee stated.

"If you don't know what the story actually revealed, then we don't know for sure if the chief even interpreted it correctly," Joe stated in a matter of fact tone.

"You're absolutely right, Joe! I hadn't thought of that. In fact, it may not even exist at all," Marlee said.

"I'm going to ask to see it today during our meeting," said Joe. "He'll have to let me see it."

Marlee nodded in agreement as the two made their way inside the police station. They approached the security window, and Lois looked at them with a blank stare. After indicating they were there for a meeting with the chief, Lois asked, "And you are?"

Marlee resisted the urge to give Lois a fake name. She recalled Bettina Crawford's assertion that Lois preferred to maintain a certain distance from everyone so they would not ask her for favors. It made complete sense, but it was still annoying.

After giving their real names, Lois motioned them into the chief's office to wait for him. "Chief Langdon called me a minute ago and said he was running a few minutes late and you were to wait in his office. He'll be here shortly," Lois said, turning on her heel and going back to her duty station to pretend she didn't recognize people she had known for years.

The chief's office looked much as she suspected it would. There was a Terry Redlin print of a pheasant in a field hanging on the east wall and a book case with a few books and procedural manuals against the west wall. Most of the bookcase was not filled with books, but rather trophies and awards. A double-sized window with partially closed tan blinds lined the south wall and the chief's desk faced the window. Three padded brown chairs were pulled in front of the chief's desk. It was a typical authoritarian room arrangement for a meeting. There was no question who would be doing the asking, and who would be doing the telling.

As they waited, Marlee's nerves got the better of her. She stood and paced around the room, stopping in front of the trophies and awards. She noted that most of them had nothing to do with police work past or present, but were for bowling, baseball, and community service. Marlee also found it curious that none of them were from Elmwood, South Dakota. They were all from Butte, Montana, which Marlee had heard was the place where Langdon was employed prior to being hired in their community. She recalled hearing that Chief Langdon was a police chief before coming to Elmwood. *Why would someone scrap their career as chief of police in one area to take the same job in another?* wondered Marlee. The only reasons Marlee could think of were that he or his wife had ties to South Dakota, or they found Elmwood a better location to live and work than Butte, Montana. Marlee did not recall hearing anything about family living in South Dakota, and she made a mental note to ask around about it. She considered the possibility that Elmwood paid their chief of police more than did Butte, but she soon rejected that notion since South Dakota was usually toward the bottom in wages at the federal, state, city, and county levels. The last explanation for the chief and his family to move to Elmwood was that he had gotten into some type of hot water at his old job and either chose to leave, or was forced out. This explanation definitely needed some further investigation too.

"Mr. Tisdale, sorry to keep you waiting, I was..." Chief Langdon entered the room and paused in his movement and conversation as he caught sight of Marlee. "What are you doing here?" he asked, glaring at her.

"Joe asked me to accompany him here today," said Marlee, trying to suppress an arrogant smile. It made her day anytime she could get the best of Chief Langdon.

Langdon paused, trying to think of a way to exclude her from the meeting. Failing to think of any excuse other than his dislike of her, he motioned for both Joe and Marlee to sit. Joe sat in the padded chair to the chief's left, while Marlee occupied the center padded chair. She pulled it up a bit closer to the chief's desk, not only to better observe him but also to put him even more out of his comfort zone. Her knees were now touching the front of his desk, and she rested her right elbow atop the desk. The chief compensated by sitting in his swivel chair behind the desk and pushing the chair back several inches toward the wall. By widening the gap between himself and the pair, he attempted to gain the upper hand in the conversation. Noticing Marlee's actions, Joe also pulled up his chair and placed his folded hands on the chief's desk.

"So, what can I do for you today?" asked Chief Langdon, looking only at Joe.

"I have a number of things I'd like to discuss today," said Joe, with an air of confidence she had not seen in him thus far. "First, I'd like to know what made you rule Logan's death a suicide. And why was I not notified prior to you making a public statement about it?"

Bill Langdon cleared his throat and blinked a few times before answering Joe's questions. He reiterated the same reasoning behind the finding of suicide that he had discussed in Stella DeVry's Criminalistics class less than an hour ago. "It was an oversight on our part that you were not contacted prior to the meeting on campus. I asked my captain in the Detective Division to inform you of the finding, but he did not follow through. I apologize. Rest assured, I will be speaking to him about this."

Way to pass the buck, thought Marlee. She felt one hundred percent sure that no conversation of this type had ever occurred between any police captain and the chief, and that he was simply using this fabrication as a way of dodging responsibility for shoddy treatment of the victim's family. In the event Chief Langdon *had* actually asked his captain to contact Joe, it was still a poor way to handle the matter. A finding of suicide should be provided to the family by the chief, not through one of his subordinates.

"Aren't you required to notify the next of kin of the findings before you make a public announcement?" asked Marlee, no longer caring if she upset the chief. The gloves were off, and she intended to get some answers from this jackass.

"Technically, Mr. Tisdale is not next of kin. He was Dr. LeCroix's same-sex partner and that holds no legal status," said Chief Langdon. "I personally informed Dr. LeCroix's sister over the telephone the morning before the announcement. Mr. Tisdale was being notified as a courtesy."

Joe leaned back in his chair as if he had been slapped. "Well, why did you tell me I could take Logan's car home if I'm not his next of kin?"

"Because you are listed as Dr. LeCroix's beneficiary of all his money, possessions, and life insurance benefits in the event of his death. He could choose to leave his belongings to anyone, and we would be obliged to release those items when they are no longer pertinent to the case. Plus, your name is on the car title, so you are a co-owner." Chief Langdon replied in monotone voice.

"We've been together for over twenty years! How can you say I'm not the next of kin? Logan and his sister have been estranged for years!" Joe shouted.

"Calm down, Mr. Tisdale. Surely you are aware that domestic partners have no legal status as next of kin," said the chief.

"Yes Chief, as a gay man, I am fully aware of the limitations that exist with domestic partnerships," Joe said bitterly. He had experienced discrimination at all levels since coming out in his early twenties. Joe and Logan took as many steps as they could to ensure their rights as a couple. Both had made the other one the beneficiary in their respective wills. Over the years, however, they had faced numerous restrictions. One that had occurred just a few years prior involved Logan and Joe being turned down for a family membership at their local YMCA, even though other unmarried couples received that discount. The difference was that the unmarried couples who received the benefit were of the opposite sex. Joe and Logan challenged the decision of the YMCA board; they refused to offer family memberships to any same-sex couples. When asked for justification on their decision, the board stated that if gay domestic partners were allowed family membership discounts, then roommates would expect them too. The board also reminded Joe and Logan that the C in YMCA stood for Christian and homosexuality might make some families uncomfortable, although they were allowed to join the gym and exercise there as long as they did not promote gay values.

"Of course," said Chief Langdon. "So you understand that we operated within the confines of the law."

Joe just stared at the chief, his mouth down-turned and his fists clenched. A full thirty seconds passed before anyone spoke. "Dr. McCabe tells me a short story was found on Logan's computer, and it led you to believe his death was a suicide. Is that correct?" asked Joe, regaining some of his composure.

"We did find a short story detailing the death of a college professor, that has a striking resemblance to Dr. LeCroix's death," confirmed Chief Langdon.

"I'd like to see it. I want to read it for myself," said Joe with conviction.

"That's not possible," said Chief Langdon. "Again, since you are not the legal next of kin of Dr. LeCroix, we are under no obligation to show you any evidence."

"That seems harsh," asserted Marlee. "As Logan's life partner for twenty years, Joe should be able to at least read the contents of the short story. Besides, if it's on Logan's computer, that would be personal property that Joe will receive as his beneficiary."

"The short story was found on Dr. LeCroix's computer on campus, so it is the property of Midwestern State University. I let Dr. LeCroix's sister know of the existence of the short story. After summarizing it for her, she seemed satisfied that it showed Logan as someone with the intention of killing himself," the chief replied.

"How in the hell would she know?" shouted Joe. "She hasn't talked to him in years, and I don't think she's even seen him in person in the past twenty-five. How could she be in a position to say the story confirms your belief that his death was suicide?"

The chief did not attempt to directly answer Joe's questions. Instead, he replied, "Regardless of their relationship, she is next of kin and gets to make the decisions. I asked her what she wanted done with the short story. She indicated that she would like it destroyed. We notified MSU of her wishes, and they deleted the short story from the hard drive. Even if I wanted to show you the story, it's not possible anymore."

"What the hell?" shouted Marlee. "Don't you think that was premature? What if you eventually find evidence proving that Logan was killed? I would think you would want to preserve all evidence in case something new comes to light."

"Why would we do that? The investigation has been closed. Now, if you will both excuse me, I have another appointment in a few minutes," Chief Langdon said, standing and motioning them toward the door.

Joe rose from his chair and faced the chief. "One more quick thing," he said. "I was wondering..."

The chief silenced Joe by raising his hand, palm facing outward. "No more questions. Look, I know this is hard to accept. Believe me, I've handled numerous death investigations and it's always hard on the family and friends no matter what the outcome. It's especially hard when it's a suicide and no one was aware the deceased intended to take his own life. Nobody wants to hear that a loved one killed himself because he couldn't stand to be alive any more. I would have a hard time accepting it myself." After Chief Langdon's uncharacteristic show of compassion, he ushered them outside his office and immediately closed the door behind them.

Joe shoved open the door in the reception area, and Marlee followed him into the hallway. "Good bye, Lois," Marlee said, with more than a hint of snarkiness. Her two conversations with the chief today had put her in a pissy mood, and Lois had the misfortune of being in the wrong place at the right time. As Marlee and Joe stepped outside the building, the front door to the station had not yet closed when Marlee yelled, "What the *fuck*?"

Joe did not say a word, but his face was bright red. She didn't know if he was going to shout, become violent, cry, or pass out. He stared at the sidewalk until he gained his composure. "That guy is the biggest jerk I have ever met. And I've met a lot of jerks."

Marlee glanced up and noticed the camera over the police station entrance. She pointed it out to Joe, and they walked toward their vehicles, not wanting anyone from the police department to see or overhear their conversation. They both wrapped their arms around themselves and shuffled their feet in an attempt to stay warm. The weather had turned noticeably colder, and the smell of snow was in the air. Marlee suggested they go for coffee to discuss the new developments. At her suggestion, Joe agreed to ride with her to the coffee shop. He grabbed a folded piece of paper on the passenger seat and handed it to her. "That's just some junk. Somebody put it on my windshield today," she said, taking the paper and unfolding it. She gave it a quick glance, expecting to see an announcement about an upcoming campus event, like the annual MSU talent show. What she saw made her jaw drop and her heart race.

Scrawled in black ink in capital block letters were the words, "STAY OUT OF THE INVESTIGATION BITCH!!!"

Doing the right thing for the right reason will land you in hot water with somebody. Almost always...

Chapter 24

"Oh my God," said Joe, reading the note as Marlee let the paper dangle from her hand. "Who would write this?"

"I don't know. Somebody does not want me asking questions for some reason, but I don't know who it could be." Marlee was still in shock after reading the note. She turned in her seat to face Joe. "The people I know who are not happy about me being involved wouldn't leave a note on my vehicle."

"Who doesn't want you involved?" asked Joe.

"Dean Green made it clear that he doesn't want me asking questions or doing any type of investigation on my own. He's a dean. He wouldn't leave a note. That guy is like a bull in a china shop. If he has something to say, he's not bashful about saying it. I think he likes ripping into people, so there's no way he's the one," said Marlee.

"Who else, then?" Joe held the note in his hands. He folded and unfolded the note in unconscious nervousness.

"Chief Langdon clearly does not want me asking questions, but he wouldn't leave a note. That seems like something that's really beneath him. He wants me to shut up, but I don't see him resorting to notes," Marlee stated.

"Is there anyone else at MSU who might be threatened by your questions?" Joe queried.

"I don't know. Maybe someone in administration? Maybe a student, or someone who has more information than they're telling? The killer?" Marlee was becoming frantic as she thought about the infinite number of people who could have left the note, and the threat it contained. Leaving a note seemed both juvenile and sinister. The two pondered the author's identity as they drove to Main Street and parked directly in front of the Coffee Bean. At least she had some good parking karma today!

Settling into the booth, Marlee ordered an herbal tea, while Joe requested a hazelnut latte. By the time the waiter returned with their hot drinks, both had decided they wanted something sweet to go with the beverages. Marlee ordered a chocolate croissant, and after some careful consideration, Joe did the same. He gazed around the Coffee Bean, taking it all in. It was small and could only hold around thirty people at a time, but it served the best coffee and pastries in town. Everything in the coffee shop was second-hand and none of it matched, which added to the funky feel of the place. They had the coffee house to themselves that afternoon, but had they arrived in the morning hours, there likely would have been a line trailing out the door and onto the sidewalk. The establishment closed at four o'clock, and Marlee knew from previous experience that there would be very few customers in the hour before it closed.

Since they had already exhausted their ideas on who wrote the note left on Marlee's vehicle, they moved toward a discussion of their meeting with Chief Langdon. "Wow, could he have made it any clearer that gay people don't have rights?" asked Joe.

"I'm sorry he said those things," said Marlee, ashamed that the head of law enforcement in Elmwood would be so crass and unfeeling.

"It's OK. I won't hold it against the town," Joe said with a half-smile.

"I was shocked when he said that anything he told you was just a courtesy, and he was only dealing with Logan's sister," said Marlee.

"I can't believe it either. What really galls me is that the short story Logan wrote was destroyed. This may be the last thing he ever wrote. I don't know a lot about solving crimes, but it seems ridiculous for the police to allow evidence to be destroyed," said Joe.

"The chief thinks it was a suicide, and doesn't think the case will be reopened. Either that or he wants to make sure it isn't reopened," said Marlee.

"What do you mean?" Joe looked up from his partially-eaten croissant, holding the ceramic coffee mug inches from his mouth.

"By having the story destroyed, the only record of what was written is what the chief tells us. He and only a few other people read the story, so it would be based on their memories and interpretations. We don't even know if what Chief Langdon indicated was true. What if he stretched the truth to back up his suicide theory?" Marlee said.

"There are legal ramifications if he falsifies information, correct?" asked Joe.

"Of course, but people in law enforcement cut corners all the time and take steps to ensure their theories are supported. Look, I'm not saying the chief did anything unethical or illegal. I'm just saying it's a possibility. He doesn't strike me as the type of guy to be one hundred percent honest," said Marlee. "By the way, did you read any of Logan's stories?"

"I read a few of them, but he was protective of his writing and usually didn't let anyone read them, except for some other aspiring writers he knew. Logan planned to put them together into a collection of short stories and look for a publisher one day," said Joe.

"He wanted to be a writer?" asked Marlee.

"Yes, that was his dream. He wrote for fun, but also for therapy and creative expression. He was sensitive about his writing and shy about people knowing his true thoughts and feelings. I think he would have used a pseudonym if he had been able to get published," said Joe.

"Who knew about his writing hobby and his hopes of getting published?" asked Marlee.

"Our friends all knew. I suppose Logan told his colleagues at the community college where he taught for years. He didn't keep it a secret," reported Joe.

"Did he keep everything on his computer or did he print it off?" asked Marlee.

"Sometimes he printed off the short stories and kept them in a folder. I know he'd been having some problems with his laptop for the last couple of months, which is probably why he used his work computer."

"So that story may be in existence somewhere in his office or home." The wheels in Marlee's brain were turning so fast, she couldn't process all the information about Logan and his dream of writing.

"I guess so. I know he kept his materials for classes on a flash drive that he carried to and from campus. It was easier than doing all of his class prep on campus or lugging his laptop around," said Joe. "This is all so strange. If the story wasn't a suicide note, then how was his death carried out?"

"I don't know. It doesn't make sense that someone else would read his short story and then recreate it as detailed in the story. Who would do it, and what would be the motivation? That's just too bizarre to even consider," said Marlee. "Do you think someone wanted something on his computer?"

"As far as I know, he only had class prep materials, some personal financial information, and maybe some of his writing on his computers. I don't know who would be so desperate to get any of those things that they would kill for them. I mean, if someone wanted his financial information, they could break into his apartment and steal his computer. They could steal his wallet to get his IDs and credit cards. Logan rarely carried much cash with him. He had enough to buy a meal or two and put a few gallons of gas in his car," said Joe.

"Did he usually carry anything else with him that someone would want?" Marlee inquired.

"He had his wallet, keys, and some books in a backpack and maybe some snacks. Otherwise, he never had much with him. Logan always preferred to travel light." Joe smiled and said, "I used to tease him about it, because whenever we went somewhere together he wouldn't bring much with him but then would have to ask me for a fingernail clipper or Band Aids. I take everything with me when I go somewhere."

Marlee smiled as she thought about what a complimentary couple Logan and Joe must have made. She was saddened that she never got to see them together. "Yeah, I think a lot of couples are like that. In some ways, opposites do attract, so they can compensate for each other's shortcomings."

"Very true. We had so many things in common, but our differences really defined who we were as individuals, and we accepted each other for that," said Joe, with a thoughtful expression on his face. They sat in silence for a few minutes, both in thought about Logan and the huge void his death caused. Marlee felt like she knew Logan better than ever, learning about him and seeing him through Joe's eyes.

"Let's brainstorm for a few minutes," said Marlee, interrupting the thoughtful silence. "Why would Logan be killed in much the same fashion as his short story depicted? It just doesn't make sense."

Joe chewed the last of his croissant and washed it down with a sip of his latte before speaking. "I don't know. This seems like some sort of premise for a far-fetched crime drama on television. If I were watching this on TV, I wouldn't believe it."

"Truth is stranger than fiction and I guess we're seeing that here. So let's start with why he would be killed in a way that mirrored his short story," said Marlee, pulling a small notebook and pen from her oversized purse. "Suicide is an obvious and easy answer, although I don't believe it, and I know you don't either. I'm still going to write it down, since we need to consider all possibilities." Joe nodded, looking none too happy to even consider that Logan had taken his own life.

"Another possibility is that someone knew about the short story and figured Logan's death would be ruled a suicide when the story was found. It would have given the killer, whoever he or she was, a way to shoot him and not ever be detected. Or, if the killer were detected, they would no longer be a suspect after the short story was located."

"This is really far-fetched too, but what if Logan was shot, and it just so happened to be carried out in the same way as this short story? You know, just a coincidence?" asked Joe.

Marlee was busy writing down their ideas. None of them held much water, but they were just thinking of all possibilities, however random they might be. "Do we know that Logan actually wrote the short story? I mean, someone else could have written it and put it on Logan's computer either before or after they killed him," said Marlee.

"No, I guess we don't know for sure who wrote the story. I guess that could be a possibility too," said Joe.

"Did Logan ever collaborate with anyone on his writing? Sometimes people have writing groups that they share some of their writing with, or they co-author articles and books," suggested Marlee.

"Not here in South Dakota. At least, not that I know of. I know he was interested in getting published eventually, but I'm sure he would have talked to me about it before he sent anything to a publisher," said Joe.

"Here's something else I just thought of. Who had access to Logan's office computer? Could someone have seen the short story and then, for whatever reason, decided to carry out the murder?" asked Marlee. She was already making a mental note to see who could gain access to Logan's office. Alice Olson, his secretary, had a key, as did the janitor, and the physical plant.

"That's a good point. I think Logan's office and computer might be a good place to look for more information," said Joe.

"Great idea. Now we just need to get a key. I think Alice Olson will help us. She thought so much of Logan and has been just devastated by his death. She'll do anything she can to find out what happened," said Marlee, confident that Alice would be on board with the plan. "Maybe we can go tomorrow night after most people have left work for the day."

Joe nodded in agreement, ready to put the plan into action.

"Are you a computer whiz, by any chance?" asked Marlee.

"No. I know the basics, but I'm no computer genius, that's for sure. How about you?" asked Joe.

"Unfortunately, no. We'll need to get a computer-savvy person to come with us," said Marlee, as the wheels in her head slowed to a pace she could follow. She didn't want to involve a student in this caper, although most students she knew were very proficient with the inner workings of a computer. Finally, the name of the perfect person dawned on her. "Sanjay Rashad!" she shouted. "He works in the Computer Center on campus, and he has a little crush on me. I think I could talk him into helping us out."

"Terrific. That's just terrific," said Joe, his mood brightening considerably.

"I'll contact Alice and Sanjay to see if we can get their cooperation. I don't have office hours or classes tomorrow, but I'll be on campus in the morning for a while to finish up some work. I'll check with them then. Of course, I'll be back in the afternoon for Logan's memorial service. Do you think you'll be up for visiting with me after the service? I imagine it's going to be really tough on you," said Marlee.

"It will be the hardest thing I've ever done, but yes, I want to meet with you after the service. The sooner we find out what happened to Logan, the better," said Joe.

After finalizing the details of their plan, Marlee gave Joe a ride back to his rental car in the police station parking lot. "Be careful, and keep your doors locked," Joe warned, fearful that the author of the note on Marlee's car might resort to violence.

As Marlee was exiting the police department parking lot, she spied Vince Chipperton, Nate Krause's probation officer, walking toward the entrance of the police department. She caught up to him, hoping he would share some information on Nate. Marlee always found herself tongue-tied around Vince Chipperton because he was so damn good-looking. He was one of those guys who was humble because he didn't realize how attractive he was, which made him even more attractive.

After sputtering out a greeting and stumbling through some small talk, Marlee asked, "I've been hearing Nate Krause's name mentioned in connection with Logan LeCroix's death. I talked to Nate, and he said you make him go to counseling sessions. I was wondering what you can tell me about him. Do you think Nate could be involved?"

"Why do you want to know? I heard it was ruled a suicide." said Vince.

"I know it's unorthodox for a professor to be asking questions about a person on probation, but I just want to make sure everything is being done to get justice for Logan. I don't think it was suicide and a lot of other people I talked to don't think it is either," replied Marlee.

Vince held Marlee's gaze with his light crystal blue eyes and shook his head. "I don't know. Nate has some violence in his background, but I just don't see him killing anyone. He's got a lot of problems, most of them mental. He acts weird. He dresses weird. It's easy for people to look at him when things go wrong."

"Thanks, Chipper," said Marlee, using his familiar nickname. They spent another minute discussing the weather before leaving the PD entrance and each going their own way.

It was late afternoon when Marlee arrived home, still thinking of Vince Chipperton and his dreamy blue eyes. Her answering machine light was blinking and showed four people had called her. The first call was from her doctor's office reminding her that it was time for her yearly physical. The second call was a recorded promotional offer from Weight Watchers. The third call was an irate Dean Green ordering her to meet with him the following morning.

The fourth call was a raspy voice, possibly disguised, that said, "Mind your own business, bitch, or you'll be sorry!"

Day Of The Dead

Cutting corners is nothing new. Since the beginning of time, people have looked for ways to do things more easily and more quickly... even if it's not entirely ethical.

Chapter 25

Could this day get any shittier? Marlee was the recipient of a menacing note, a threatening phone call, and a whole lot of condescension by the chief of police. To top it all off, she was on the dean's radar again and she guessed it was not for positive reasons. Marlee was surprised at herself. Usually any one of those things would have ruined her day, but today she was focused on finding out who killed Logan LeCroix and why. She was getting closer to the truth. She could feel it in her bones.

Too bad it hadn't reached her head yet.

Marlee placed a call to Bettina Crawford at the police department to follow up on their conversation over supper from a few nights ago. It was her day off, so Marlee called her at home. "So how was the hot date?" Marlee asked after Bettina answered the phone.

"Awful. He chewed with his mouth wide open; he talked about himself constantly; and, I think he farted at the table while I was eating," groaned Bettina.

"Gross! Are you going on a second date?" Marlee teased.

"Hell, no!" shouted Bettina. She was looking for a boyfriend, but she wasn't desperate–at least, not *that* desperate.

Marlee laughed and launched into some questions about the suicide ruling. Bettina did not believe it herself and was quick to say so. "There are a lot of us at the station that are furious over this. There wasn't enough conclusive evidence to indicate this was a suicide, and the chief should know better."

"Do you know anything about a short story that was found on Logan's desktop computer at work?" asked Marlee.

"No, I haven't heard anything about that. Why?" Bettina's voice rose an octave, suggesting that she was puzzled but intrigued.

Marlee filled her in on the details revealed by the chief earlier that day. Bettina let out a long slow whistle. "Wow, that's just crazy. I don't know what to make of it."

"If this is part of his conclusive proof, then why wasn't this information known around the police station? I get why maybe the chief wouldn't release it publicly, but it's outrageous that it wouldn't be released to other members of the department," said Marlee.

"He knows a lot of us don't support his decision. It seems to me that, if this story propped up his theory of suicide, he would want us all to know," said Bettina.

"Hey, did you find out anything about the guys I told you about who said they would beat up men who rejected their romantic advances?" asked Marlee, realizing that she hadn't heard anything more on this rumor.

"From what I've heard, these guys were probably just telling Logan that to scare him. No one I talked to has heard of a group of gay men beating up other gay men," said Bettina.

"So, you think it's safe to cross that theory off the list?" asked Marlee.

"Yeah, I think so," said Bettina. "I think they were just giving the new guy in town a hard time. They probably had a good laugh at Logan's expense over that one."

"Um, I had a threatening phone call and a threatening note on my car today." Marlee filled Bettina in on the circumstances, at which time Bettina went through a checklist of safety precautions for Marloo to follow.

"What can you tell me about Chief Langdon?" asked Marlee, after they had finished with the topic of threatening communications.

"He's a dick," said Bettina without a moment's hesitation.

"Um, I already know that. I mean, why did he come to Elmwood if he held a chief of police position in Butte, Montana? Why leave one chief's position for another? Did he have family here or some sort of ties to the area?" asked Marlee.

"I've never gotten a clear answer on this. There were a few different explanations, but one thing that was mentioned three or four times was that the chief got in some trouble at his old job," reported Bettina.

"In legal trouble?" asked Marlee.

"No, I think it was trouble over how he did his job. Apparently it was a huge scandal and he left shortly afterward, according to the people at the station who told me about it. I bet if you look on the Internet you can find some details on it," suggested Bettina.

"That's a brilliant idea, Bettina! I'll do that right now." Marlee said, excited to find out some dirt on the chief of police. She knew she was being childish, wanting to find some negative information on him, but she couldn't help herself. They said their goodbyes and Bettina reminded Marlee to be careful since she was on the radar of someone who either killed Logan or knew who did.

Marlee went into her home office and sat before her computer. She went to a search engine and typed in the name of the town and state where the chief lived along with his first and last names. Bingo! The local newspaper had article after article on William "Bill" Langdon, and it was evident he had been embroiled in a scandal at his previous place of employment. According to the newspaper, a young gay man was found dead in Franklin Park in Butte, Montana. He had a bullet wound to his head, and the firearm was found at the scene. After a brief investigation, Chief Langdon ruled it a suicide and closed the case. Evidence was brought to light by the deceased's parents that suggested it was a hate crime. The chief refused to reopen the case. The deceased's parents were politically well-connected and were able to get the state attorney general's office to look into the matter. An investigation initiated by the AG's office located two suspects, who later pled guilty to shooting the young man because he was a homosexual. The city was in an uproar, and Chief Langdon resigned before he could be removed from office. Two months later, he was employed as the chief of police in Elmwood, South Dakota.

Logan LeCroix's death wasn't the first time that the chief had ruled the questionable death of a gay man as a suicide.

After supper, Marlee pulled some files out of her book bag. She needed to go over some information for a meeting that she had just realized she had the next morning. Cheating on college campuses was nothing new, but a new type of cheating was running rampant at MSU, and most other colleges throughout the nation. It involved buying and selling papers over the Internet. There were several websites devoted to selling term papers to students, who through a lack of ability, time, or work ethic, were unable to write them on their own. Students merely had to indicate the topic, the length of the paper and the manner in which the sources had to be cited. Upon acceptance of their credit card payments, the students would receive "their" term papers within a few days. For students who had waited until the last minute and were willing to pay more, papers could be emailed to them in a few hours. Students could even indicate the grade they wanted on a paper, knowing that if they were failing the class, turning in an A paper would bring undue scrutiny. Online paper mills were earning big bucks by selling the same papers over and over, sometimes to students at the same university.

In addition to some students at MSU buying papers, others were selling them to paper mill websites. Students who were proficient at writing could submit their work to one of the paper mills and earn over $100 for it. It was rumored that some students were paying for a large portion of their tuition by selling papers. Not all of them actually wrote the papers they submitted to the paper mills. Students apparently made copies of their friends' and roommates' papers, unbeknownst to the actual authors. The matter had been exposed at the end of last semester when two students were caught submitting identical papers in an English Composition class, papers that the professor had actually recalled from the semester prior. When confronted, these two students eventually came clean and provided limited details on the cheating scam. Unfortunately, the two students who were caught refused to name anyone else on campus who was involved in buying from or selling papers to paper mills.

Before Marlee went to bed, she re-checked all of her doors to make sure they were locked. She was not overly worried about the note and the call, but there was no point in tempting fate. The night did not bring the sleep she needed, as she tossed and turned for hours. As soon as she heard the newspaper slide into the mail slot on her house at 5:30 a.m., Marlee bounded out of bed to check what the local news reporters had discovered. There was a recap of the chief's announcement of suicide, along with an editorial about Chief Langdon failing to notify the Elmwood Examiner of major news items, like findings in a death investigation. The editorial further called into question whether or not there was something that the chief did not want the citizens of Elmwood to know. Hell hath no fury like a newspaper scorned.

Her house was a pig pen, so Marlee did some cleaning and washed an overflowing sink full of dishes before going to campus. Her career and many other aspects of her life were in chaos, but at least she had a clean and orderly house. She arrived on campus shortly before 8:00 a.m. and tried to decide what to do first. She needed to meet with Alice about a key to Logan's office and also with Sanjay from the computer center about helping to untangle some of the computer nuances that she and Joe knew nothing about. What she dreaded the most was the meeting with Dean Green. She decided to get it over with, so she marched to his office.

The dean's secretary, Louise, was at her desk organizing piles of paperwork that the dean and faculty members left for her to sort, mail, and process. She indicated that Dean Green was in early this morning and motioned Marlee toward his office. The dean would expect her to act meek and mild, exactly how she normally acted around him. She preferred to fly under the radar rather than call attention to herself. Since Logan's death, Marlee did not hold steady with that philosophy. She had been asking a lot of questions and making a pest of herself on campus and around the community.

Marlee knocked on Dean Green's door and when he barked for her to enter, she said, "You rang?"

He swiveled around in his office chair and glared at her, stunned for a moment by her flip greeting. "Shut the door and sit down," he barked, moving toward the small round table across from his desk. He pulled out a chair and sat so close to Marlee that their knees nearly touched. *Another technique to get the upper hand,* thought Marlee to herself. "I had a call from Chief Bill Langdon yesterday. He told me you were asking him all kinds of questions about LeCroix's death when he was a speaker in Dr. DeVry's class. Then he said you came to his office with Joe Tisdale and had even more questions," Dean Green spat out.

"That's true. Stella invited me to sit in on her Criminalistics class to hear the chief speak, so I did, because I teach Crime Scene Investigation, which as you know, is a prerequisite for Criminalistics. The chief was answering other questions, so I asked some too. Then I saw Joe Tisdale, and he asked me to go to a meeting he had set up with the chief," reported Marlee, knowing full well that her recounting of the events was not completely accurate.

"You think you're real funny, don't you?" growled Dean Green.

"Uh, no," Marlee said, ready to be hit with the full wrath of Mean Dean Green.

"Langdon told me the questions you were asking. He said you got everybody in the class all stirred up and asked questions he wasn't about to answer. Then he said you managed to get Joe Tisdale all riled up too. We talked about this before, and I told you to stop asking questions and interfering in the work of the police department," Dean Green said, regaining a smidgen of composure.

"But the police aren't investigating any more. Chief Langdon ruled it a suicide, and the case is closed. Nothing else is being done. It's obvious to everyone that this is *not* a suicide!" shouted Marlee, aware that she wasn't helping herself with her answer or her tone.

"It is not obvious that this was a murder. The police conducted a full investigation. Just because you have some law enforcement experience and teach a few criminal justice classes does not mean you know more than the police!" shouted Green.

"I don't agree with the chief's ruling, but I never said I was smarter than–" said Marlee before being interrupted.

"Shut up! That's enough! This is your second year here. You don't have tenure, and you need a positive review from me to get your contract renewed next year," stated Dean Green.

"Are you threatening my career just because I've asked some uncomfortable questions?" Marlee asked, looking him straight in the eye.

"No. When I talked to you about this before, I was threatening your career. Now, I'm telling you to look for another position, because your contract won't be renewed for next year. You are under contract for the remainder of this semester and next semester, but after that, you're on your own. And let me remind you that, if you leave before next May, when your contract is up, you can be sued for failure to fulfill its terms. Now, get out!" Dean Green shouted.

Marlee stumbled out of the dean's office, her head spinning and her legs all of a sudden made of lead. Ten minutes ago, she was a respected assistant professor on the tenure track with hopes of a long career at MSU. Now she was facing unemployment in six months. Shock took over, and Marlee began to shake uncontrollably. She made her way to her office, shut the door and sat down. What was she going to do? She loved teaching, and her heart belonged at MSU. Marlee did not want to start over in her search for a teaching position. Not having her contract renewed would make it difficult to secure a new tenure track position in criminology. Word would get out that she was let go, which would tarnish her reputation. Her life was about to take a dramatic turn. She was facing not only a new job search, but most likely a move to another town or state.

Needing to process what had just happened, Marlee picked up the telephone and called Diane. Upon hearing the news, Diane rushed to Marlee's office. The two sat quietly in the darkened office for a few minutes, listening to the background music meant to drown out their conversation from anyone attempting to eavesdrop. Finally, Marlee felt calm enough to recount her conversation with the dean.

"Do you think he'll cool down and change his mind?" Diane nervously adjusted her dark framed glasses.

"I doubt it. He hates being wrong and wouldn't have said those things unless he knew he could get away with it. I think he's dead serious and will do whatever it takes to make sure I'm done teaching at MSU," Marlee stated.

"There must be some sort of appeal process. He can't fail to renew your contract because he doesn't like that you disobeyed his direct orders. Christ, this isn't the military!" exclaimed Diane, getting more furious by the minute.

"It might as well be the military. Unless you have tenure, the whole process is very political. I don't know where I could appeal the decision," Marlee said.

"How about the union?" asked Diane.

"I didn't join. I know I talked about it, but when it came right down to it, I couldn't afford the hefty membership dues," Marlee said. "What am I going to do?"

"Maybe you could at least talk to Harry Hesnar. He's the president of the union here on campus. Even if he can't help you, maybe he can give you some advice. It's worth a try," Diane brightened with the realization that there may be a solution to Marlee's dilemma.

"Yeah, it's worth a try," Marlee said, blowing out a long sigh. "I have to start thinking about getting my curriculum vitae and references ready so I can go out on the job market. Oh, God. Who's going to give me a good reference after this?"

"Let's not even jump that far ahead yet. I think the first step is to talk to the union president for some guidance. You know what strikes me odd about this whole thing?" asked Diane. Marlee shrugged and she continued, "This seems like a total overreaction by the dean. There were no intermediate sanctions levied against you. He told you not to do something, you did it, and then he fired you. The other thing is, why is this such a hot-button issue for him? He used to be in administration at a university much larger than MSU, so I imagine he's dealt with police investigations of various tragedies on campus before. Why has Dean Green been so adamant that faculty and staff stay out of the LeCroix death investigation?"

"Wow, I hadn't thought of that," said Marlee pondering Diane's comments. Why indeed had Dean Green gone off the rails when Marlee continued asking questions? Many of the people she talked to were not even on campus and therefore, fell out of the dean's scope of authority. Did Dean Green have something to hide, or was he merely taking directives from his superiors? The more she thought about it, the angrier she became. Marlee would not accept Mean Dean Green's decision without a fight. A big fight!

Taking matters into your own hands is the only remedy.

Chapter 26

After Diane left to teach class, Marlee spent a little time licking her wounds. She was an over-achiever, and getting fired was not an option. It wasn't just a matter of ego. She truly liked the MSU campus, the students, and her colleagues. Marlee was challenged in her position and loved that she was learning right along with her students. She vacillated between shock, sadness, embarrassment, and anger. Shock, sadness, and embarrassment were emotions she would have to deal with another time; anger motivated her, and that was what she needed right now. She would use her rage not only to keep her teaching position, but more importantly, to find out what had really happened to Logan LeCroix and why the dean was so anxious to keep her from it.

While the background music was still playing in her office, Marlee called Harry Hesnar to set up a meeting. As president of the MSU branch of the professor's union, he was charged with ensuring that faculty contracts and faculty rights were not violated by the administration. Harry had made a convincing pitch at the fall in-service for faculty members to join the union. Listing the many benefits that union membership provided, like advocacy and representation in disputes, he also noted that the union was not able to assist faculty who were not members. Marlee made a mental note to join the union at MSU immediately if she ever got out of this predicament.

Harry picked up on the fourth ring and suggested, rather unenthusiastically, that Marlee come to his office right away. He had some free time before teaching his Art History class later that morning. Marlee made her way over to Harry's office in the Fine Arts Building, which had the prestige of being the oldest building on campus. The building had a lot of character but had narrow stair ways, no elevators and small bathrooms. MSU had been recently advised that they would need to make the building more handicapped accessible or else close it altogether. Marlee hoped that they would make the necessary renovations so that everyone could move freely about the building. Unfortunately, the campus had a history of tearing down old buildings and replacing them with shiny new structures. Paintings, statues, and other works of arts, handcrafted by faculty and students, adorned the interior of the building. Under normal conditions, Marlee would have spent time looking at the new pieces in the constantly rotating display of artworks. Today, she was all business and stormed into Harry's office on a mission.

"So, I checked the records, and I see that you are not a member of the union," Harry said pointedly after he had motioned her into the office. Harry Hesnar was a small, bespectacled man in his late sixties. The few strands of gray hair he had left were pulled from one side of his head to the other and plastered down in the world's worst comb-over. He wore a cream colored cable knit sweater that had pilled up from many years of washing and wearing. His brown corduroy pants were a new addition to his wardrobe and made a swishing noise with the slightest bit of movement.

"That's right. I didn't join the union because I didn't feel like I could afford it," Marlee said.

"And now?" queried Harry. He seated himself in his office chair behind a desk that looked as if it were ready to collapse at any time. The chair he sat in did not look too sturdy either, and creaked as he rolled up closer to his desk. Tenure and seniority were important on a college campus, but they didn't necessarily ensure new furniture.

"I think it would have been the wisest money I ever spent," said Marlee, realizing that she actually meant it and was not just blowing smoke up Harry's skirt. "If I get through this, I promise I'll join."

"Uh huh," said Harry. This wasn't the first time he had heard a professor in hot water promise to join the union once their predicament was solved. "So tell me what happened."

Marlee recounted her meeting this morning with Dean Green and also the previous admonitions he had given her about asking questions regarding Logan LeCroix's death. "Do you think he has grounds to have me terminated?"

"As you know, an untenured professor can face not having their contract renewed at any time. Often these reasons have more to do with personality conflicts than anything work-related. That's why tenure is so important. It allows faculty to have the freedom to express their thoughts without fear of being fired," Harry stated.

"I know it's political and the dean is pissed because I talked to people about Logan's death when he advised faculty to stay out of it. I never talked to the press and I never made official statements on behalf of the university. I talked with students, professors, and staff on campus, Logan's partner, and some people who knew Logan. It seems to me that Dean Green's insistence that faculty stay out of the investigation pertains to making public statements and should not involve what I do personally," Marlee said.

"Where you run into a problem is that you asked questions on campus. You talked to students. I'm guessing you may have used some of your office hours and other work time to find out information. Is that correct?" asked Harry.

"Yes, it is," Marlee said, looking down, realizing that Dean Green might have a stronger case than she had originally thought.

"Even though I'm not supposed to become involved in helping non-members, I'll do some checking around on this and see what I can find. This isn't the first time that Dean Green has issued a faculty member their walking papers based on not following his directives. I'd like to nail that SOB to the wall," said Harry, becoming more interested in Marlee's case by the minute.

On her way back to her office, Marlee stopped in to chat with Alice Olson. She still needed to get the key to Logan's office so that she, Joe, and Sanjay could get in there tonight. At this point, she didn't have much to lose if she got caught, but she wanted to make sure Alice and Sanjay didn't get punished for helping her. Marlee proceeded down the hallway and into Alice's office. She wasn't there, but her work study student, Jeremy, was sitting in front of Alice's computer. When he saw Marlee, he quickly turned the monitor so she wouldn't see what he was doing. Marlee laughed, "It's okay, Jeremy. I won't tell anybody that you're playing games on the computer when you're supposed to be doing work for Alice."

Jeremy's look of shock softened into a smile. He was shaped like a barrel, standing five foot four inches high and weighing well over three hundred and fifty pounds. He sported a light brown crew cut covered with a black knit cap. Jeremy was dressed like most students on campus, wearing sweatpants and an MSU sweatshirt. His backpack was dropped near Alice's desk and was partially open. "Hey, Dr. M. What's up?"

"I'm looking for Alice. Is she around?" asked Marlee.

"Yeah. She had to go to the dentist but said she would be back in an hour," Jeremy said.

"I'll check back then. Oh, wait, I have that faculty meeting on cheating to attend, so it will be sometime after two o'clock before I make it back to see her," said Marlee.

"A meeting on cheating?" Jeremy asked, curious about the topic.

"There's been a bunch of cheating happening on campus. You've probably heard about it. Students have been buying papers and passing them off as their own. Other students are selling term papers they wrote to paper mills and making some decent money on it," recounted Marlee.

"Uh, no. I hadn't heard about that," Jeremy said, shifting uncomfortably in his chair. His body language betrayed him, screaming out that he indeed knew something about cheating on campus.

"Really? That's kind of hard to believe. I thought everyone had heard about it. Not that everyone was involved," Marlee said hastily, not wanting Jeremy to think she was accusing him of cheating.

"I guess I heard some people talking about it in the dorms, but I didn't hear any names mentioned," Jeremy said, looking a little less uncomfortable.

Marlee had no intention of putting Jeremy on the spot by trying to get him to rat out his classmates. He probably knew more than he was saying, but she didn't think it was the time nor the place to ferret out further information on cheating. She made a mental note to check back with him to see if he might be a bit more forthcoming at a later time. "Yeah, I haven't heard any names specifically mentioned either. I think, basically, we're just going to talk about how to detect if a paper was plagiarized."

Jeremy nodded, still looking uneasy about the conversation. As Marlee made her way out the door, she turned and looked over her shoulder to tell Jeremy goodbye. She noticed tears welling up in his eyes. "Jeremy, what's wrong?" she asked, genuinely concerned about his well-being.

"Oh, it's just some family stuff going on," Jeremy said, waving her off. Marlee knew it would probably just embarrass him if she pushed to find out what was going on in his family. She tried to maintain a professional distance with students, but that wasn't always possible. A born helper, Marlee had difficulty seeing someone in pain and not doing anything about it.

Marlee nodded and said, "Hey, if it's anything you want to talk about, you know where my office is. Stop in any time." Jeremy gave her a half smile as she walked out of the room.

The faculty meeting that morning was held in the Angus B. Stewart Conference Room of the administration building. With the donation of enough money, one could get a room or even a whole building named after them. The conference room was a plush office with a large oblong table in the corner, surrounded by leather chairs. Marlee took a seat and marveled at the burgundy drapes, the chocolate brown carpet with burgundy designs, and the opulent furnishings. This was where the president and vice president regularly held their meetings. The room was made to impress those in attendance, whether they were from the board of regents or other universities. On rare occasions, the lowly faculty was allowed to meet there, but only under the direct supervision of the president or vice president.

Marlee seated herself on a leather chair and noted the contrast of this soft, squishy leather chair with her own wooden office chair, with a seat cushion she had bought herself at Kmart. It paid to be in administration. The room soon filled up with professors from most of the disciplines. She was there representing the disciplines of Criminal Justice, Sociology, and Political Science. Seated on her right was Bunny Adams, a new professor in the math department. How anyone with the name Bunny would get respect from her colleagues and students was beyond Marlee's comprehension. Richard Ramos, a professor of Sports Marketing sat on her left. He was in his fifth year of teaching at MSU and was going up for tenure soon. While they waited for the meeting to start, Richard talked about his progress in getting his tenure application finalized. In addition to writing an application letter and submitting references, an applicant had to assemble a binder or a box full of supporting material that demonstrated aptitude in teaching, research, and service. Syllabi, course projects, papers, and any honors received were all painstakingly organized in hopes of securing tenure. Marlee wondered if she would ever get to go through this process at MSU, given her current situation with Dean Green.

Ten minutes past the scheduled start time, President Ross entered the room and took his seat at the head of the table. He chatted amiably with those nearest him and, with a loud clearing of his throat, started the meeting. The president was courteous in thanking everyone for their time and introduced the nature of the problem, which was wide-spread plagiarism and cheating at MSU.

"What we're here to do today is to come to a consensus on how we will handle instances of plagiarism and cheating in classes. In the past, faculty members have had discretion on what they will do in their individual classes. Given that this problem seems to be growing, especially with students buying and selling papers to paper mills, I believe we need an agreement on a common course of action when a student is suspected of or actually caught cheating," President Ross said.

The faculty members looked at each other. Some nodded in agreement, while others remained stone-faced, secretly objecting to any attempt to curtail their academic freedom as it pertained to grading and cheating. All professors were against cheating and plagiarism, but some believed in handling it informally and giving students a chance at redemption.

Richard Ramos was the first to speak. "What I've done in the past is to try to assess the degree of the plagiarism. It the whole paper is written by someone else, I will fail the student. If there are a few passages that they did not cite correctly or at all, then I have a discussion with them about what they did wrong and give them another chance to make it right. I don't think all cheating and plagiarism should be punished equally." Two professors nodded their heads in agreement.

President Ross said, "I agree that not all cheating is equal, and not every instance should be treated the same. What I hope to accomplish is to at least some sort of faculty reporting system. It would be a cheating clearinghouse where we could determine if a student had been cheating before this incident. In other words, we are interested in whether the student is a first time offender, which might result in a lighter punishment, or a repeat offender who perhaps can be severely sanctioned or even expelled."

The meeting lasted for another hour in which the issue of how to handle cheating and plagiarism was discussed *ad nauseum*. The main question concerned who would have access to the database. Some were in favor of reporting the information to administration to deal more harshly with repeat offenders. Others were concerned that, once a student was labeled as a cheater, it might be difficult to overcome the stigma, especially if all professors could view the names of students who were previously reported. Coming to no consensus on the topic, the meeting was adjourned, and a follow-up meeting for further discussion was scheduled for the week after Thanksgiving.

Walking out of the meeting, Marlee and Bunny Adams were grumbling about the lack of progress accomplished. "Are meetings always this unproductive?" asked Bunny, new to the campus, and to teaching.

"That was actually a very productive meeting compared to some I've attended. Even though we didn't come up with a decision, we had a good discussion. No one got into a fight, there wasn't any name calling or mudslinging, and we didn't get off on totally unrelated topics. Nope, this was a fairly good meeting," Marlee stated. The horrified look on Bunny's face made Marlee wish she hadn't been quite so candid in her remarks to the newbie. Everyone knew you had to sugar-coat the truth for the new professors, or else they would flee at the first opportunity. "Just kidding," Marlee said with a smile, hoping to mask the reality of the situation.

Bunny smiled back, relieving Marlee of the burden of having scared a new professor into running home and applying for a bunch of positions at other universities.

When Marlee reached her office, it was almost noon. She knew Alice would be gone over the lunch hour, so she needed to wait around campus for a while to speak with her. Marlee tried to busy herself with class prep for the following day, but her mind kept floating back to the details of Logan's death and the people she had talked with about it. When she tried to force herself to focus on something else, she worried about the dean's comment that her contract would not be renewed after May. She knew there was little she could do right then about her career, so she plunged headlong into sifting through the details and accounts of Logan's death. She pulled her notebook from her book bag and turned to the first page of her writings and charts on Logan's death. Maybe, by sifting back through the information and her written thoughts, she would be able to uncover some connections that still eluded her.

After an hour of sorting through her notes, Marlee was no closer to an answer, but she felt certain that there was something to be learned from gaining access to Logan's office computer. Noting the time, she made her way back to Alice's office. Alice had just returned and was hanging up her coat. Her cheeks were still pink from the chill of the outdoors. "Hi, Marlee," greeted Alice.

"Hey, Alice. I was wondering if we could talk for a few minutes in private?" asked Marlee, looking around to make sure there weren't any work study students engaged in projects or other students taking make-up tests.

"Sure," said Alice, looking at Marlee with curiosity. Alice moved toward the open door and shut it for privacy.

"Here's the deal," Marlee said in a low voice as she moved to sit on the edge of Alice's desk. "I was wondering who had access to Logan's computer in his office?"

"The people from the computer center were up here installing new software, and they are constantly up here fixing computers or helping the professors work through some type of computer glitch. The protocol is that they notify the professors that they will be working on their computer, so there are no surprise changes or fixes. Cecil, the janitor, has access to all the offices, but he's been talked to about using the computers. He got into some trouble over it last year. Other than that, I can't think of anybody else," said Alice, searching her brain to think of anyone else who might have entered Logan's office.

"You have access, right?" asked Marlee.

"Well, yes, I have keys to everyone's office, but I wouldn't use Logan's computer. I have my own right here, so there would be no need. Plus, I have a computer at home," Alice said.

"Who has access to the keys you use to get into everyone's office, besides you?" asked Marlee.

"No one. I lock up the drawer with the keys every day when I leave for home," said Alice. She motioned toward a desk drawer and pulled it open to show the ring of keys laying on top of a stack of envelopes.

"But that desk is unlocked during the day, so someone could come in when you're not around and grab the key to Logan's office, right?" Marlee pushed.

"I guess so, but I don't know who would do that. Somebody could probably grab the key if I were in the restroom or had run over to the campus post office. Work-study students are here throughout the day, but there are times when the office is unstaffed for a brief period. Besides, what's the big deal about his computer? Have you found out something?" Alice asked.

"Sort of. The Chief of Police told me that Logan wrote a short story in which a college professor kills himself on campus. The details are eerily similar to Logan's real death, so the police used that to support the theory of suicide. Joe and I met with the chief and asked to see the short story, but he said it was deleted from Logan's office computer at the request of his estranged sister," Marlee recounted.

Alice's mouth was wide open, and her eyes bulged. "What?"

"I know, it's a lot to take in. Did Logan ever talk to you about writing short stories or wanting to be a writer?" Marlee queried.

"No, he never said anything to me about it," Alice said.

"Do you know about someone coming to erase some things from Logan's hard drive a day or so ago?" asked Marlee.

"The computer center people sent up one of their work-study students to do some work, but I don't know his name. He's a friend of my work study student, Jeremy. When Jeremy comes in, I'll ask him his friend's name," Alice replied.

"Alice," Marlee said, lowering her voice to a whisper, "Joe and I want to get into Logan's office and take a look at what's left on his computer. I don't want you to get into any trouble, but we need to get the key tonight."

It didn't take long for Alice to get on board with the idea. "I'll leave my desk unlocked tonight when I leave. You have a key to get inside my office, just like the other faculty, so it will be easy enough for you to get in here, grab the key and go to Logan's office."

"Thanks, Alice. I appreciate it so much. If we happen to get caught, we won't say a peep about where we got the key," said Marlee.

"I don't care if I do get into trouble. It's for a good cause," said Alice. "What exactly are you and Joe looking for on Logan's computer, besides the short story he wrote?"

"Joe said Logan wanted to be a writer and was hoping to get published at some point. I just want to see if his stories are on the computer and what they're about. I also want to see if they've been viewed by someone other than Logan, either before or after his death," said Marlee.

"Do you know how to find that out?" asked Alice, knowing Marlee was not the most computer savvy professor on campus.

"No, but Joe and I lined up a third person to help us. He's proficient with computers and can tell us if things have been deleted, copied, or moved to another area of the computer. I'm not going to tell you his name, because the less you know, the better. Just in case we get caught, and you're questioned by Dean Green," said Marlee.

"Hey, before I forget, I was in here earlier today and your work-study student seemcd upset. I asked him about it, but he didn't want to talk. Just thought I should let you know, since I know how close you are to the kids that work for you," said Marlee.

"It's awful. His mother has stomach cancer and it's inoperable. Jeremy has been torn up over it, but he always comes to work and is keeping up in his classes too. I don't know how he does it," said Alice.

"Wow, I had no idea," said Marlee. "Does he have other family at home to help him? Does he have friends here to support him?"

"It's just he and his Mom. She lives about an hour away in Cassaway. He drives there at least twice a week to see her and care for her. I gather that money is very tight for them, and Jeremy has to put a lot of his time toward working various jobs," said Alice.

"Ah, the poor kid. Has anyone looked into having a fundraiser for Jeremy and his family?" Marlee knew benefits had been held on campus in the past to assist students with medical issues.

"He hasn't talked much about it. I guess I could ask him. That might be something we could do for him here on campus," said Alice.

"Yes, let me know. I'd be happy to help. And don't forget to leave your desk drawer unlocked tonight. I'll let you know if we find anything," said Marlee, as she opened the office door and walked out.

DAY OF THE DEAD

Truth, like danger, hides in the shadows.

Chapter 27

Marlee drove home for a quick lunch and to change clothes. She was wearing jeans and a navy sweatshirt with the MSU logo, along with brown fur-lined clogs. Normally she would have no need to change midway through the day, but Logan's memorial service was being held that afternoon, and she wanted to dress up a bit. She microwaved a frozen diet meal and wolfed it down without tasting a bit of it. Then she changed into a long black skirt, topped with a purple and black sweater, and completed the outfit with black low-heeled boots.

Back at campus, she had difficulty finding a parking spot and had to check in three lots before finding an open space. A few classes were still being held, and the regular employees were not due to leave for another two hours, so many of the parking spaces would have been occupied without the memorial service on campus. Making her way to the entrance of the Quinn Building, she nodded to a few people she knew. The mood was somber and soft classical music filled the lobby. Students were standing at the entrance handing out memorial booklets and Marlee took one before entering the room. She found an open chair near Diane and sat down. Diane looked at her with red-rimmed eyes and offered a small smile in greeting. Marlee reached into her purse, pulled out two packages of tissues and handed one pack to Diane. She knew that Diane would forget to bring Kleenex.

Looking around, Marlee noticed four large bouquets of flowers on the stage. In the center of the stage was a tripod, which balanced an enlarged photo of Logan. He was smiling and looked truly happy, with the skin crinkling slightly around the corners of his eyes. Joe Tisdale entered the room just before the service began. He sat in the front row along with the president, vice president, the deans and other bigwigs from the MSU administration. A non-denominational pastor had been selected by Kendra Rolland, the Director of Student Affairs, to handle the service. Pastor Pam Striden made her way to the stage and began the farewell ceremony for Logan. Given that Joe Tisdale was the only one in the room who had really known Logan well, the service was generic, but well done. It included singing by two faculty members and a reading by another. Pastor Striden ended the service by encouraging everyone to sing "Tears in Heaven" by Eric Clapton.

Marlee wasn't one to cry. She had attended the funerals of all four of her grandparents in the past twenty years and had never shed a tear. Not that she wasn't sad; she just wasn't a crier. This was different. The tears ran down Marlee's cheeks as she thought of Logan coming to Elmwood alone, working to make a new life for himself, and then having his life taken from him. As she walked out of the building, she wiped her tears just as a loud sob escaped her mouth. She covered her mouth, walked to her car and drove home. In this state, she wasn't even able to process her feelings with Diane. It was just too sad.

When she arrived home, Pippa greeted Marlee at the door. She scooped the fluffy kitty into her arms and hugged her for comfort. Pippa finally struggled free after receiving the amount of attention she wanted. Marlee changed out of her dress clothes and back into the jeans and sweatshirt she had worn earlier. She stretched out on the couch and flipped through television stations as a way of distracting her from her feelings. After two hours of complete inactivity, she called Joe to see how he was feeling after the service and to set the plan for that evening. Joe appreciated the effort MSU had put into Logan's memorial ceremony, and felt that his life was celebrated as well as it could be by people who didn't know him very well. They agreed that Marlee would pick Joe up at his hotel at 11:00 p.m., and they would go to Scobey Hall to search Logan's office computer.

At 10:40 p.m., Marlee left home to pick up Joe at the Ramkota Hotel. Although she arrived a bit early, he was already waiting outside the front door. He seemed shaken and Marlee wished she had the words to comfort him. If she hadn't been such a mess herself after the ceremony, she would have made sure to speak with before leaving. "Did you talk to Alice at the memorial?" asked Marlee.

"Yes, I did. We went for coffee right afterwards, so we were able to lean on each other for support. Logan would have been so happy to see the huge turnout at the service and the positive words that were said about him," said Joe.

They drove the remainder of the way to campus in silence. Marlee had contacted Sanjay earlier that evening to confirm a time to meet him as well. He agreed to be waiting by the east door to Scobey Hall at eleven o'clock. Marlee parked her car two lots over, so that it would not be readily recognized by anyone who was in or around Scobey Hall at that time of night. Joe and Marlee made their way to Scobey and waited for Sanjay. "He should be along shortly," said Marlee, trying not to become impatient. They waited in silence for over five minutes, Marlee becoming more irate by the moment as her blood pressure rose. A crackling of leaves caught her attention, and she turned just in time to see a dark figure jump from behind a tree. It was Sanjay dressed all in black and wearing a black knit cap. "Holy crap, Sanjay! Why are you dressed like a cat burglar?" said Marlee, more loudly than she intended.

Sanjay Rashad just flashed a wide grin at Joe and Marlee, proud of himself for sneaking up on them.

Marlee used her building key to let them inside. As they walked up the stairs, Marlee introduced Joe and Sanjay, since they had not yet met. The three walked to Alice's office, and Marlee used her key to let herself inside. Once inside, she used her small flashlight to locate the desk drawer and find the key to Logan's office. Marlee slid the key to Logan's office off the keychain, returning the other keys to the drawer. She pulled the office door closed behind her, and the three made their way to Logan's office. Once inside, they closed the door behind them and left the light off so as not to attract undue attention. It was a Friday night, so most faculty and staff would not be on campus at this late hour. The students who lived on campus were more concerned with other matters and most likely would not notice if lights were on in an office in Scobey Hall. The police had an officer stationed on-campus during the overnight hours, so it was that person she was trying to avoid. She also worried about the cameras supposedly hidden around campus.

Logan's desk was sparsely furnished, and three boxes of books sat on the floor. A desk chair was pulled up to a computer monitor placed on a stand. Sanjay leaned over and turned on the computer. As it booted up, Marlee wondered how Sanjay would be able to get information from the computer if he didn't have Logan's password. Joe stood behind Sanjay and held the flashlight.

Sanjay sat in front of the computer and typed in characters upon request. The system paused for twenty seconds and then allowed him in with a greeting of "Welcome, Logan."

"We're not supposed to announce it, but we can get into anyone's computer anytime we want. The computer center knows that will cause ill-will with faculty, so we pretend to wait and get their permission to enter their offices and mess with their computers," Sanjay said, looking pleased. He was enjoying the attention Joe and Marlee were giving him. He had suddenly gone from computer nerd to superhero.

For the next five minutes, Sanjay typed on the keyboard, moving from one screen to another. He muttered the whole time, but it was unintelligible to Marlee, since it was all techno speak. "Can you see yet who accessed Logan's computer and when?"

Sanjay continued tapping away on the keyboard and muttering to himself. "Here we go!" he nearly shouted. Marlee shushed him and pointed to the door, reminding the computer whiz that they wanted to keep this break-in a secret. "Okay, I found some of Logan's short stories. They had all been deleted. I can also see the days they were accessed. It looks like some of them were last viewed before his death and some afterward."

"Can you make copies of them?" asked Marlee, pointing to the small printer sitting on a table next to the computer.

"I can do better than that. I'll just forward all of them to my computer and yours. Then we will both have a copy," Sanjay replied.

"Sanjay, you're a genius," said Marlee, fully meaning it. "Can you also copy the log showing when the computer was accessed? And also, who accessed it, if you can?"

Sanjay beamed with delight. Normally he was one of the most overlooked people on campus. Even though universities were overrun with geeks and nerds, the people from the computer center seemed to occupy the lowest rung on the academic social ladder. Tonight, possibly for the first time in his life, Sanjay was a rock star. "Sure, I can get all that." He typed a bit more on the keyboard and turned his chair to face Marlee and Joe. "We're done here. I've got everything we need."

"Good," Joe and Marlee said in unison. "Let's get out of here," Marlee said. Even though there was no indication of anyone in Scobey Hall to see them, she was still worried about getting caught. The dean had made it clear that her career was in the toilet, but she still held out a little hope that it could be salvaged. Getting caught entering an office which, up until just two days ago was sealed with crime scene tape, would not help Marlee breathe life back into her career.

The three quickly exited Logan's office, locking the door behind them and pulling it closed. Marlee made her way to Alice's office and returned the key to the drawer where it belonged. She pushed the lock button on the desk drawer and locked Alice's office behind her. As long as they could exit the building without being seen, they would be in the clear.

Joe put his fingers to his lips as Marlee approached him. "Shh... I thought I heard footsteps coming up the stairs."

"Oh, my God. We have to get out of here, ASAP!" Marlee whisper-shouted. The three turned and race-walked softly down the back stairwell. It was on the opposite side from the stairs they had taken earlier, but that was fine. Both stairways led to the first floor exit doors. Nearing the first floor, Marlee said, "Sanjay, it's not safe for us to go to your office right now. We don't want anyone seeing us together there. Let's wait until tomorrow to meet. I'm done with class at noon. Can we meet sometime after that?"

Sanjay nodded and suggested they meet right after Marlee's classes in his office. Exiting the building, Marlee waved to Sanjay as he took off in another direction and disappeared before their eyes. Maybe wearing all black wasn't such a dumb idea after all. Joe and Marlee walked around the building and over to the lot where her car was parked. They were in such a hurry to escape from campus that they didn't even notice the figure of a person behind a tree, watching their every move.

Lies, prejudice, and threats. All in a day's work. Don't be too quick to dismiss the obvious.

Chapter 28

It was a fitful night. Marlee tossed and turned, anxious to see what the information from Logan's computer would reveal. What if this was the key to the whole case? What if it was a dead end and she had to pursue one of the other leads? What if she were nowhere near an answer? She had more questions than answers as she lay awake. Her alarm jolted her out of a deep sleep at 7:00 a.m. Typical, she was awake all night and then fell asleep just an hour before the alarm went off.

She stumbled out of bed, groggy from lack of sleep and stress. She started the coffee and hopped in the shower. Within a half hour, she was pleasantly caffeinated and ready for the day. She dressed hurriedly and spent minimal time on her hair and makeup. After drinking a protein shake and packing a quick lunch of yogurt and an apple, Marlee was out the door and off to campus for what she hoped would be a most revealing day.

Prior to her first class at ten o'clock, Marlee sat in her office and prepared for her lecture. The first class was Intro to Criminal Justice, and they were talking about the correctional system, which was one of Marlee's main areas of interest. Working as a probation officer for seven years had given her unique insight into jails, prisons, probation, and parole. Today she would lecture for half of the class period on justifications for imprisonment. Then she would involve the class in an activity in which they would be required to apply these justifications to scenarios. Her students tended to like the hands-on activities in the class, so she knew the class would be fun. In her Policing class at eleven o'clock, she had just finished lecturing on police ethics, and today this class would also be doing an in-class activity in which they had to determine what actions were and were not ethical, based on the standard of ethics she provided them. Most students knew stealing by a police officer was unethical, but many of them were unsure if they could accept a free meal while on duty. The exercise provided for some in-depth discussions of what was right and wrong for police officers while they were in uniform and off duty.

Marlee nearly broke her leg getting out of the Caldwell Building fast enough and over to Sanjay's office at noon. She could not wait to hear what he had uncovered about Logan's computer and the short stories he wrote. Joe was already in Sanjay's office when Marlee arrived. She shut the door behind her, and they all spoke in hushed tones. "So, what did you find?" Marlee asked before she even took off her coat or set down her bag.

"I sent copies of everything to you at your personal email address," Sanjay said, nodding in Marlee's direction. "I didn't make hard copies of anything, other than the short story and some access information." Sanjay handed them each a small stack of papers, clipped at the top. "First, the short story is just as you detailed it. It's based on a gay professor at a small campus who kills himself. Logan's death really does mimic many of the details from his story. The other stories I read were on a variety of topics, and none of them seemed particularly autobiographical. Finally, from looking at the system restore files, I was able to determine the file access dates for other users."

"So what does that mean for those of us who don't speak computer geek? Uh, sorry. I mean..." Joe faltered, looking for the right words as a blush crept up his cheeks.

"Hey, no offense, man. What it means is that someone other than Logan had access to his computer from the time he started work here in August until after his death," said Sanjay.

"Sure, we know the computer center had access, had loaded some software for him and had helped him with a couple glitches. We also know that the police looked at his computer after he died," said Marlee, with a hint of impatience.

"Here's where it gets interesting," said Sanjay, speaking faster and faster as the momentum of his story increased. "One other person accessed his computer more than once. And, I also see someone with computer center credentials accessing Logan's computer when they were not authorized to do so. This happened on at least two occasions before Logan died and once again after he died." Sanjay looked at Joe and Marlee with a sense of satisfaction, still enjoying his role as superhero.

"Someone from inside the computer center accessed Logan's computer when they weren't supposed to? When was this?" asked Marlee.

"Well, let's see," said Sanjay, scrolling through documents on his computer. "Here it is. The first time was about a week before he was killed, and the second was the Saturday before his death. The last time was the same day that the crime scene tape came down. The unknown person, not affiliated with the computer center, accessed Logan's computer twice, on the same day. It was the Friday before Logan died."

"Could any of these accesses have been police related? Maybe someone from the PD or their forensics lab?" Joe asked.

"Nope, these are all non-police accessed-dates. What the police did is easy to find and label," said Sanjay.

"Who from the computer center would access Logan's computer without authorization?" asked Marlee. "Is there ever a reason to do that?"

"Like I said last night, we can do a lot of things, but it's not an accepted part of the protocol. We can actually get sanctioned if we access information from faculty or staff computers, even though the computers are technically government property and the faculty member has no right to an expectation of privacy. Just because we have the know-how to do it, doesn't mean it's acceptable," said Sanjay.

"Who has the ability and the credentials to do this?" asked Marlee. "And, can you tell who did it?"

"Several people have the ability in the computer center to go into a computer and access whatever they want. According to the protocol, each of us needs approval from our supervisor before we can take any action," Sanjay reported.

"Who's in charge of the computer center now?" asked Marlee. She knew there had been some turnover during the semester, but she had never heard who had finally secured the position.

"Alan Haskell is the new director. He just started in September. He comes from somewhere down south. Alabama, maybe? I don't remember. I can't stand the guy," Sanjay said, with a disgusted shake of his head.

"Why is that?" Joe was intrigued by the strong reaction Sanjay had toward his supervisor.

"He totally changed everyone's duties when he started, so that put everyone against him right away. He must have figured out that he'd gotten on the bad side of everybody in the computer center, so he had us all over for a party at his apartment. It was one of the worst experiences of my life. Al got really, really drunk and started saying really harsh things about people. I think he may have gotten into some trouble over it," said Sanjay.

"Why do you think so?" asked Marlee. She knew people at MSU associated with each other socially, but she'd never heard of a supervisor getting sloppy drunk and alienating all of his employees.

"A couple days after the party, he sent around an email to all of us, apologizing for his intoxication and the insensitive comments he had made about people of other races," reported Sanjay.

"Al made racist comments?" asked Marlee.

"He was telling jokes. The problem is that his jokes all have punch lines that are derogatory to blacks, gays, women, and other groups too. He's a jerk. I think someone from the party talked to someone in administration and he was reprimanded," said Sanjay.

"Ugh, that's horrible," said Marlee. It would be bad enough to hear those types of comments from anyone, but hearing them from your direct supervisor put the employees in a precarious situation.

"Yeah, we all walk on eggshells around him. After hearing some of his drunken comments, we all know what he really thinks of most of us," said Sanjay. "He doesn't have anyone's respect anymore and I think he knows it."

"Do you think he'll stick around at MSU very long?" Marlee couldn't imagine Alan Haskell's blatant racism, sexism, and homophobia would be tolerated for long at the university.

"I don't know. I guess he was anxious to take this job because his brother lives here. Oh, he was at the party too and was just as much of an asshole as Al," said Sanjay. "He's been acting weirder than usual and keeping to himself more the past few days, so maybe he knows he will be given his walking papers by the administration and is looking for another job."

"Can you think of any reason he would want to access Logan's computer? Did he even know Logan?" Marlee asked.

"No, I don't know why he would do that. I'm not sure if he knew Logan, but they lived in the same apartment building," said Sanjay.

Marlee's jaw dropped as she realized that Al Haskell was the man from Logan's apartment building who had harassed him with gay slurs. She turned to Joe, who had just come to the same conclusion. Sanjay looked at them quizzically, and Marlee filled him in.

"Yeah, that sounds like Al. He's a jerk, alright," Sanjay grimaced, baring his startlingly white teeth.

"Based on what you know of him, do you think Al would kill Logan?" asked Joe.

Sanjay thought for a few moments. "It never felt like he was violent. He seemed like a big blowhard, but not somebody who would physically hurt another person. Of course, do we ever really know people?"

"What if he was with his brother and maybe another like-minded person or two, and they'd all been drinking? Do you think they could become violent toward someone they didn't like or didn't approve of?" asked Marlee.

"It's possible. I guess people do things in groups all the time that they wouldn't do alone," concluded Sanjay.

"That's right. Sociologists call it groupthink. People act in ways in groups that they would never do alone. They get swept up in the group enthusiasm or anger. This is how peaceful demonstrations can turn into riots so quickly," Marlee stated.

Joe and Sanjay both looked at Marlee, their eyes glazing over. It was a scene she saw regularly in her classes when the students were losing interest. Marlee backed off lecture mode and asked, "So who is the non-computer-center person who accessed Logan's computer?"

"That's a bit trickier, because I haven't tracked the person down yet, but I can tell you it came from someone on campus. I'm trying to figure out the building and then the office or dorm room. Then I should be able to narrow it down to the person. All this takes time, but maybe I'll have it by later today." Sanjay leaned back in his swivel chair and interlaced his fingers behind his head.

"Thanks, Sanjay. This is awesome work. We couldn't have made it this far without you. Just give me a call when you find out the building, office or person it came from," said Marlee.

"Will do!" exclaimed Sanjay, as he flashed Marlee a wide smile.

As Marlee and Joe left Sanjay's office, Joe said, "That guy's really into you."

"I know. He asked me out before, and I lied and said I had a boyfriend. I feel kind of bad flirting with him now so he will help us," said Marlee.

"That was flirting?" asked Joe. "You talked to him professionally. That was all. There was no flirting."

"It felt like flirting." Marlee was confused. She felt like she had really turned on the charm with Sanjay.

"You'll still go out on a date with him, like you promised, right," asked Joe, feeling a bit sorry for Sanjay.

"Of course I'll go through with it. I just don't think it will turn into anything more. He's a nice enough guy, but not really my type," said Marlee, trying to remember why she thought they didn't have anything in common. Sanjay was a few years younger than Marlee, but that didn't matter. It wasn't as if she would be labeled a cougar for dating him. He was weird, but not in a creepy way. Marlee brushed her thoughts aside. She didn't have time to contemplate dating right now. She had a murder to solve!

Marlee walked to the parking lot and angled toward her vehicle. When she was two rows away, she could see a flyer underneath the driver side windshield wiper. She quickly looked at the other cars in the lot. None of them had flyers, so it was not an advertisement. Marlee's stomach tightened as she neared the car and reached for the folded paper. Written in block lettering was, "BACK OFF BITCH! THIS IS YOUR LAST WARNING."

With a rapidly beating heart, Marlee grabbed the flyer and put it on the passenger-side seat in the car. The first note was somewhat threatening, but this one certainly held a dire message. Marlee's hands shook as she put her vehicle in reverse and backed from the parking lot. Who would be so brazen as to put notes on her car during the light of day?

Joe and Marlee had a quick lunch, and she told him about the latest note. Both were at a loss as to the identity of the author. It had to be somebody on campus who felt very comfortable being in the parking lot during daylight hours. They rehashed what they now knew about the case after their meeting with Sanjay. Marlee felt fairly certain that Alan Haskell, the new Director of the Computer Center, was Al the homophobe from Logan's apartment building. She felt equally sure that he was the person from inside the computer center who had accessed Logan's computer before and after his death. Marlee still struggled with what motivation he would have to access Logan's short stories. She also didn't know why he would want Logan dead. Being a homophobe did not necessarily translate into murder. Other than disliking Logan because of his sexuality, was there any other motive for killing him? Besides Al, who was the person on campus who accessed Logan's computer? Were Al and this person in cahoots, or did they have two unrelated motives? Maybe the second person had a benign reason for accessing Logan's computer without his permission and was not involved in his murder. If not, what could this second person's motive be for wanting Logan dead?

Marlee didn't have office hours that afternoon, so she didn't need to return to campus, but she did so anyway. She wanted to correct the quizzes she had given in Intro to Criminal Justice after they finished the hands-on activity in class that morning. There were 45 students, and it would take some elbow grease to grade all of the quizzes. If she finished them this afternoon, it would be one less thing to worry about over the weekend. She went to her office and shut the door behind her, knowing she would be better able to concentrate if she were distraction-free. Marlee was in deep concentration while grading but heard some rustling outside her door and then an envelope slid underneath. *Another threatening note,* she thought. She jumped from her chair and flung the door open to see who was responsible. The only person visible was Jeremy, Alice Olson's work study student. He held an armload of papers and was attempting to pin something up on a bulletin board.

"Jeremy, did you see who put this under my door?" Marlee shouted, waving the folded piece of paper.

"Some older guy was by your door, but I didn't see him put anything under it," said Jeremy, as he continued his attempt to tack an announcement on the bulletin board with one hand.

"Which way did he go?" asked Marlee.

Jeremy pointed to the hallway that led the opposite way from where they stood. Marlee tore off in search of him, fully expecting to find Al Haskell. The only older man she saw as she followed the hallway down the stairs was Dean Green. He gave her the stink eye, and she glared back. At this point he had already told her that her career was over at MSU. There was no need to play nice with him anymore. Marlee raced past the dean and stopped at the exit on the first floor. She flew out the door and looked in all directions before deciding to head toward the computer center. She ran as fast as she could, stopping to catch her breath twice. When she arrived at the computer center, she was told by the secretary that Alan Haskell was in a conference call and had been for the past half hour. It was at that point that she realized she didn't know what Al Haskell looked like. She ran to Sanjay's office.

"Do you know if Al is in a teleconference right now?" asked Marlee.

"I'll check," Sanjay said, walking out of his office and around the corner. He returned thirty seconds later and shook his head. "Yeah, he's in there. Why?"

"Somebody put this note under my office door while I was in there. A work study student told me an older guy was near my door, so I thought maybe it was Al with another note warning me to keep out of the case," said Marlee.

"Couldn't have been him," said Sanjay. "He's been in his office for a while on that call. What does the note say?"

Marlee unfolded it and read the now familiar block letters: "IF YOU ASK ANY MORE QUESTIONS BE PREPARED TO DIE!" Her hands shook. This was the second threatening note she had received in less than two hours. Somebody was deadly serious about wanting her to stop asking questions.

"Well, if it wasn't Al, then who was it?" Marlee muttered more to herself than Sanjay.

"Did you see any other older guy as you came over here?" asked Sanjay.

"Just Dean Green, but it couldn't have been him. He's not subtle enough to use notes to convey his messages. He would just barge in my office and start yelling if he had something else to say," said Marlee.

"Are you sure?" asked Sanjay. "Maybe he's leaving you the notes knowing you wouldn't suspect him, since it's not his usual style. Besides, he can't exactly threaten to kill you when he talks to you face to face. That's illegal, I think."

"It is illegal, but I just don't think Dean Green would do this," said Marlee. "If he thought I was an actual threat to the safety or reputation of MSU, he could probably have me suspended, pending some type of investigation. He wouldn't need to leave cryptic notes. I guess I'll track down Jeremy and have him give me a description of the man by my door. Have you had any luck figuring out who from outside the computer center accessed Logan's computer? "

"I haven't figured out who did it, but I know it came from within Scobey Hall. I'm not one hundred percent sure, but it looks like it was somebody with administrative clearance," said Sanjay.

"The dean? That still doesn't make any sense. What would possibly be his reason for secretly accessing Logan's computer? And if he did, what connection does that have to Logan's death? Why would the Dean want him dead? This is getting more and more confusing all the time," said Marlee. With every step forward, this investigation seemed to take two steps backward. On her way out of the computer center, she stopped to look at the photos of those who worked for that department. Front and center was Alan Haskell. He was very non-descript, of medium build, and with medium brown hair and hazel eyes. Nothing about this guy stood out. He would be able to move around in public and go unnoticed because everything about his appearance was unremarkable.

Marlee went to Alice's office in search of Jeremy. When she got there, Alice said that Jeremy was out hanging up flyers on bulletin boards all over campus. The flyers advertised the upcoming English Club meeting, a Speech and Debate contest, and the first annual MSU Holiday Dinner. Alice indicated that Jeremy would be back within the next few minutes.

Marlee sat down on the edge of Alice's desk and briefly updated her on the findings on Logan's computer. Alice seemed happy for the distraction and eventually chatted on about her plans for the weekend. Logan's death still weighed heavily on her, but Marlee was glad to see that Alice was able to focus on other things, at least occasionally.

"I have a scrapbooking conference this weekend. It starts tonight. I thought about cancelling my registration. Since Logan died, I just didn't feel up to it. My daughter talked me into going to get my mind off Logan. I think she was right. I'm actually leaving work a little early today so I can get some supplies for tonight's first session," said Alice.

"Will Jeremy lock the office for you if you leave early?" asked Marlee.

"Oh, yes. He will make sure the mail is delivered to the campus post office, turn off all the lights, log both of us off the computers, and lock the door. He's very dependable. I really don't know what I'd do without him. He's been so helpful, especially since Logan died," said Alice.

"It's great that you can depend on him, especially since he has so much going on with his mother's illness," said Marlee.

"He does all that, plus he has another job on campus. He works for the safety department and issues tickets to people who don't have campus parking permits or who park in restricted areas. Jeremy is one of only three students who hand out all those tickets, so he's very busy," said Alice.

"I always wondered who handed out those tickets. I've never seen anyone actually doing it. Do they have uniforms?" asked Marlee, reflecting back to her own college experience where campus ticketing officers wore brown uniforms and fake badges to justify their positions.

"No, they don't have to wear anything like that. Jeremy was disappointed that he didn't get a badge or anything. They give them a ticketing booklet and that's it," said Alice, laughing. It struck Marlee that this was the first time she had heard Alice laugh since Logan's death. She was glad to see the old Alice coming back.

As the two were chuckling, Jeremy walked into the office and set down a much smaller stack of papers than she had seen him with earlier. "Alice, I hung up as many of these as I could, but there were too many fliers and not enough space on the bulletin boards," said Jeremy.

"That's okay, Jeremy," said Alice. "Just put them back in the mail slots of the professors who asked that they be posted. They can use the extra ones to post on their doors or to hand out in classes." Jeremy nodded, relieved that Alice wasn't going to force him to go out to hang up the remaining flyers.

"Jeremy, can you describe the guy you saw by my office door a little bit ago?" asked Marlee.

Jeremy looked down at the floor, trying to recall every detail of the man's appearance. "He was an older guy with glasses."

"How old? Like my age, or really old?" Marlee asked. Just this year she had realized that her students considered her an old person, even though she was only in her mid-thirties. The term "old" was indeed relative.

"Older than you, maybe fifty," Jeremy replied. "He was average height and weight with brown hair." Marlee realized that description ruled out Dean Green, who Jeremy would have been able to identify by name anyway.

"Have you ever seen him on campus before? Does he work here?" Marlee asked.

"I don't know. I didn't see his face very well," said Jeremy.

"Would you recognize him if you saw him again? Could you identify him from a photograph?" asked Marlee.

"I don't think so. Maybe?" said Jeremy.

"Was he a white guy? What was he wearing?" Marlee continued.

"Yeah, a white guy," said Jeremy. This didn't narrow the suspect pool at all, since over 95 percent of Elmwood's population was Caucasian. "He had on black or dark blue pants and a gray sweater."

"What exactly did you see him doing by my door? Did you see him put an envelope underneath it?" asked Marlee.

"He was just standing there. He wasn't doing anything. I kept hanging up flyers and then you came out and he was gone," said Jeremy.

Marlee left Jeremy and Alice, wishing them both a good weekend. She was disappointed with Jeremy's description of the man by her office. He could have been Alan Haskell from the computer center, but he also could have been one of any number of men on or off campus. She went back to her office, hoping for some inspiration on the next steps to take.

Are words or actions more harmful?
It depends on the situation.

Chapter 29

Drumming her fingers on her desk, Marlee pulled her notebook from her book bag and looked at her notes on the case. She felt certain that a few of the previous leads were no longer viable explanations for Logan's death. Marlee didn't think Joe had enough of a motive to harm Logan, so she crossed him off the list. According to Bettina Crawford from the Elmwood Police Department, the theory about groups of gay men assaulting one gay man if he rejected the romantic advances of one of them, was probably untrue. Marlee crossed this motive off the list. A hunting accident didn't make any sense either since the gun used was not a hunting rifle. Marlee scratched that idea from her list. The remaining explanations were: a hate crime, an accident, a robbery, a crime of passion or a reason that she had not thought of yet.

Marlee started a new page, assigning motives and people possibly responsible for killing Logan. Al Haskell, a known racist and homophobe, could have killed Logan with the help of his brother. An accident could include innumerable scenarios and perpetrators. If Logan were shot during a robbery, it would have been by someone who wanted money or something else they believed he possessed. A crime of passion could have been committed by someone who loved, hated, or was obsessed with

Logan, such as Nate Krause, the mentally ill student who went to Logan's apartment.

Two other questions kept coming back to the forefront of Marlee's mind. What made the chief of police ultimately decide that this was a suicide? Was it just the short story found on Logan's computer? Was it because of his bias against gays and not wanting to expend further energy on the matter, or was it to save his own reputation because the PD could not locate the real killer? The second question dealt with Dean Green and MSU Administration. Why were they being so secretive about what they knew? Why was the dean threatening faculty and staff if they talked to the press or asked too many questions?

After putting together her new assessment of the case, Marlee realized that she didn't have any fewer possible explanations than she'd had before. They were just different. She pulled out her campus telephone book and started making a list of all the men who fit Jeremy's description of the man by her door earlier that day. After listing ten names, she was not even a quarter of the way through the phone book. Deciding that this exercise was going nowhere, she thought about her next move.

Marlee made her way over to the computer center and asked to meet with Alan Haskell. She was shown into his office just as he was getting off the phone. Marlee introduced herself and explained that she happened to be in the building and thought she would meet him since he was new to campus. This was an absolute lie, since she rarely had anything to do with the computer center and really couldn't care less what went on over there as long as her office computer and the computers in the classrooms worked well.

Al held out his hand and smiled at Marlee. He gave her the creeps and chills ran down her spine. The older she became, the more she learned to trust her instincts about people. Her whole body was telling her that Al was not a good guy. Marlee sat down in a chair near his desk and the two discussed Al's adjustment to MSU and Elmwood.

"Did you buy a house when you moved here or are you renting?" asked Marlee. This was a frequent question asked of newly hired faculty and staff. It was a roundabout way of assessing if they had a family and if they planned to stay at MSU for more than a year.

"I rent an apartment on the east end of town," said Al, enjoying the chat.

"Oh, one of the new apartments?" Marlee pried.

"I'm in the Newsome Apartments," said Al. "It's small, but that's OK, since it's just me. It'll work until I buy a house. I'll probably start looking this spring."

"The Newsome Apartments?" Marlee asked. "I think that's where Logan LeCroix lived. You know, the professor who died on campus a couple weeks ago?"

"Yes, it was," Al grimaced as he shifted in his chair.

"Did you know him?" inquired Marlee.

"Sort of. I knew who he was, but I wasn't friends with him or anything," said Al.

Marlee took a deep breath. It was now or never. "I heard that you knew him well enough to know he was gay," she said.

"Who said that? I'm not gay!" Al shouted, jumping out of the chair.

"I know. I heard you don't like gays and called Logan names and made other slurs about him being homosexual," Marlee stated.

"So?" said Al, not even trying to deny his actions.

"So... why did you kill him? Was it because he was gay?" Marlee said.

"I didn't kill that little fairy! I wouldn't waste my time on him. Who are you anyway? Get the fuck out of my office!" Al shouted, pointing toward the door.

Marlee left the office, shaken by the encounter with Al. She hadn't gained any new information by the confrontation, but she had the sense that he was not the killer. He seemed like someone who would hide behind mean words, but would not be brave enough to physically assault someone. By the way he reacted to her accusations, she saw that he was all bark and no bite.

While she was in the computer center building, she decided to stop back at Sanjay's office to see if he had any new developments. Sanjay was on the telephone when she poked her head in his office, but he waved her in with an excited gesture. He finished his phone conversation without even saying goodbye before he put down the receiver. "I tracked down the identity of the person from the computer center who accessed Logan's office computer. It was Zack Gable. He's a work-study student here and definitely does not have authority to be doing anything other than what we tell him. How he got into Logan's office, I don't know. Zack is incredibly gifted in his understanding of computers, so I totally understand how he was able to access Logan's short stories and delete them. He just didn't go quite far enough in deleting them," reported Sanjay.

"How long has Zack worked here?" asked Marlee, thankful to be able to put a name to the computer center employee who accessed Logan's computer before and after his death.

"This is his second year. He started as a freshman, which is odd, but like I said, he has top notch skills," said Sanjay.

"Did you check to see if he was ever asked by anyone to do some work on Logan's computer," asked Marlee.

"I did check, and in the two years he's been here, he was never authorized to go to any professor's office in Scobey Hall. He just handles tech problems in the classrooms and computer labs," said Sanjay.

"Do you have his class schedule?" asked Marlee.

"No, but he's scheduled to work here this afternoon from two to four o'clock. I suggest you wait here in my office until then. We can talk to him together," said Sanjay.

"I just talked with Al Haskell a few minutes ago and asked him why he killed Logan," Marlee stated, worried that hanging around the computer center for any length of time was probably not a good idea.

"You did what?" screeched Sanjay, turning in his chair so violently that he nearly fell to the floor.

"It started as a fairly friendly chat. We talked about how he liked working here, and then I asked where he lived," Marlee relayed the rest of the conversation with Al, including her accusation that he killed Logan because he was gay.

"Are you insane?" Sanjay screeched again. "He could have hurt you!"

"He confirmed that he knew Logan and didn't deny using a gay slur when talking to him. He did deny killing Logan and then yelled at me to get out of his office," said Marlee.

"So, all that and you didn't get anything from the confrontation with Al," Sanjay said.

"Nothing could be further from the truth. Al confirmed he knew Logan and had called him names. He also showed that he is a homophobe. By the way he reacted when I confronted him, I'd say he was not responsible for Logan's death," reported Marlee.

"How so?" asked Sanjay.

"He uses his words to intimidate people, but I really don't think he's violent. Al seems much more the type to incite violence in others through his slurs," said Marlee. "Of course, I can't swear to it that he didn't kill Logan or was there when it happened, but I just don't think so. My intuition tells me this guy is an asshole, but he didn't kill Logan."

"Maybe you shouldn't hang around the computer center," Sanjay said, peering over his shoulder to make sure Al wasn't walking by his office.

"Can you think of some reason to send Zack over to my office to fix my computer when he gets here?" asked Marlee.

"Yes, I'll have him come over right away, and then I'll come over a couple minutes after that. We can confront him with what we know and ask why he accessed Logan's computer. He might be able to give us a clue to the whole case!" said Sanjay, rubbing his hands together in anticipation of the confrontation.

Marlee left the computer center and made her way over to Scobey Hall as quickly as her feet could carry her. Once she was in her office, she called Alice's office to follow up on something they had previously discussed. After she had her answer, Marlee kicked back in her chair and started putting together her questions for Zack when he would arrive within the half hour.

As the puzzle pieces fall into place the full picture is revealed, much to the chagrin of those in authority.

Chapter 30

A soft tapping on the doorframe of her office alerted Marlee that Zack was there. She turned to look at him. Zack was of average height and had a slim build. He wore athletic pants and a lined Columbia fleece jacket zipped up to the chin. His feet were clad in something that looked similar to plaid bedroom slippers. Zack's dark blond hair was slicked back, either from styling products or from lack of washing, highlighting the acne on his forehead, cheeks and chin. He looked vaguely familiar, although Marlee was positive he'd never been in her classes.

"Dr. McCabe?" he asked.

"Yes. Are you from the computer center," asked Marlee.

"Yeah. I'm supposed to fix your computer. The note I got said you were having trouble logging in," Zack mumbled.

"There are a few different problems with it. I turned it off, so have a seat while it reboots," Marlee said, turning the desktop computer back on and motioning for him to sit down. She was taking her time, waiting for Sanjay to arrive so he could help with the questions. Given Marlee's lack of computer prowess, Zack would be able to talk techno geek to her and she wouldn't have the faintest idea what he meant. Sanjay would be able to poke all kinds of holes in Zack's story.

The computer warmed up and went to the login screen. Marlee held her breath because if Sanjay didn't hurry up and get there, she was going to have to confront Zack by herself. As Zack moved to sit in the chair in front of the computer, Sanjay appeared at the door and marched in, shutting the door behind him. Zack looked at Sanjay, wondering why he had been sent to Marlee's office too. This was a one-person job, and Zack would not need assistance on something as simple as this.

"Zack, we have some questions for you," Marlee began. "We know you accessed Dr. Logan LeCroix's computer before he died and also after. We also know you didn't have authorization to do it."

"No, I didn't. I've never even been in his office," said Zack, with a level of defensiveness saved for the truly guilty.

"That's not true, Zack. I accessed the system restore files, and I found out that you were in Logan's office and accessed his computer on more than one occasion. I can show you step-by-step how you did it too," said Sanjay, looking him square in the eye.

"Okay—before Dr. LeCroix died, he asked me personally to come over and look at his computer because he was having problems. He thought it would be quicker than reporting the problem to the computer center and then having them assign someone to come over," said Zack.

"Why were you on his computer after he died?" asked Marlee.

Zack looked at the floor, concocting an answer that would be both plausible and would not incriminate him in any wrongdoing. "Look, I don't know what you mean. I helped him before he died, but I was never in his office afterward. It must have been somebody else."

"It wasn't," said Sanjay. "It was you, and we have all kinds of proof. We also know you accessed Dr. LeCroix's short stories. Why?"

"It wasn't me! It was not me!" Zack shouted.

Marlee heard some noise outside her closed door and went to check. There stood Jeremy, just as she had requested. When Marlee had called Alice Olson earlier, she had asked that Jeremy report to her office at exactly two-thirty. Marlee motioned him inside, and his face went completely white as he saw Zack sitting before the computer. Jeremy and Zack looked at each other with their mouths hanging wide open.

"Spill it! Why did you two break into Dr. LeCroix's office and access his computer?" asked Marlee.

Neither student spoke for a full minute. Marlee resisted the urge to start speaking, knowing that silence was a powerful interrogation tool. When she couldn't take the silence any longer, Marlee said, "Look, we know you were both in Logan's office. We know Jeremy got the key from Alice Olson's office, and that Zack used his computer know-how to get into the computer and try to cover his tracks. We know you both accessed Logan's documents, specifically his short stories. Now tell us why!"

Silence continued between the students for another thirty seconds until Marlee noticed Jeremy's chin trembling. She stared right at him, and he said in a wavering voice, "We didn't mean for him to get hurt. We just wanted to scare him so he wouldn't turn us in for selling his work to a paper mill."

"Shut the fuck up, Jeremy!" Zack started to stand, but Sanjay firmly pushed him back down into the chair.

"You two killed Logan." said Marlee. She had only come to this conclusion half an hour earlier, after Alice Olson confirmed that Jeremy Driscoll's friend from the computer center was in fact Zack Gable. After that, the pieces of the puzzle fell together.

"We just meant to scare him. Zack said the gun didn't even work," said Jeremy.

By now, everyone was standing except for Zack, who still sat in front of Marlee's desktop computer. Jeremy began to sob, but Zack looked defiantly at the floor.

"So why kill Logan?" asked Marlee "I can't believe it was over theft of his short stories just so you could sell them."

"He wasn't supposed to die," Jeremy said between sobs. "He told me about wanting to be a writer and how he had a bunch of short stories that he might try to get published one day. I told Zack, and we came up with the idea to take them off his computer and sell them to an online paper mill."

"Have you both been selling other papers to paper mills?" asked Marlee.

Jeremy nodded while Zack continued to stare at the carpeted floor. "I needed the money. My mom has cancer and I needed to help her with her bills. I was already working two work-study jobs and couldn't put in any more hours working and keep up with my classes. I didn't know what to do. Zack told me about selling papers to the paper mills and how much money I could make from it, so I did it. I told myself I would only do it a few times, but my mom needed more and more medical help. We had to pay for someone to care for her at home. The insurance wouldn't cover it. I didn't know what else to do." Jeremy said, as he broke down in sobs that made his whole body heave. He held his head in his hands as tears ran down his face.

"When did you first access his computer?" Marlee asked.

"The week before he died," Jeremy said between sobs. "We didn't think he would ever find out that we copied one of his short stories and sold it. Somehow he found out and said he was going to the dean with the information. I knew we would probably be kicked out of school, so we waited for him one night outside his office. I knew he worked really late into the night most days, so we waited and waited for him to come out. When he didn't come out, I called his office from my dorm room and said we wanted to talk right away. He came running out of the building, and Zack pulled the gun on him and told him not to tell a soul about what we did. Dr. LeCroix grabbed for Zack's arm and the gun went off. We didn't know what to do, so we threw the gun in the dumpster and ran off. A few minutes later, we decided we needed to make it look like a robbery, so we came back and took out his wallet to make it look like we took his cash. Then we got the gun from the dumpster, wiped off our finger prints and put it back in there under a pile of garbage."

"How did his death mirror his short story?" asked Marlee.

"I didn't realize it did until after the accident," said Jeremy.

"It's seems very coincidental that the story basically matches up with the crime scene and the manner of death," said Marlee. "And I don't believe in coincidences."

"Zack grabbed Dr. LeCroix's keys and got back into Scobey Hall and then into his office. He accessed the computer and changed Dr. LeCroix's story around to match the death. He tried to make the story look like it was a suicide note. Then Zack wiped the keys off and left them on Dr. LeCroix's desk and came back outside. Then we got out of there because we knew Dr. Dole came into the office really early."

"Where did the gun come from?" asked Marlee.

"It belonged to Zack's grandpa. He has an antique gun collection and Zack didn't think he would notice it was gone. It was so old that we didn't even think it would work and Zack told me there weren't any bullets in it anyway," said Jeremy.

"So, you two are the ones who have been leaving threatening notes on my car?" asked Marlee.

Jeremy nodded. "We knew you were going to figure it out eventually, so Zack tried to scare you away from asking so many questions by leaving a message on your home phone. I put the notes on your car when I was writing out parking tickets for my other job. I put the note under your door when I was out hanging up flyers. We were never really going to hurt you."

"Kind of like you never meant to hurt Logan LeCroix?" Marlee asked looking Jeremy straight in the eye.

"We never meant to hurt him!" Jeremy shrieked, the sobs overtaking his body again.

A knock at the door interrupted further conversation in Marlee's office. She pulled open the door to find Bettina Crawford and Sean Yellow Tail from the Elmwood Police Department. Marlee had alerted Bettina to her belief that Jeremy and Zack had killed Logan LeCroix and asked that she come over with backup. The two police officers crowded into the already packed office. Bettina and Sean read both Zack and Jeremy their rights and handcuffed them before leading them out of the office and down to the police station. Jeremy was still sobbing, but Zack continued to look down at the floor, stone-faced.

After the two students were taken from campus, Marlee tended to the first and most important order of business. She called Joe Tisdale at the hotel and said with a quivering voice, "We got 'em, Joe. We got 'em." Joe broke down in sobs as she relayed the details of the murder as the story had just unfolded in her office. They both wept as they discussed the senselessness of Logan's death.

After a long, heartfelt conversation, Joe said, "I guess this now means your career is safe at MSU."

"Whoa, I hadn't even thought about that. I hope it does. After all, the reason the dean said I was not going to have my contract renewed was because I disobeyed him and asked questions about the investigation. Since my questions helped bring about the arrests of those who killed Logan, he should think twice about firing me," said Marlee before hanging up the phone.

Marlee then marched down to Dean Green's office. Louise said he was on a phone call, but Marlee didn't care. She barged into the dean's office and hit the receiver on his telephone, cutting off his call.

"What the fuck do you think you're doing?" bellowed the dean, leaping out of his chair.

"Sit down and listen for once!" Marlee yelled, adrenalin coursing through her system and giving her super powers. "For your information, two students were just arrested in the murder of Logan LeCroix. They killed him because he was going to turn them in for stealing his written work and selling it to online paper mills. I suspect you know some of this already and that's why you threatened my career!"

"How would I know anything about it? Why would I want it covered up?" the dean shouted, with an air of righteous indignation as he sat back down in his swivel chair.

"Because MSU had cameras that captured part, if not all, of the murder. You and others in administration destroyed the tape because you didn't want it to tarnish MSU's reputation any further. A suicide on campus can be easily explained away and quickly forgotten, but two students killing a professor would seriously impact MSU's current and future enrollment. You and others in administration did it to protect your asses!" Marlee yelled, banging her fist on the dean's desk.

"Not true! None of this is true!" yelled Dean Green, standing from his chair in an attempt to use his height and girth to intimidate Marlee. As much as the dean protested, Marlee could see in his eyes that she had hit upon the truth.

"How much did you know about the cheating scandal on campus? Did you know that was part of the reason for the murder?" asked Marlee, unfazed by the dean's attempts to shut her down.

"Get your ass out of here now before I call campus security!" yelled Dean Green, banging his fist against the bookcase near his desk for effect.

"I assume my career here is in good standing and that I won't need to find a teaching position elsewhere," Marlee said smugly over her shoulder as she left the office.

"Don't fucking count on it," sneered the dean.

Afterword

Jeremy admitted everything to the police as soon as he was questioned at the station. Zack remained silent and requested an attorney right away. After conferring with his lawyer, Zack realized that pleading guilty was his only option, given Jeremy's admission. The two pleaded guilty to voluntary manslaughter and were sentenced in Sheehan County Court in Elmwood, South Dakota, on February 5th, 2005. In exchange for their guilty pleas, the charges against them for threatening Marlee through the telephone and notes were dismissed.

Zack was held more culpable than Jeremy, since he was the one who provided the firearm and actually shot Logan LeCroix. The judge sentenced Zack to twenty years in the South Dakota State Penitentiary. Jeremy's sentencing hearing was particularly heart wrenching, as his terminally ill mother testified on his behalf and pleaded with the court to let her only child remain out on bond until she died. Although moved by her pleas, the judge sentenced Jeremy to fourteen years in prison with the term to begin immediately. Jeremy was dragged from the court room in handcuffs while his mother shrieked his name over and over. Jeremy's aunt grabbed his mother's small frame in an embrace before she collapsed to the floor. She died less than a month later. Jeremy was not allowed to attend the funeral.

The buying and selling of papers at MSU seemed to decline after Jeremy's and Zack's involvement were disclosed. Whether it actually declined was anyone's guess, since students may have just moved on to other forms of cheating and plagiarism that had not yet come under fire. It came out during the sentencing hearing that Zack was making $2,000 per month by selling papers to online paper mills. Much of his money was spent on alcohol, hard drugs, and online gambling. Jeremy became involved in stealing and selling papers when he became financially desperate due to his mother's cancer.

After Zack's and Jeremy's arrests and convictions for the murder of Logan LeCroix, Dean Green was forced to backtrack on his previous threat that this would be Marlee's last year teaching at MSU. Relieved that she would not have to leave MSU and Elmwood to look for a new career, she knew her position was far from secure. Marlee needed the recommendation of her dean to earn tenure and she knew that Dean Green would like nothing better than to see her fail. She wasn't sure how far he would go to make that happen. Her relationship with the dean, who was supposed to be her advocate for the tenure process, was on very shaky ground. The video footage from outside Scobey Hall on the early morning of Logan's murder was never found. MSU's statement was that the videotape was accidentally destroyed before anyone could view it to see what it contained. Administrators from MSU, including Dean Green, swore this in written statements to the Elmwood Police.

Much to Marlee's surprise, Chief Langdon did not have anything to do with the cover-up of Logan's murder. She thought that perhaps the chief and the dean were in cahoots, but later came to realize that was not the case. The chief sincerely thought the matter was a suicide and was satisfied with a quick resolution to the case. When

Jeremy and Zack confessed, the chief immediately backtracked by indicating that the investigation was still ongoing, but that the PD needed the real killers to let down their guard. Bettina Crawford and Sean Yellow Tail both received commendations for arresting Jeremy and Zack. Bettina was promoted to detective, and Sean Yellow Tail was given the coveted special project of working to develop a diversity committee in Elmwood.

Alan Haskell left MSU two weeks after the incident in his office with Marlee. The official reason given for his departure was that he had found a job closer to his home in Alabama. Unofficially, Al was terminated due to his racist, sexist and homophobic comments both on- and off-campus.

After the real perpetrators were identified, suspicion was lifted from Nate Krause. To his credit, he did not hold a grudge and even seemed to blossom after the investigation. He continued with counseling and became actively involved in campus activities. Nate re-enrolled in Intro to French and passed with a B. He later decided to add French as his minor.

Even without her dean's support, Marlee started a Criminal Justice Club. The founding members were Dominic Schmidt, Donnie Stacks, and Jasper Evans, but the membership grew to over twenty within a short time. Since the club was not sanctioned, Marlee could not hold meetings on campus, but that did not prevent her from holding the meetings at various eating establishments in Elmwood. She was also not allowed to advertise the Criminal Justice Club on campus, but she announced the upcoming meetings in her classes anyway. She made good on her deal to go on a date with Sanjay, as promised. They went to dinner at Apollo's. Marlee ordered a garlicky pasta dish with extra garlic and spent most of the time talking about her cat. There was no second date.

Joe returned to California. He drove Logan's car, packed full of Logan's belongings from campus and his apartment. Joe sold the large home where he and Logan had lived for the past several years. There were just too many memories. He and the dogs moved to a small house with a big back yard in the nearby city of Petaluma when he found employment in the engineering field. Joe spread Logan's ashes near the Mendocino National Forest where they used to go camping with their dogs.

Midwestern State University returned to normal, at least as normal as it could get after a murder, following Zack and Jeremy's sentencing hearings in February. Students went to classes, and professors continued to teach them. Spring came early with warm days that melted the snow. The early arrival of spring brought hope to a campus that had experienced a dismal fall and winter. Joe Tisdale donated money for an annual scholarship in Logan LeCroix's name. The stipulations of the scholarship were that the student must be minoring in French and have dealt with some type of barrier in his or her life.

The first recipient of that scholarship was Nate Krause.

The Day of the Dead, celebrated on November 1st, is a time for the living to remember and pay tribute to the deceased. It is believed that on November 1st, the spirits of the dead return to Earth to be with their loved ones for 24 hours. For Joe and my friends in both California and South Dakota, November 1st will forever remind them of me. It was the day I died.

The End

Did You Enjoy This Book?

Reviews are the most important way to get my books noticed by other mystery lovers. If you've enjoyed this book I would love for you to leave a review on the book's Amazon page. The review can be as brief or as detailed as you like.

Without reviews from readers like you, my books will be less visible on Amazon. Honest reviews of my books help bring them to the attention of other mystery lovers.

Thank you so much!

About The Author

Brenda Donelan is a life-long resident of South Dakota. She grew up on a cattle ranch in Stanley County, attended college in Brookings, and worked in Aberdeen as a probation officer and later as a college professor. Currently, she resides in Sioux Falls. *Day of the Dead* is the first book in the University Mystery Series.

Also by Brenda Donelan

Holiday Homicide

Criminology professor Marlee McCabe is thrust into a criminal investigation when a janitor is murdered at Midwestern State University. Marlee's sleuthing leads her to the Lake Traverse Indian Reservation and into the dangerous underworld of trafficking Native American artifacts and sacred cultural items. Those involved are not afraid to use threats, violence, and even murder to keep their secrets buried. What will they do to keep Marlee from exposing the truth?

Murder to Go

On the second day of a week-long class trip, a body is discovered in a motel room. Criminology Professor Marlee McCabe struggles to continue the tour of prisons and juvenile correctional facilities while uncovering the truth behind the life and death of the victim. As she protects her students from harm, Marlee begins to suspect the killer has ties to her university. What steps will the murderer take to hide the truth and prevent Marlee from revealing it?

Art of Deception

A million-dollar antique is stolen from an art show in Elmwood and Professor Marlee McCabe jumps into the investigation when her cousin, Bridget, is arrested and thrown in jail. Marlee steadfastly defends her cousin until secret details of Bridget's life call that loyalty into question. As Marlee struggles between dedication to family and the pursuit of justice, she is forced to make decisions which may destroy the rest of her life.

Fatal Footsteps

Get ready for a wild ride as Criminology Professor Marlee McCabe looks back to her earliest adventure as an amateur detective. It's 1987, the time of acid wash jeans and big, permed hair. When a college dorm mate is found dead in the snow outside a party house, Marlee puts her newly-learned Criminology knowledge to use as she strives to find out who killed the co-ed and why. The more involved Marlee and her roommate become in the investigation, the more deadly it becomes for them and their friends. As the body count rises, Marlee fears she's next on the killer's hit list.

Made in the USA
Lexington, KY
17 October 2019